Called for Icing

CANADIAN PLAYED
BOOK TWO

CYNTHIA GUNDERSON

Copyright © 2023 by Button Press

All rights reserved.

No part of this book may be reproduced in any form or by any electronic or mechanical means, including information storage and retrieval systems, without written permission from the author, except for the use of brief quotations in a book review.

With Gratitude

Editing and Critique
Scott Gunderson, Jordan Truex

Cover Design
Mitxeren

Author Note

While I gain inspiration from real life, all the characters in this book are entirely fictional, as are the players and hockey teams referenced. Though I use real NHL team names for world building, the team set in Calgary has been changed to the Blizzard since that NHL team comes into play in books three and four of this series. No spoilers...but keep reading :).

xo Cindy

Find extended author notes in special edition copies at www.CindyGunderson.com

Because recovery and healing is real.

CHAPTER

Penny 3:42pm

> On my way over now. Is that ok?

Brett 3:46pm

> Yep. Not doing much today. I'm flexible

Penny 3:47pm

> I'll be quick

Brett 3:49pm

> Refer to previous statement

PENNY STOOD at the doorstep with her hand raised. Yes, she was currently desperate, *but was she really this desperate?* To consider moving in with a complete stranger and trade professional services for rent?

That sounded . . . dirty. *Trading services for a free room.* Especially because the roommate in question was a hockey player who was twice her size and presumably pumped full of testosterone. She shouldn't make assumptions, but she'd spent time around her brother's hockey friends. She knew their inner thoughts. Granted, that was in high school, and she was now in her thirties, but did hockey players really change that much?

This guy Brett had looked the part on Sunday with his faded jeans and tousled sandy hair. Somehow, the brace on his knee only made him look more badass.

Penny exhaled through her teeth and rocked on her feet. How was she going to explain this? She'd have to find a creative way to present this situation to her family when she talked to them next.

Andrea, her older sister, could *never* see what Brett looked like, that was for damn sure. Andrea noticed too much. She knew Penny's type, and it was, in a word, Brett. Injured wing and all.

Most recent case in point: Danny. He was an athlete on the mend when she'd met him, and look how that had turned out. She needed to go for . . . an engineer or something. Someone with a dad bod. An introvert. A guy who was attractive but didn't know it, a male version of that girl from She's All That before she took off her glasses.

Focus, Penny. She dropped her hands from her hips and clenched them into fists. *She should knock.* Just a quick rap on the door, then she could see the place and get back to Kelty's. She didn't have to say yes to this arrangement.

At the team barbecue the other night, even Kelty's father-in-law had pointed out that this proposition had disaster written all over it. The guys on the team had insisted it sounded like a match made in heaven, but of course they'd take that stance. They wanted Brett healed and back on the team for next season more than they cared about a perfect stranger's emotional welfare.

Kelty hadn't been fully candid, even after Penny pressed her back at the house last night. She was a good friend. A good listener. Not one to give advice. She'd never pushed for Penny to leave Danny, even though she'd expressed her personal opinion about his personality more than once.

When Penny eventually called in tears, Kelty hadn't asked questions. She *had* insisted Penny crash in her guest room. The guest room that was only available until mid-June when her niece was moving in for a month-long summer internship.

When Penny scoured the internet for apartment options, she'd quickly realized she'd have to make a deal with the devil to find something affordable or somehow find a couple of roommates. Since she'd put all her eggs in Danny's basket and hadn't built other relationships in Calgary, that was depressingly unlikely.

Then Penny tagged along to Sean's team Sunday Supper and a hockey player, of all people, had offered her an olive branch.

She lifted her hand to the door for the second time. Maybe this wouldn't be a disaster. Maybe this was exactly what she needed—a platonic roommate who happened to have a beautiful face and wasn't at all invested in her life. She would offer her services, and he'd let her stay in his extra room. Simple. *Note to self: she had to find a different word for services.*

The door swung open before she could knock, and Penny jumped back.

Brett stood in front of her in a white T-shirt and grey sweatpants, the same brace she'd seen Sunday clamped over his right knee. "I was wondering how long you would stand there before knocking."

Penny looked toward the window. The blinds were still closed. "How did you know I was here?"

"Cameras."

Penny's eyes shot up with alarm. Had he been sitting on the

couch watching her war internally with herself for the past ten minutes?

Brett chuckled and moved out of the way for the door to open wider. "I'm kidding. I only have cameras in the bedroom."

Penny's eyes widened further, if that were possible, and Brett's face went slack. "Also kidding—I'm sorry, I don't know why I said that. I don't have any cameras in the house. At all. I'm just—" He exhaled. "I don't normally do this."

Penny stepped over the threshold and slipped off her shoes. "What, invite random women over to scout out the place? Ask complete strangers to move in?"

Brett closed the door behind her and ran a hand through his hair. "No, that used to be Tyler's job." He shook his head. "Sorry, you probably don't know him yet. Emma finally made an honest man out of him."

Penny stepped away from the door and folded her arms in front of her. "I met them at the barbecue. They seem nice." She wouldn't say it out loud, but the moment she saw Tyler, she'd drawn some . . . conclusions. Then she'd crumpled up those assumptions and tossed them in the bin. When Emma walked into the room, Tyler was a man crossing the desert, and she was a glass of fresh spring water. He'd barely been able to look past the stars in his eyes to find the toppings for his burger. That guy was *not* a player. At least not anymore.

"You're serious about this, then?" Penny asked, relieved that she likely wouldn't have to worry about a revolving door of weekend sleepovers for the summer. If she said yes to this, which was a big *if*.

"Yeah." Brett fiddled with the hem of his shirt. *Why wouldn't he be nervous?* He'd barely said two words to her at dinner on Sunday before blurting out the idea of them rooming together. *After* hearing she was a physical therapist. "I'm serious. For sure."

He'd had a few days to think it through, so Penny decided to take his answer as truth. On Sunday, after Brett's idea echoed around the back patio, he explained that he'd been looking for a physical therapist for weeks. The only ones he could find who had openings were down south and private pay.

She knew from personal experience that Danny's office had been one of them. Brett had texted her a few weeks ago in the midst of her life crisis, and she'd given him the information to schedule. She hadn't given it a second thought or connected that friend-of-Kelty's-Brett and this guy were the same person until they'd been sitting across from each other at the Thompson home.

Penny scanned the living area, taking in the wood floors, clean decor, and updated kitchen. "This place is nice. You could get a lot more in rent than what I charge for physical therapy."

"You aren't very good then?"

Penny's eyes flashed. "Yes, I'm good. But one appointment a week isn't—"

"I don't want to do one session a week. I want to do three."

Penny considered that. "You're motivated." She glanced down at his knee. "Didn't you just have surgery?"

Brett hobbled over and sat down on the couch. "It's been a week."

Penny blinked. "A week? So you were at supper on Sunday a day after you got out of the hospital?" He shrugged. "Those drugs must've been good," she murmured.

"I didn't take any drugs."

"You—"

"I only have five months until the next season starts," Brett cut in. "The doctor said it would probably take six months to recover, but I figure with more aggressive therapy—"

"That's not always how it works. Doing more to help your body progress can be helpful, but you can't force your body to heal."

"I realize that."

Penny crossed her arms in front of her. "You seriously didn't take any pain meds?" A muscle flexed in Brett's jaw, and he shook his head. "Before or after?"

"Why does it matter?"

She stumbled on her words. "I don't know, maybe the fact that it's insane not to take something after you tear through the inside of your knee, and then someone slices through your skin and muscle to fix it?" Her eyes narrowed. "Are you one of those people? Who refuses anesthesia and—"

"I was knocked out for the surgery, but I'm curious what you mean by 'those people.'" Brett's eyebrow lifted.

"I just meant . . . you know. The people who think they can cure cancer with crystals or something." Her cheeks warmed. If he was one of those people, then she'd just done an excellent job of alienating her would-be roommate. *If.*

That word pulsed in her head, but it was becoming less insistent. Three PT sessions a week was a low price to pay for a private bedroom and bathroom in Northwest Calgary. She'd started her search for rentals three weeks ago when she decided to leave Danny, but it hadn't taken her long to exhaust the available options—at least the liveable ones.

"Maybe they *can* cure cancer with crystals." Brett's face was deadpan, and Penny was about to apologize when a wide smile split his features. "I'm kidding."

Penny's heart seemed to climb up into her throat. *Had she seen him smile like this before the other night?* She didn't think so because she definitely would've remembered it. Penny dropped her eyes but couldn't keep a grin from creeping onto her face. "First the cameras, then the crystals? A regular comedian."

Brett exhaled and leaned back on the couch, lifting his left arm behind his head. More dark ink peeked out beneath the sleeve of his T-shirt. "I hang out with my hockey team, and that's about it. I think I've forgotten how to have a filter."

Penny held up three fingers. "Three brothers, remember? Once I'm convinced you're not a creep, you can say whatever you want."

Brett's blue eyes sparkled. "How long will that take?"

Penny's stomach flipped. "It took my brother Theo at least four years to convince me." She walked into the kitchen and inspected the appliances. She'd been oblivious to the housing crisis when she moved out from Vancouver. Danny owned an apartment down south, and it had all seemed so idyllic.

Penny loved Van City, but she'd been itching to get out. Ever since her older brother Lucas . . . She shivered and rubbed her arms. The city hadn't felt the same since he'd passed. Her family hadn't felt the same. Like a dark cloud had been hovering over them the past three years.

Danny had been a cloudless blue sky and moving to Alberta a fresh spring breeze. She hadn't known then how hard the wind would blow on this side of the Rockies.

Penny rounded the island. "You might have to get used to the idea of not playing next season, even if we do extra PT."

"Not an option."

Penny blew out a breath. She wasn't going to argue with a guy she'd just met. He wasn't family, her boyfriend, or even her friend, and she didn't owe him anything. If he wanted to ruin his knee, so be it. "Can I see the bedroom?" Her cheeks flushed. "I mean mine. My bedroom. The room that would be—"

"Just down the hall on the right. Mine is the room at the very end of the hall. Tyler left his bed frame and mattress, so you can use that or replace it with your own stuff."

She didn't have her own stuff. *So stupid.* Danny's apartment was already furnished, so all she'd brought with her was her PT equipment, clothing, and personal items. Thankfully, she'd purchased her equipment before getting together with Danny, so he couldn't claim that in their split. Not that he could force her to give anything up since they weren't married . . . yet somehow she'd still left her gourmet coffee maker and favourite bowls.

Penny opened the door and looked in. *Nice. Clean.* Still smelled a little like male aftershave, but she didn't mind. Most of her childhood had smelled like that growing up with older brothers and her adult life? Up until three weeks ago, she'd been with Danny for nearly three years. Before that, she'd been with her yoga instructor for a year and a half, and before that, her college boyfriend, Jeremy, for four. Penny didn't do short-term relationships. Or being single.

It had taken her eighteen months to call things off with Jeremy because she couldn't bear the thought of his puppy dog eyes when she told him she was done. Even his lack of a job and refusal to contribute to their bills each month wasn't enough to make her pull the plug. *It had taken his more than friendly interest in their neighbour Monica to do that.*

She wanted to make people happy. Even when she wasn't. That was the perfect logline for her life from age twenty-three to thirty-one.

Penny took a peek into the bathroom, which also looked put together, then walked back out into the living room. "It's great." She searched for something to follow up with, but her thoughts jumbled into a knot. What else was she supposed to say? 'I'm leaning toward servicing you for free rent?' She almost snorted. *Therapy. She would agree to administer therapy.*

"Yeah. It's a good place." Brett ran his hand over his knee brace.

She should've brought Kelty with her. At least they knew each other and could shoot the breeze or something. *Did she even remember how to shoot the breeze with someone?* Brett didn't seem overly talkative, and she couldn't tell if that was a good or bad thing. On the one hand, he probably wouldn't be in her way as a roommate. On the other, would every day feel like this? Standing there staring at each other awkwardly?

"I get up early to work out at the gym. Right now, I can't do much, mostly upper body. Then I'm working from home since I can't drive." Brett tapped his knee.

"Still painful?"

He nodded. "Another week or so, and I'll trust it."

"How do you get to the gym?" Penny asked. Brett pointed to a crutch against the wall by the door. "You walk?"

"It's only a few blocks. Part of this community. So if you wanted to go—"

"I don't work out at the gym," Penny scoffed. She hated everything about those places. The clinical machines. The smell of rubber and sweat. The guys who bent over next to you and kept making aggressive eye contact.

"You're one of *those* people?" Brett smirked.

Penny shot him a look. *Smart aleck.* "I didn't mean it like that. I think it's great if people go to the gym, I just prefer to get my exercise other ways. And I get up early, too, so that shouldn't be a problem." Brett nodded but didn't ask any follow-up questions. Penny was glad not to elaborate. "So, three PT sessions a week."

"Right."

Penny pursed her lips. "Only for the summer. Maybe not the full summer, honestly. My parents have a thing at the end of July. I still haven't decided what I'll do after that." She'd considered bailing immediately and heading back home after leaving Danny, but what would she do there? She didn't have a place or a job in Vancouver either, and her parents had tried to convince her not to move here in the first place. She wasn't quite ready to limp home with her tail between her legs.

Brett nodded, and her heart thrummed in her chest. *This would be fine, wouldn't it?* It was only a couple of months, and Kelty and Sean had known Brett for years. He was a stranger to her but not to them.

Saying yes to this meant she could save money all summer. Get her feet under her. Then, if things still weren't looking up, she could do the drive of shame over the Rockies at that point. "Okay, then. I can write up a contract."

CHAPTER
Two

BRETT CLOSED the door and clomped into the kitchen. *Cameras in the bedroom?* Why the hell had he said that? He'd been spending too much time with the boys if he thought that was a charming opening line.

Not that he wanted to be charming. *Amiable. Normal.* That was the goal, even though these days he felt anything but. His knee still ached at night, and he couldn't remember the last time he'd gotten a full night's sleep.

Brett's phone vibrated on the counter. He exhaled and flipped it over. Tony. Impeccable timing, as usual. He seemed to have a sixth sense for when Brett was at his lowest. "Hey, buddy."

"Lovely afternoon, eh?" Tony's voice sounded like it was being dragged by a pickup truck down a gravel road. Courtesy of twenty-plus years of smoking.

Brett perched on the stool and splayed out his leg, wincing at the throb of his heartbeat behind the brace. "I wouldn't know. How's Leanne?"

Tony sighed, and Brett couldn't help but smile. Tony and Leanne had only been married six months, and their relationship was more volatile than a shaken-up Molson. "She's fine. We're fine."

"Sounds like it."

"I forgot our anniversary."

Brett laughed out loud. "Again?"

"Last one didn't count. That was the anniversary of our first date, and we've agreed that doesn't need to be celebrated."

"Who agreed?"

Tony exhaled. "Right. Why aren't you leaving the house?"

"I'm not *not* leaving the—"

"It's over twenty degrees out there, and you're sitting inside feeling sorry for yourself?"

Brett wanted to snap out a rebuttal. *I'm slammed with work. I'm taking a day off. I'm taking it easy like the doctor instructed.* None of that would fly. Tony called him on his shit, which was why Brett had asked him to be his sponsor four years ago. Even now that Tony lived in Kamloops, they still talked at least once a week.

Brett glanced up at the clock on the stove, then stood and lumbered to his bedroom. Tyler would be over to pick him up in thirty minutes, and it might take him that long to change into shorts. "I'm stuck, bud."

"I know. That's why I'm calling. Are you still going to practice?"

Brett sat on the bed and pulled at the velcro straps of his brace. "Heading there in a few."

"Going into work?"

"Nope. Won't be able to drive for another week or so. I still can't bend my damn knee."

"Mmhmm. You could ask—"

"I'm not going to ask." Brett set the brace next to him and tugged at the compression wrap underneath.

Tony cleared his throat. "I wish I was still there."

He wasn't the only one. A few of the guys from the team, Tyler included, had come along to AA meetings, but he missed having someone in his life who understood why they were such an integral part of his life. All the Snowballs were supportive, especially since they'd seen him at his worst when he first joined the team, but none of them were in recovery.

Brett put the call on speaker phone as he stood and balanced on his left leg to pull off his joggers. "No, you don't. You hate Calgary."

"I hate the provincial sales tax in BC more," Tony grumbled. Brett barked a laugh and hobbled to the dresser to pull out his athletic shorts. "This is where we grow, eh? Go back to the basics. Let go of the things you can't control. Give it to God."

Brett rubbed his forehead. *God, grant me the serenity to accept the things I cannot change, the courage to change the things I can, and the wisdom to know the difference.* How many times had he repeated the Serenity Prayer? A year ago, he would've said he'd mastered it. Hell, even a month ago, he would've said he was solid.

"Right. I know, bud. Thanks for the reminder."

"You're going to kick ass on the ice again in six months."

Brett tied the string on the waistband of his shorts, then sat and re-wrapped the bandage and attached the brace. "Four."

"Four, what?"

"Four months. I found a physical therapist."

"Well, shit, buddy. Lead with that!"

Brett chuckled and reached for his deodorant on the nightstand. He'd been requesting appointments for months with no luck, which was why he'd asked a near stranger to move in with him without a second thought. "Hopefully she's good."

"Did you offer Alberta Health your first-born child?"

"Sperm donation. So they can make as many of me as they want."

Tony laughed, then broke into a coughing fit.

"No, she's a friend of Kelty's." Brett hesitated. He and Tony told each other everything, but the words "she's moving in with me" died on his tongue. *It wasn't a big deal.* Penny needed an apartment, and he needed PT. That fact didn't explain the swoop in his stomach at the thought of her taking up residence in the room next to his.

"Do you have to drive far?" Tony asked.

"Nope, ah . . . " *He had to tell him.* It would come up eventually, and *it wasn't a big deal.* "Actually, she's moving in here."

"Here? As in—"

"My apartment. Since Tyler moved—"

"Your physical therapist is moving in with you?"

"Not like—yes, not *with* me. In the other room—her own room, it's—we're trading for—"

"Buddy. Are you paying her in—"

"*Rent.* She's living here free in exchange for physical therapy so that I can get in extra sessions—"

Tony howled with laughter on the other end of the line. "Defensive about that, eh? I thought you were a winger?"

Brett ran a hand over his face. "Don't give up your day job." Tony guffawed, and Brett turned off the speakerphone, tucking the phone between his cheek and shoulder as he grabbed the strap of his hockey bag. He didn't know why he took this with him to practice since he hadn't been on the ice in weeks, but it felt wrong to leave it at home.

Tony wheezed as he finally caught his breath. "No, this is perfect. I won't have to worry about you choking on a piece of steak or something."

Brett scoffed. "You think I eat steak for dinner?"

"Didn't your company hit a million in contracts already for the year? Plenty of cash to buy Grade A Alberta beef."

Brett grinned and hobbled down the hall. Through the window, he saw Tyler's truck pull up next to the curb. "Tyler's here to chauffeur me to practice, buddy."

"Give him a kiss for me."

"With tongue?"

Tony snorted. "Only way to do it. Love you."

"Love you, bud. Go buy Leanne some chocolate."

"It's past chocolate at this point. I'm heading to The Bay."

"They have more than a 7-Eleven in Kamloops?"

"Asshole."

Brett laughed as Tony hung up, then shuffled to the door and swung it open to reveal Tyler's grinning face.

"There's my favourite invalid."

Brett looked him up and down. "Where's your monkey suit?" Tyler shook his head and started down the steps. "No white gloves or a bottle of sparkling water? What kind of service is this?"

"I'm not helping you down the stairs." Tyler descended the steps with annoying agility.

Every time Brett even came close to straightening his knee, a zing of pain shot through his thigh to his hip. He knew he was going to have to work through it eventually and was already dreading it. *He would have to work through it with Penny.* The dark void in his middle deepened as he swung his leg wide with each drop. There were only five stairs, but that was plenty.

Tyler turned back at the sound of his bag hitting the railing. "I was kidding, I can—"

"I'm fine, bud. It's good." Brett was already sweating when he made it to the passenger door.

"Gorgeous day." Tyler slid into the driver's seat as Brett threw his bag in the back.

Brett hoisted himself up, wincing as his knee knocked against the dash. "That it is." He rolled down the window as Tyler drove down the street and turned left at the stop sign. Something as simple as the summer breeze slipping over his arm made him long to move. To run or even just walk faster than a geriatric.

"You okay?" Tyler asked.

Brett nodded. "Haven't been out of the house much. Feels good."

"You know I'll swing by whenever."

Brett picked at a loose string on the sleeve of his shirt. "I know." Tyler was serious, no doubt, but Brett wasn't going to ask him for anything else. Since Tony moved, Tyler had come to as many AA meetings with him as Sean had, and he was already picking him up for practice on top of it.

Brett asked about the property renovations Tyler and Emma were overseeing, successfully keeping the spotlight off himself and his lack of coping skills until they reached the ice arena and parked.

Tyler insisted on walking next to him, even though Brett was slow. It wasn't like they were late for practice, but he still hated holding him back. He despised everything about being a charity case. At least his surgery wasn't in the middle of the season when he'd truly be letting the team down, especially after that last loss to Stiff Sticks to finish out the tourney. They'd lost the cup in the last minutes of that game because he'd gone down and left his team a man short. All the Snowballs were dead-set on redemption.

Tyler held the door for him as they walked into the atrium. "I'll take the elevator." Brett adjusted the strap of the bag on his shoulder, expecting Tyler to take the stairs, but instead he walked with him.

"What plans do you have this weekend? Want to come out on Friday to the Perch?" Tyler asked as the elevator doors opened.

Brett shuffled in. "Friday? Not sure."

"Your calendar's all booked up, eh?"

Brett chuckled and ran a hand over his days-old stubble. "Like a sexy librarian." All of this felt strange. As roommates, Brett had felt like the stable one. Consistent with his routine while Tyler was constantly rebounding from his late nights and sleepover guests. Now Tyler was in a committed relationship and running a business. He still went out on the weekends but was spending more time with guys like Curtis, Fly, and Suraj—all either married or with long-term girlfriends.

More than once, Tyler had texted to invite him out with Sean and Kelty, which wasn't surprising. Now that he and Emma were together, Sean and Tyler had buried their proverbial hatchets, but if they thought Brett was going to come out as their fifth wheel, they didn't understand the only camping he did was in a tent under the stars.

When the elevator doors opened, they walked to the dressing room. Half the guys were already there, and Brett took up residence in the corner so he wouldn't get in their way. He didn't have to change, but being here with all of them made not getting out on the ice almost bearable.

"How's Gimpy?" Darcy called out.

"Ask your mom, Winfield," Brett shot back. "Pretty sure with only one working leg my performance was still more than satisfactory."

Boyd chortled, and André stripped off his shirt with flare. Darcy punched André's shoulder, knocking him into the locker.

"Missed you, buddy." Country clapped Brett on the back.

"Country, what the hell is this I hear about you getting on TikTok? Isn't that for young bucks?" Fly pulled up his socks.

Country's face coloured as he dropped his bag on the bench. "I didn't *get on* TikTok."

"I saw the video. It was hilarious." Curtis glanced up as he wriggled into his pads.

"My brother posted it. I didn't know he was filming!"

Brett pulled out his phone, more than a little intrigued. He occasionally spent some time scrolling on TikTok, but he'd never seen one of his teammates' faces pop up on the app. "What's the handle?"

Country muttered under his breath as he started stripping. "I told Cole to take it down."

Curtis scoffed. "He can't take it down. It has almost half a million views!" He leaned past Country to hiss, "It's @MapleStickHandler."

Country knocked him back next to the bench, but not before Brett had already started typing. "Cole made it up—I had nothing to do with this."

"Bud, you have to look at his followers. They're all hot

women—" André started, and Country threw a glove at his head. "What? That's a compliment! You don't want hot women sliding into your DM's? What's wrong with you people in western Canada?" André tossed the glove back, but missed the bench entirely.

Brett picked it up off the floor and handed it to Country. "You're not enjoying all the attention?"

Country's lip twitched as he strapped on his cup. "I was watching hockey, not performing for the internet."

"The 'internet?' What is this, nineteen-ninety?" Fly teased. "I can say that because I was around when the internet was invented." Everyone laughed. Fly talked like Brett's dad even though he was only thirty-nine. Everyone on the team was between the ages of thirty and thirty-nine, but no matter where they all landed on that continuum, they all felt the same age. He kept forgetting that Fly was hitting the end of the line for the Snowballs, and that realization sobered him even as Country appeared on his phone shirtless.

Sean pushed through the door and hadn't even gotten past Curtis when Suraj said, "Last year with the team, eh, Fly?"

Fly sighed and stuffed his folded clothes into his locker. "Aging out. On to Masters."

The room went quiet, and Brett felt a pang in his stomach. Fly had started with the Snowballs nine years ago. None of the guys had known this team without him.

"Well. Thanks for that downer." Sean stalked past André and Darcy and dropped his gear. Brett shot Tyler a look. Sean wasn't good with change in general, but especially not when it came to the team. "What are you all waiting for? We've got four minutes till we should be out on the ice."

Brett stood and drew a deep breath. Probably not the best time to razz Country about his profile picture, but he couldn't help himself. "Country, if you take your jersey off, I could film—"

Country snatched his phone and turned off the screen, then

handed it back to him. He didn't say a word, but there were splotches of red on his cheeks.

Brett worked to keep from breaking into a laugh. "See you boys out there." He made his way to the stands and started his upper body workout as the rest of the guys pushed through the door in the boards. The sound of skates slicing through the ice and pucks smacking against the boards was both music to his ears and a shard of glass in his gut. He gritted his teeth, pushing himself harder with each tricep dip.

Only a few more months. Not even. He wouldn't be able to get on the ice in less time than that, but he would at least be able to drive in a few weeks once he could straighten his knee. He was about to mentally rehearse the timeline to stave off the angst when he paused mid-rep. Penny's face filled his head, and warmth flooded his chest.

What the hell was that? He dropped and pushed up, his arms on fire as sweat beaded on his brow. *Was he excited for Penny to move in?* Of course, he was. He needed the PT, and she was solving that problem.

But that feeling . . . That wasn't an "I finally got an appointment after calling around Calgary for weeks" kind of emotional response. That was a "she's hot and I want her to notice me" kind of solar flare.

Brett swallowed hard. He'd spent the past four years working to pay attention to how he felt. That wasn't something he readily admitted to people who weren't in recovery, but it was the only way he knew how to cut off the spiral that used to make him want to numb. *Feel the feelings.* He used to be terrified of that. Now, he let them roll through him without much thought, but the idea of Penny made his insides twist.

Brett's heart sped as he pushed harder, his arms on fire. He was lonely. He missed Tyler as a roommate. That had to be it. He doubted Penny would be interested in spotting him for bench at the gym or eating wings for breakfast on Sundays, but it would be nice to have someone at the house. All the unknowns of bringing in a new roommate and the fact that all his normal coping skills were moot had to be the source of the tightness in his chest.

Then, as if in rebuttal, the image of her looking around his living room while he sat on the couch flickered in his mind. The way she tucked her black wavy hair behind one ear. The pinch in her brow, her teeth tugging on her lower lip. Brett's hand slipped on the metal bench, and he barely caught himself before dropping to the rubber floor.

He dragged himself up and sat. *Okay.* It wasn't only the newness and lack of control. He was attracted to her. That was also normal. She was a beautiful woman, and besides a few short-lived relationships, he'd been single since getting sober. Normal response. Expected even. He would accept it and let it pass through, just like everything else.

"Slacking, eh?" Country grinned as he skated over to the edge of the rink, leaning against the boards.

"You can't jaw until your arms are bigger than mine." Brett smirked and pulled up the sleeve of his shirt.

Country scoffed. "My pads and jersey, they're obscuring everything or I'd show you up right now."

He probably would. Country worked on his family's ranch, and after showing up with the team to help repair a fence last summer, Brett had never teased Country again for being a hick. "Look who's slacking now?" Brett motioned at the rest of the team, dropping their sticks for line skates.

Country cursed under his breath. "Sean's pissed because Darcy and Suraj missed conditioning last week. This'll be a thigh burner."

Brett folded his hands behind his head. "Make it look pretty, bud."

Country held up his glove and did his best to flip him off even though the thick padding didn't move much.

"I'm watching that video as soon as I get home!" Brett chuckled and flipped over, carefully positioning his legs, then dropping into a plank as his teammates' skates scraped against the ice.

He wanted to be out there dashing toward the blue line in unison with them. He'd gladly take a thigh burner any day of the week instead of sitting here letting his heart, lungs, and muscles atrophy. No matter how much weight he lifted or reps he pushed, it wasn't the same.

"Faster!" Sean barked.

Brett dropped his chest to the ground and pushed back up, keeping most of his weight on his left toes. He wouldn't stop working until they did.

Penny grunted as she pulled another duffel from the garage. "I think there's only that long bag with the poles and straps and then my toiletries left," she said as Kelty passed her on the driveway.

"Sean texted. He said Tyler's on his way with the truck."

Penny nodded and dropped the bag next to the others on the curb. After seeing the apartment Saturday morning and emailing back and forth with Brett over the weekend, she didn't see any reason to wait before moving in. It hadn't taken her long to pack up since she was still living out of her suitcases.

Penny put her hands on her hips and stared at the pile of bags on the concrete. This was it. All she owned in the world besides a few pieces of furniture she'd tetrised into her parent's storage unit before leaving Vancouver.

It wasn't that she wished she had more belongings. She'd never been one to pine after things, but when she'd imagined her life at thirty-two, it never involved being transient. That was for college—for when you didn't know what you were doing. How long was that phase supposed to last?

"There." Kelty set down the last two bags and brushed off her hands. "Who needs a boyfriend?"

Penny grinned and breathed in the scent of lilacs drifting from the blooming bushes along the fence. "Should we just walk it all over? Prove we don't even need the truck?"

Kelty snorted. "You're on your own on that one. Do you want some water?"

Penny shook her head. "I'm good. Thanks for everything, Kelt."

"I'm so glad it all worked out."

Penny gritted her teeth against the twist in her stomach. She didn't have a job and was moving in with an injured hockey player who she was pretty sure thought he could play God with his own soft tissue. Or assumed she could miraculously heal him. *Definitely all worked out.*

She'd tried not to think about Brett the past two days, but it had been virtually impossible. How could she not wonder about him? Whether he'd regret his decision to let her move in— whether he'd like her. Not *like*, like. But like . . . like. As in, not regret this arrangement they'd agreed upon, or at least feel like it had been worth it for him.

Standing in his living room, his relaxed manner had both put her at ease and unnerved her. The way he'd sat all nonchalantly in his white T-shirt on the couch, his tattoo barely poking out the bottom of the sleeve. How she'd seen more of it when he lifted his hand to push his blond hair out of his piercing blue eyes.

That was the unnerving part. How his eyes seemed to want to smile but couldn't.

Penny's phone buzzed in her pocket. She stepped away from Kelty and pulled it out. Her sister Andrea's smiling face pulsed on the screen. "Hey, I can't—"

"I know you're moving tonight, but I just wanted to touch base about the anniversary dinner. We have a date!"

"Oh yeah? When?"

"July twenty-eight. We had to take mid-week because everything on the weekend was booked."

"Makes sense." Penny put Andrea on speaker and flipped to her calendar. "Twenty-eighth. Got it."

"I've already booked the house over there, but it has a thirty-day cancellation."

Penny saved the calendar entry and put the phone back to her ear. "You got the one with the blue doors?"

"Oh, definitely. It's way closer to the beach, and Aunt Z said there's a little market there with restaurants." Andrea squealed. "Everyone else is going to stay with her in the guest house. It's going to be incredible. You're still good for your part, right? I think we'll need to nail down flights for sure next week. I'm worried prices are going to go up."

Penny's ribs tightened. "Yeah, definitely." There was nothing definite about it. With only five of her six siblings available to contribute to this anniversary surprise trip for her parents, they had run the numbers, and each agreed to come up with six thousand dollars. Once they arrived in Greece, Aunt Zaneeta and Uncle Anthony would no doubt insist on contributing to the cost of food, but they weren't going to ask for it. Thirty thousand would ensure they were covered from anything unexpected.

The only problem? She'd agreed to all this when she had a salaried position. When she wasn't living for free with no job prospects in a city where her only professional connections came through her ex.

"Great, 'kay. I just wanted to make sure you were in the loop. I want to see pictures of your new roommate and house and stuff. No rush. When you get a chance."

Penny imagined herself dropping her bags in the entryway and sitting down next to Brett, asking if she could take a selfie. Nope. That would not be happening anytime soon. Mostly because she knew exactly how Andrea would react to his smile and athletic build. "Mmhmm."

"Talk soon. Love you."

"Love you, Dre." Penny put the phone back in her pocket and turned to find Sean's car parked in the garage where her belongings used to be.

Sean gave a small wave. "Tyler should be here—" He looked past her and raised his arm. Penny turned to see a truck pulling up the street. She recognized Tyler, but her eyes were immediately drawn to the face in the passenger seat. *Why was Brett here?*

Penny turned and hurried to her things, not quite sure why she was rushing when he hadn't even parked yet.

"We've got this." Sean waved her off as she leaned down to grab a bag.

"But Brett can't—"

"You think it'll take more than me and Tyler to load this stuff? You have less boxes and bags than Kelty packs for a weekend trip."

"Hey!" Kelty smacked him, and Sean smirked. He grabbed her arm and pulled her in for a kiss.

Penny looked away and still tried to snag a duffel, but Sean snatched it off the ground.

"I'm serious."

"I'm supposed to just stand here?" Penny frowned.

"No. Go get in the truck. It'll take two seconds."

Kelty rolled her eyes as Sean loaded up his arms and whisked past them both. "Just let him do it. It's his dad's fault. He made him believe he wasn't a real man unless he took care of the women around him."

Penny looped her thumbs in her pocket and pursed her lips. Pressure built behind her eyes, and her chest suddenly felt like it was wrapped in a corset. *Why was she getting emotional?* Standing on the sidewalk while some guys she barely knew loaded up her belongings?

She hadn't cried when she left Vancouver with Danny. Not even when she left South Calgary to come here. Penny started to hyperventilate. Maybe because both of those times, she'd had at least an inkling of a plan? A familiar face on the other side?

Kelty pulled her into a hug, oblivious to her current existential crisis. "I'll see you at Sunday Supper. This'll be great, Pen."

Penny nodded and pushed back, willing the pressure behind her eyes to dissipate. She needed to walk away. To take a lap around the block. To do anything but—

"All set." Tyler pushed the tailgate up with a clang. "Ready?"

Penny nodded, her heart pounding hard enough to make her heady. Without her permission, her legs moved, sending her around the front of the truck to the passenger door. She reached up to pull on the handle, but the door was already opening toward her.

Brett moved to the middle seat, and she stepped up, gripping the handhold, then sat next to him. She glanced over and caught the side of Brett's profile as Tyler jumped into the driver's seat. Brett was so close, she could smell a hint of warm spice and pine on his skin. His hair was damp, and Penny noticed the subtle variation in the colour of it, making it look as if he'd gotten highlights. *He didn't dye his hair, did he?* No. It looked too natural to—

Brett looked over and met her eyes. Penny pretended to search for her seatbelt as Tyler started the truck.

"Alright, let's get the two of you home, eh?"

CHAPTER Three

HOME.

That word felt like a punch to the gut, but Penny held it together only because Michael Jackson was playing on the radio. Her mom had been obsessed with him all growing up, and listening to the eighties' synth felt like she'd wrapped her arms around Penny and squeezed. She doubted anyone had ever had that reaction to Billie Jean in the history of humankind, but she was grateful to avoid a full mental breakdown in the cab of Tyler's truck.

But she would break down. It was coming, which meant she needed to get settled in fast so she didn't look like a crazy person on her first night. Alone. In a stranger's apartment.

Penny clenched her jaw and jumped out of the truck the second Tyler parked, then started unloading from the back.

"You're in a hurry." Tyler pulled down the tailgate and motioned for her to move to the back instead of contorting herself over the wheel well.

Penny hauled a duffel full of PT equipment over her shoulder and followed him behind the building. They made a few more trips, then finally loaded everything into a single-car garage behind the small complex. "You realize this doesn't count as an apartment if you have your own garage, right?"

Tyler laughed. "It's not big enough to fit Brett's Jeep, so I don't think it counts as a garage. It would probably fit your car, though." He dropped the other two equipment bags and stepped back. "Did we get it all?"

Penny nodded. "Just a few more things to take into the house." Tyler closed the garage, and they walked around the building to the front door.

The complex was nice. On a quiet street. Only six units. A driveway back to an open parking area with six, albeit small, garage units that were most likely all being used for storage like Brett's.

"Trying to injure the other knee?" Tyler barked as they rounded the building, and Penny's head shot up. Brett was hoisting one of her suitcases up the steps in front of the house, balancing on the handle so he could take the next step with his good leg.

Brett grunted as he lifted the bag up the last three steps and set it on the landing. Penny didn't *not* notice the way his arms bulged against the sleeves of his T-shirt. Salmon pink today. She loved it when men wore pink. It said both *I'm confident in my masculinity* and "eff you" to societal norms. If it also had a floral pattern on it, she was sunk.

Thankfully, Brett's was plain, but watching him hobble to the door with her bag in tow made something twirl in her midsection. *He was probably just annoyed that Tyler was getting all the credit.*

"Thank you," Penny called out as she jogged to the truck to grab her toiletries. Tyler followed, muttering something under his breath as he checked the bed and closed the tailgate. "Thanks for the ride and for helping me unload."

Tyler wiped his hands on his jeans. "Happy to help. Emma instructed me to give you her number and tell you she's expecting to see you back at Sunday Supper."

"I know, I didn't go Sunday because I was packing." Penny pulled out her phone and opened the contacts, then passed it to him so he could enter it in.

Tyler's thumbs tapped on her phone. "Well, don't let Brett keep you away." He handed it back to her.

Penny frowned. "Why would he?" He was there the week before when she'd gone with Kelty, days after his surgery no less. Otherwise none of this would've happened.

Tyler rubbed the back of his neck. "He's not feeling great. Understandably. He doesn't want to be a burden."

Penny nodded, not sure exactly how going to Sunday Supper with his team would be a burden. It wasn't really any of her business. "Thanks. You've all been so welcoming."

Tyler smiled and rounded the truck. "We'll have to get together once you're settled. We're headed to the Perch this weekend. I gave Brett the details, but you can text Emma, too."

Penny waved as he got in the truck and started it, then she turned and walked to the steps. So, she'd judged Tyler unfairly when she first met him. He was a nice guy who just happened to look like a bro marketer or prescription drug rep. Maybe her whole worldview was skewed toward the cynical. *Maybe she was wearing Danny-coloured glasses.*

When she looked up, Brett was standing in the doorway. "Oh. Hey. Thanks for bringing in my bag." Penny ascended the steps. Brett moved back, leaving room for her to enter, and she thought back to Saturday when she'd met him for the first time.

She took off her shoes, ignoring the way her heart picked up speed, and looked down at the bags in the entryway. Her eyes narrowed. "I don't think that's mine." Penny pointed at a black duffel with letters on the side.

"Oh, no, that's my hockey stuff." Brett shuffled past her and bent over to pick it up. "I was just at practice. Got a ride with Tyler, that's why . . ." He trailed off when he saw the look on her face. "What?"

"You were at hockey practice?" Her eyes flicked down to his

brace. That explained the damp hair and clean scent. But even if he was only standing on the ice and practicing stickhandling, the chances of him slipping or—

"I work out in the stands." He shifted his weight, and Penny met his eyes. "While the team practices, I do calisthenics on the bleachers."

Penny looked back at the bag. "And you need your equipment for that?"

He shrugged and turned, walking toward the hall. He was wearing jeans today with the brace tight around his right knee.

"I'm sorry I'm taking up so much space in your garage." Penny grabbed the handle on her bag and rolled it down the hall after him.

"It's fine, it's not like I was using it anyway."

Brett entered his room, and Penny opened the door to hers. She rolled the bag in and set it next to the wall then went back out to retrieve the rest of her belongings. As Penny shuttled her things, the day crashed into her. This was her life now.

She was hyperaware of Brett moving around outside her door, but didn't want to make anything awkward by walking out into the kitchen. It was getting late, and her eyes felt like they'd been rubbed with sandpaper. The leftover lasagna she'd had at Kelty's was making her stomach unsettled on top of it.

Penny made a mental deal with herself to unpack her bathroom items and put one suitcase of clothes away, then she was going to curl up and go to bed. She could deal with the rest of the stuff in the morning.

A knock on the door startled her, and she looked up. "Come in." Penny sat up on her knees as her pulse quickened.

Brett pushed the door open but didn't take a step past the threshold. He leaned his shoulder on the door frame and slid his hands into his pockets, which only accentuated his musculature under that damn salmon pink shirt.

"I just wanted to check if you needed anything."

"No, I'm good. Just trying to unpack."

Brett nodded, wrapped his knuckles on the wood, then turned and hobbled back out into the kitchen. Penny wanted to say something. A part of her wished he would stay and keep her company, but what would they talk about? Just like any roommate, it would take time for them to get to know each other and feel more comfortable.

She only knew that theoretically since she'd never *had* an actual roommate. Housemate. Whatever they were. From the time she left her house, she'd been in a relationship, bouncing from one guy to the next. Sure, there had been a few times when she'd crashed with a friend, but she'd never lived with a complete stranger before.

Penny threw a stack of underwear and socks in one of the top drawers of the dresser Tyler had left. How had she gotten to her early thirties without ever having a traditional roommate experience? She thought she was going to have to figure something out after Lucas died, but then Danny had come along and her whole world had shifted.

A thought occurred to her for the first time. Had she jumped in so hard and fast with Danny because of what happened to Lucas? That was kind of her MO, so it shouldn't have felt surprising.

Feeling sad?

Find a boyfriend.

Frustrated?

Boyfriend.

Unsure what to do next?

Having a boyfriend was the obvious solution.

Even if the relationships weren't ideal, being with someone was easier than admitting she didn't know what she wanted to do in her life. Being a physical therapist was great. But she'd always assumed that once she graduated, her path would be more clear.

Wasn't that how it was supposed to work? Get an education,

get a job, settle somewhere, and enjoy life? That was certainly how it had worked for two of her older siblings.

After Lucas, her parents had been less than subtle about where they thought her life should be headed. On the one hand, they'd poured out more love in the past three years than the rest of her life combined. On the other, Penny had never felt more pressure to make them proud. To prove that they weren't terrible parents because one of their children hadn't made it.

They hadn't been big fans of Danny, and she couldn't blame them. Even when they'd asked her to reconsider moving to Calgary, she was blinding herself to the red flags. All Danny talked about was himself, his practice, his goals. She could count on one hand the number of times he'd ever asked her what she wanted or what she was interested in.

He just assumed her interests were his. But she'd been more than happy to hide behind someone else's ambitions because she had none, and the pressure to make her parents proud was crushing.

What was the point? She'd done everything she could to help her brother, and it hadn't changed a damn thing. She'd been the one he called when he was high and couldn't get home at three in the morning. She'd been the one to pick him up and watch him overnight when he couldn't remember what he'd taken or how much.

She'd gone to therapy with Lucas, had talked on the phone with him for hours in the middle of the night while he sobbed into the speaker. She'd seen his face grow gaunt, his eyes shadowed. She'd watched him waste away and pick at his skin. She'd sat on pins and needles during work hours just waiting to get a call that he hadn't made it home.

When that call finally came, despite all the imagination and mental practice, she still wasn't ready for it. So when Danny had shown up at her office after a lunch meeting and asked her out, she had no hesitation. Yes, she would go to dinner. Yes, she would go dancing.

Yes, yes, yes. Anything to keep her from having to go home, from talking to her parents or seeing the look in their eyes reminding her that she had failed at her *one job*.

She'd been unofficially tasked with taking care of Lucas because she was the one he always called. It had been as simple as that. Penny loved and hated him for that. She hated how he hurt her. How she was constantly anxious. And yet, she wouldn't have wanted him to rely on anyone else.

She loved being the one he trusted, the one who was supposed to make him better. But every time he fell deeper, her own shame and disappointment in herself grew deeper roots.

Penny swiped at the tears in her eyes and gave up on emptying her suitcase. She stood, stalked to the bathroom, and splashed cold water on her face. The tears that had been close to breaking out all day were finally here, and she didn't want to face this standing up.

She hurriedly brushed her teeth, pulled her hair into a braid and was about to jump into bed when she remembered she hadn't put her sheets or comforter on yet.

She cursed under her breath, realizing she'd brought her sheets, but her quilt was still at Kelty's. They'd been cold the night before while watching a movie and had pulled it off her bed. She was *not* going to go out and ask Brett for a blanket looking like this, so she spread her sheets over the bed with trembling hands and pulled on a sweatshirt, then curled up, clutching her pillow.

At least living with Danny had taught her one thing.

She knew how to cry without making a sound.

CHAPTER
Four

AT EIGHT, the sun was already well on its journey across the sky. The summer days were longer here than in Vancouver, but not by much. She was going to have to get some blackout curtains for this room. That or a sleep mask, which was probably easier than putting holes in Brett's wall.

Penny rolled to her side and stretched, then listened for any sound outside of her bedroom door. When she heard nothing, she crept from the bed, went to the bathroom, and rinsed her mouth out with water.

When she walked back into her room, her phone screen lit up. A message from Danny. Penny's heart leaped into her throat as her thoughts fragmented. Why was he texting? Did he regret how he'd treated her? Was he going to digitally cuss her out for leaving?

She swiped up and started to read.

> Having trouble finding the blue foam roller. Any thoughts? Tim thinks you were the last to use it

Penny re-read the message twice, her heart sinking like a stone. *No, she didn't know where the damn foam roller was.* What a narcissistic prick. She clicked off the screen, and her stomach grumbled as she strode to the door.

Fantastic. She'd forgotten to think about groceries in all the hubbub the night before, which meant she was going to have to brave the store this early in the morning or find breakfast somewhere to tide her over.

The version that did not include both shopping and cooking sounded like the more pleasant option, given her current bleary vision and mildly murderous thoughts. Kelty had helped drop her car off yesterday afternoon before Tyler came to pick up her things. It had seemed so smart at the time since Kelty had to stop at the bank just down the street. If she'd been thinking though, she would've driven separately and hit the grocery store on the way over.

No point rehashing it now. It wasn't the end of the world. All she had to do was sneak out the front door without waking Brett up. Simple enough. She grabbed her keys off the dresser and tiptoed down the hall. Penny stopped in the kitchen to get a glass of water and nearly slammed into the counter when she heard rustling behind her.

She dropped her phone, and it clattered onto the wood floor. Thinking she could somehow reverse the noise that had already echoed through the apartment if she moved fast enough, she bent down and picked it up. Thankfully she hadn't been already holding a glass. When she stood, she saw Brett shooting up on the couch. Shirtless.

He winced and fell back against the armrest, the blanket he'd slept with puddling at his waist. "I'm sorry. I didn't mean to scare you."

Penny's heart jumped into her throat at the sight of his bare torso. He was thick. Sturdy. Not cut like one of those guys that counted their macros, which was actually more attractive in Penny's books. She'd gotten enough of that self-obsession with Danny, and it wasn't like his muscle was useful for more than entertaining himself in the mirror. When she caught herself wondering how Brett's weight would feel on top of her, she shook her head and gripped the edge of the counter.

No. She scolded herself like a toddler or disobedient dog. Penny was onto herself. She was feeling vulnerable and stressed, and she was not going to do what she always did. She was not going to seek validation and purpose in someone's arms. She was going to figure this out on her own for once.

Brett dropped an arm over his face, and Penny pressed back into the corner, trying to hide in the shadows since her eyes were puffy and she probably looked like she'd had an allergic reaction to shellfish.

"It's fine. I was just getting a drink of water and thought you were still in bed. I didn't want to wake you."

Brett rubbed his eyes. With his hair mussed around his face, he looked like a rock star who'd woken up confused to find the hot model he'd spent the night with wasn't next to him. "Do you always get up this early?"

Absolutely not. "Do you always sleep on the couch?"

"It's a recent development." Brett dropped his arm, and Penny noticed his right leg was propped up on the armrest. She leaned forward to try and parse out the tattoo on the underside of his bicep now that it was on full display.

"Knee bothering you?"

Brett exhaled. "It's not bad."

It was bad if he was opting to sleep on a couch that was approximately two feet too short for his tall frame. Penny didn't want to continue the conversation since it would likely require her to make eye contact, but she couldn't help herself. "Taking an NSAID before bed would help with that."

"I don't take pain killers." Brett sat up, which only made his pecs look larger. He straightened the chain on his neck. *Have mercy.*

Penny turned back to the cupboard and pulled out a glass since her mouth now felt like it had been held up to a blow dryer. *Right.* Brett hadn't taken anything after surgery, which was borderline insanity, but he was a hockey player. He was probably convinced real men didn't need meds. That his testosterone and machismo could pull him through. Well, that and her physical therapy, of course.

Penny gulped water from the tap, then set her glass in the dishwasher and made her way to the door. *Don't look at him. Don't—*

"Where are you going?"

"To get breakfast and go grocery shopping," she answered too quickly.

Fabric rustled behind her. "You don't need to do that at the crack of dawn. I doubt Timmie's is even open yet, and I have plenty of stuff here."

"I don't expect you to—" Penny started, but Brett cut her off.

"No, let me make you something. You can go shopping later."

Make you something? Penny froze with her hand on the door. She didn't want to be rude, but the last thing she wanted was for Brett to feel that he'd accepted a charity case.

"It's fine, I'll—"

"Stop. I'm making myself breakfast anyway. It's no big deal."

Penny stood, conflicted. On the one hand, she did not relish sitting in a parking lot waiting for a restaurant or grocery store to open. On the other, the idea of turning around and letting Brett see the bags under her eyes made her squirm.

With each of her boyfriends, she'd woken up and gotten ready before they did so they'd never had to witness her morning breath or her less than perfected face. Danny had always slipped out of bed and gone on a run, which had given her ample time to make herself presentable.

But Brett wasn't a boyfriend. He wasn't even a friend. So why did it matter if he saw her looking terrible? It was probably best she ripped off the Band-Aid early. Plus, if he was going to make eggs shirtless, who was she to say no to that?

She turned just in time to see him pull a black T-shirt over his head. Damn. He grimaced as he pushed himself to his feet, then reached for a crutch standing against the wall.

"Why didn't you use that last night?" Penny asked.

"It's always worse in the morning. By mid-afternoon I can usually put pressure on it."

Penny nodded. Most patients were highly motivated to stop using a crutch when their armpits got chafed and sore. "You really don't have to do this."

Brett set his crutch against the counter and reached into the fridge. He pulled out a carton of eggs and a container of spinach. "I made Tyler shakes all the time. I always have extra."

Penny made a face. "You use eggs in your shake?"

Brett laughed. "No, those are separate."

She sat on the stool, twisting her key ring and trying not to think about what Brett would think when he turned around and saw her swollen face. "You like protein."

Brett turned and set the eggs on the counter. The fridge door closed behind him as he met her eyes. Something flickered in his expression before one side of his mouth pulled into a grin. "Gotta fuel all of this somehow."

Penny smiled and rolled her eyes. "So tell me about yourself, Brett." She folded her arms and leaned over the counter.

"You already know everything there is to know."

Penny snorted. "All I know is that you play hockey, you're friends with Kelty and Sean, and you tore your ACL."

"Exactly. That's me in a nutshell."

Penny ignored the comment. If he was avoiding talking about himself, she was too adept at hiding her own personal details to let someone else get away with it. "Does your family live close?"

"My parents have a house in the Northeast, and they travel overseas quite a bit. My mom's a business consultant. She started a company fifteen years ago and has been really successful. Now she gets hired by corporations to troubleshoot their operations."

It took Penny a moment to respond to that. It wasn't often

she heard about women in positions of power like that. "And your dad?"

"He quit his job about two years into that business and has worked for her ever since." Brett turned to pull a banana from the counter and grinned at the expression on her face. "I know. I'm intimidated too."

Penny breathed a laugh. "That's amazing."

"They're incredible people." Brett peeled the banana and threw it in the blender along with a handful of spinach and two scoops of protein powder from the container on the counter.

"Siblings?" Penny asked.

"One. My sister. She's getting her master's in psychology at U of A."

Penny exhaled. "So what are you, a rocket scientist?"

Brett laughed out loud. "Alas, I'm but a lowly contractor."

Her cheeks warmed, and she was grateful for the sound of crunching ice from the dispenser, then the whir of the blender motor when Brett turned it on. This wasn't fair. Brett was funny and attractive and in the same house as her while she was supposed to be standing solidly on her own two feet for the first time in her life? It was like this was some kind of cosmic joke. *You think you want to be single for once? Well how about now . . .*

Brett turned off the blender, and Penny cleared her throat. "What kind of contractor are you?"

"Commercial builds. Apartment complexes, hotels, office spaces. It varies by project." He poured the shake into two cups and handed her one.

"Do you have a straw?" she asked. He raised an eyebrow as if to say, *Oh, you're a princess?* Penny scoffed. "What? I have sensitive teeth!"

Brett turned and reached into a drawer behind him, then handed her a stainless steel straw. "Sorry, that's probably going to hurt your teeth, too. I don't have any plastic ones."

Penny waved him off. She wouldn't complain about him

trying to save the environment. "This will be perfect. Thank you so much for breakfast."

Brett opened the carton of eggs. "Scrambled or over easy?"

Penny shrugged and took her first drink. It was chocolatey and good. "However you like them is fine. Do you want me to make the eggs, though?" She hated sitting there while he waited on her hand and foot. Especially since he only had one foot to work with.

Brett shook his head and reached into a cupboard under the counter to pull out a pan, exposing a strip of his lower back. "I don't mind."

Penny forced her eyes back to her shake. "Yeah, but I feel bad sitting here while you do all the work."

He stood and shot her a glance. "You can do the dishes."

Penny laughed. "I don't know if that's a fair trade."

He set the pan on the stove and reached for the olive oil and salt and pepper next to the fridge. This kitchen was outfitted, which meant either Tyler was a cook and he left everything here when he moved or Brett was more cultured than he looked at first glance.

Brett grinned as he tipped the oil into the pan. "Hey, you're the one who said you felt bad."

"Fair enough. I'd be happy to." Penny watched him while he cooked. He heated the pan and cracked four eggs, then tossed the shells in the trash bin under the sink. "Do you work from home?" she asked when he leaned back against the counter.

"Right now, yes, for the most part." Brett motioned to his knee.

"Do you prefer that?"

"Honestly, it's gotten a little old. I'm usually on-site for at least half the week."

Penny nodded. She understood that. When she was seeing patients, those moments alone felt like gifts instead of perpetual servitude. It was tedious living in her own head twenty-four seven without any distractions.

Brett exhaled. "Hopefully won't last for too much longer, though." He shot her a knowing glance.

"If you're hoping I'm a miracle worker, I'm going to be a huge disappointment."

Brett coughed. "I don't think that's possible." He turned and splashed a little water in the pan, then set it back on the stove and topped it with the lid. Penny's insides warmed. What had he meant by that? Was she already exceeding any expectations he'd had for a housemate?

He turned and braced himself on the counter, and she suddenly wished she'd done something to smooth the hair that was half pulled out of her braid.

"What kind of job are you looking for?" Brett asked.

"Something that pays the bills."

"You don't really have bills at the moment."

Penny laughed. "You know my finances now?" The corners of Brett's mouth twitched. "I only have free rent for the next few months, so I better take advantage right?"

Light streamed in through the window behind her, making Brett's blue eyes sparkle. "Fair. If you could have your ideal job, then what would it be?"

Penny considered his question as she sipped on her shake. "Probably signing on with a team, being on salary, getting to travel while building long-term relationships."

"You don't build relationships with your clients?"

"I do, but they're usually short-lived. I help them through something, and then they move on. With a team, it seems like you become more a part of the family, so to speak."

Brett's expression sobered. "Is your family from here?"

"No." Penny shook her head. "I'm from Vancouver."

Brett nodded. The way he was leaning toward her made his shoulder muscles squeeze under his shirt. "Siblings?"

Penny took another long drink. She never knew how to answer this question. If she said six, then inevitably the topic of

Lucas would come up. If she said five, she'd feel sick to her stomach. "Six. Three brothers and two sisters."

Brett's eyes widened. "Where are you in the mix?"

"Second to youngest." Penny licked a drip of shake off her lower lip. "One younger sister and then the rest are older."

Brett nodded and turned back to the eggs. Satisfied that they were finished, he removed the pan from the stove and took two plates out of the cupboard.

Penny's ribs felt like they were shrinking against her lungs by the time he passed her a plate. "If you don't mind, I think I'm going to take this to my room. Get started on some applications."

Disappointment flashed briefly in his eyes, but he nodded and smiled. "Of course. I've got to get ready for work anyway."

"Thank you so much for breakfast. I'll replace the groceries."

"No need."

Penny stood and rounded the counter to grab the pan and blender, but Brett stood, blocking her path. She backed up a step. "I was just going to wash—"

"I was kidding about doing the dishes. Just go do what you need to do."

"But I want to—"

"There will be plenty of dishes to do, I promise." He smiled, and there was that sadness again sitting right behind his eyes. "You barely moved in. I've got this."

Penny should have fought him on it. She should've insisted he let her help. But that might have been the first time in years that someone had offered to do something for her without expecting anything in return, and it felt so uncomfortable, she was momentarily stunned. So, to avoid standing there gaping at him, she nodded once, then grabbed her eggs and protein shake and retreated to her room.

She couldn't concentrate at first, so she focused on eating. The eggs were perfectly cooked, which didn't help with the current *Brett's sitting out there in the kitchen and what the hell does he have tattooed on his arm?* situation, but as soon as the sound of dishes in the kitchen settled down, her heart rate returned to normal. She finished her food and started searching the job boards.

She had a collection of listings already from the few days she'd been at Kelty's, but a few more had popped up over the weekend. One looked particularly promising. A chiropractic office that was looking to expand its services by offering PT.

Penny was about to buckle down and submit applications when she realized she needed to update her résumé which was currently outdated. She popped open the file and started to adjust her work dates, tamping down the anxiety that came with listing her office as a past employer. Not her office. *Danny's office.*

And that's when she saw the email come through.

With Danny's name as the sender.

CHAPTER
Five

BRETT SAT at the dining room table, the first of three makeshift workspaces he'd made since he'd been forced to work from home. When he purchased this apartment, he hadn't even thought about needing an office space. Not that he planned on his current situation being permanent. Both the apartment and the remote work.

His teams and contractors were doing good work, but he hated not having his eyes on the sites and troubleshooting in-person with clients. He'd never been good at digital communication, though this was forcing him to improve at it.

It was slow going. He'd been staring at a blank email for the past three minutes. Even though writing down his thoughts wasn't his forte, it didn't normally take him this long to figure out what he needed to say to a client. This morning he was more than a little distracted.

Brett glanced up at the closed door in the hall. Penny had walked into her room after breakfast, and he hadn't seen her for a couple of hours. Why couldn't he stop thinking about what she was doing in there? Unpacking? Sitting on the bed working on her laptop with her legs crossed and her hair draping over her shoulders?

He ran a hand over his face. He couldn't visualize the words that needed to appear on his screen, but he had no problem visualizing her. *Was she crying?* The thought clenched around his stomach. He wasn't the most observant person in the world, but since he knew she hadn't gone out drinking the night before, that was the only explanation for her red-rimmed eyes that morning. They weren't bloodshot like she'd smoked a joint or something, they were puffy and raw. Exactly like he remembered his sister Cameron's had looked more or less every day of grade ten.

Seeing anyone in pain wasn't fun, but seeing it directly in front of you first thing in the morning was more poignant. Was Penny upset about moving in? Had something happened last night and she needed help? *Had he done something to upset her?*

He didn't see how that last one would be possible since they'd barely strung a few sentences together last night before she'd disappeared to unpack. He'd asked if she needed help. Could that have set her off?

Brett forced his fingers to the keys and typed. *Hey.* Too informal. *Good morning.* Better. Penny obviously had plenty of family, though if they were in Vancouver and she was here, maybe their relationships were strained at the moment. Even if that was true, she and Kelty were on good terms. Kelty and Sean were only an eight-minute drive away.

But something niggled at him. Something about the way Penny talked. It wasn't tangible, but more like an underlying belief. Like she had zero expectations from the people in her life.

Some people talked about their struggles like they knew they had a safety net. They had people that understood them, that they could call at any second if they got desperate. Brett didn't think most of his friends recognized it, but since he had to exist in the world after burning those bridges, he knew what it felt like to be isolated. Even if he'd never been truly alone, he'd been convinced he was too many times to count.

He'd worked the past three years to build himself into a person who could hold relationships and not just abuse them.

Thankfully, he had his people now. People who understood him, even if they didn't all live close. People he could count on, even if they didn't fully get him to his core.

He could pick out any sad soul who believed they were an island from a mile away. Penny seemed to believe she was Cape Breton through and through. But that wasn't something you brought up with a woman you'd barely met a week ago and only talked to a handful of times. At least his communication skills had come that far. So he'd made her breakfast. That was a start. It was the first time he'd felt useful in weeks.

The door to Penny's room cracked open and Brett's fingers jolted into action. He'd only managed to type a single sentence of pure nonsense when Penny brought her dishes to the sink, rinsed them, and loaded them into the dishwasher.

"I'm going to head to the store. Anything I can get for you?" Her jaw was tight as she opened the fridge and peeked in. "It doesn't look like you have much in here."

Okay, ouch. Brett turned in his chair. "Don't need much for myself."

Penny ignored the self deprecation. "I wanted to ask you how this would best work for you. Do you want me to take a few dinners throughout the week, assign a few days? I could prep lunches or . . ." Penny opened the freezer.

Brett wanted to stand and walk closer for this conversation, but his knee was already complaining from the activity that morning. Which meant he likely needed more activity, not less. PT, whenever they started, was going to be brutal.

"Yeah, I think that would be great," he answered. Penny slammed the freezer closed, and Brett frowned. That was a bit aggressive. "I'm not a terrible cook. Why don't you take Monday, Wednesday, Friday, and I'll take—"

"No, I'll take four days. You can have three." Penny spun and planted her hands on the counter. Her eyes flashed. "My mom is from Greece, and she forced me to learn how to cook before I went to kindergarten."

Was this a competition? He had no clue what he was competing for, but he jumped in anyway. "Well I learned to cook an egg in preschool."

Penny's lip twitched.

"Your family's from Greece? Have you ever been?"

Penny nodded, her shoulders still tensed and lifted next to her ears. "We're actually planning a trip this summer."

"Oh, yeah?" He swiveled further in his chair. She didn't respond to the preschool comment which meant he definitely won that round. *Was he really throwing down his mitts over cooking age?* He needed to slam something against the boards and get it out of his system.

"For my parents' fortieth anniversary."

Brett whistled. "Forty years. Impressive."

"Glad my family can intimidate you, too." Penny pushed back and reached for her keys on the other side of the island where she'd left them earlier. "How long have your parents been married?"

He shrugged. "I honestly have no idea."

Penny spun and opened a cupboard, closed it with more force than was necessary, then moved on to the next.

"Are you alright?" Brett asked. Although he was sure his kitchen could handle the mild abuse, it didn't seem like normal behavior for her. But who knew? He'd only spent a few hours in her company.

"Fine. Just getting the lay of the land. Why?"

"I don't know, maybe because you're shaking the cupboards down like they stole something."

Penny's cheeks coloured as she walked to the door to slip her shoes on. Brett didn't know whether to pretend to be working and let it go or wait.

"What?" Penny held out her hands, and for a second, she looked like a defensive teenager. *That was it.* Something pained behind her fierce expression. He'd always been able to read people, which hadn't always been to his benefit. It made friendships easy to come by, but the burdens were heavy to carry.

Brett exhaled and stared out the bay window. "Looks a little windy out there today."

Penny scoffed. "Can you say that in good conscience?"

Brett eyed her curiously. She was picking a fight. He knew that feeling, too. Where you were so fired up you had to beat something to get it out of you. He had no problem being a sparring partner. "What do you mean by that?"

"I'm just saying. When the wind in this province gets to hurricane levels, I don't think this can be labeled windy."

"Says the woman who moved here when?"

Penny's gaze sharpened. "Two years ago."

"Hardly counts."

Penny blew out a breath and adjusted her shirt over the waistline of her pants. The wide-legged jeans looked comfortable, hitting her perfectly at the waist and flaring over her hips. Brett's skin warmed, and he looked down at his screen.

"I'm sorry. I got an email a few minutes ago, and it wasn't great."

Brett was curious, but he held back. If she was ready to talk about it, she would. "I'm sorry," he said instead of asking another question. "Hopefully grocery shopping will take your mind off it."

Penny's expression softened. "Is that what grocery shopping is supposed to be? Cathartic?"

"I used to think so." Brett finally found the words he needed for his email and hammered them out before they left his brain. When he finished the few short sentences, he saved the message to drafts. He'd gotten in the habit of giving himself a half hour or so before sending just in case he missed something. When he looked up, Penny was still watching him with her brows pinched together.

"Used to?"

Brett leaned back in his chair. "I haven't been to a grocery store in a few weeks, for obvious reasons. I've been getting my food delivered."

Penny nodded and twisted the key ring in her hand. She'd done that earlier when she was sitting at the stool. He'd noticed then that her fingers were slender, and she had nails that were painted a pale beige. He liked them. Not too long. Simple. The color looked good against her olive skin. He wondered what they'd look like against his.

Brett coughed and reached for his water bottle. "Good luck." He took a sip and was about to set the bottle back on the table when Penny spoke up.

"Do you want to come?"

Brett hesitated, then set the water down. "To the grocery store?"

"No, on this road trip I was thinking of taking. Thought I'd leave right now."

Brett quirked an eyebrow. "Ah. You're a smartass."

Penny grinned, all the frustration seeming to seep out of her for a moment.

Brett's insides fizzed as he closed his laptop. "Yeah. It would be good to get out of the house."

"You're okay taking a break right now? I can wait if—"

"No, now's fine."

Brett pushed up from the table and grabbed his crutch then hobbled to the front door. He positioned himself to reach for his shoes, which he would then have to take back to the table to sit and put on, but Penny stopped him.

"Here, I can help you." She crouched down and pulled his shoes in front of his feet then wrapped her hand under his right foot and guided it toward the shoe. Electricity shot up from his ankle where the tips of her fingers with those beige nails grazed the sensitive skin.

"Penny, you don't have to—"

"Don't be stubborn. This will be faster, and I'm not a patient person."

Thankfully, his shoes were slip-ons, so she didn't have to work at it. Though now he was wishing they were high-tops.

Once the shoe was on, he stepped tenderly on his right leg, gritting his teeth as he lifted his left and gripped onto the crutch for balance.

"There." Penny pushed up and stood in front of him. "Was that so bad?"

Brett pursed his lips. "I don't like feeling like an invalid."

"Well, you are one for the time being, so you should probably get used to it."

"Harsh."

"But true. C'mon, haven't you ever helped anyone else when they were injured?"

Brett thought back to the time Country dislocated his shoulder. How he needed help putting his pads and jersey on for at least a few weeks when he still insisted on practicing, the stubborn bastard. Then there was the time that Curtis broke two of his fingers and his thumb.

Brett had taped him up more than once before a game. Again, because he wouldn't miss it even when his hand was swollen to the size of a bee's nest.

"I'll take that as a yes." Penny reached for the handle and pulled the door open. "By the way, I think we should probably do our first PT session soon. I don't like how stiff you're looking."

"Here I thought you were only paying attention to my leg." Brett snapped his mouth shut as he raced to form an apology before Penny burst out laughing.

"What the hell, Brett! Is that how you talk to all your roommates?"

His face had to be the color of a tomato by how hot his cheeks were. "Actually, yes." That was, in fact, the problem. That was exactly what he would've said to Tyler. "I'm sorry. I'm not used to being around pretty—" He caught himself again. Maybe not the only problem. He needed to reign in his tongue, which was turning out to be impossible around this girl. And now he was thinking about his tongue . . . What the hell *was* his problem?!

Penny's cheeks turned pink. "I don't know, Tyler's one of the prettiest boys I've seen in a long time."

Brett snorted and used his crutch to navigate the stairs, then followed Penny to her car. He owed her one for that save. *Nothing stiff. No tongues.* He worked to envision pictures from his surgery. Hairy men. Phil Kessel's face. Anything to get his blood to drop back from Formula 1.

So she knew he thought she was pretty. At least that was the word that came out of his mouth. Gorgeous was more like it. She had to already be aware. A woman didn't get to her mid-thirties without understanding a basic fact like that. And hey, at least she wasn't rage slamming fridges and cupboards anymore.

Brett slid into the passenger seat but kept his right leg dangling on the curb as he tried to figure out how to bring it in without forcing his knee to bend in ways it wasn't ready to.

"That seat should push back a ways." Penny motioned to the side.

Brett felt along the edge of the seat until he found the handle then pushed his seat back as far as it would go. It allowed him to make enough space to slide his leg in with only minimal discomfort. Was it bad that his first thought was that Penny couldn't be dating anyone since no guy would have sat here with the seat pushed so far forward?

He mentally berated himself. He did *not* need to be having thoughts like that right now, though he shouldn't have been surprised by any of this. It wasn't that a relationship was the worst idea for him at the moment, it was just . . . that it was a really effing bad idea.

He wanted to believe that at some point he would be in a better place—ready to date again—but he'd been telling himself that for the past two-plus years and hadn't gotten there yet. Tony kept telling him he was going to have to jump in at some point, but Brett still didn't trust it. There was always something that cropped up in his life that made him feel off-kilter. Didn't he need to be more stable before he could make a commitment to someone else?

He'd messed up with enough people in his life, and he didn't want to add more to the list. He and Cameron were barely repairing all the damage he'd done. His parents were veritable saints and had stuck with him through it all, but he had plenty to make up on that front, too.

He needed to be someone others could rely on, and right now he couldn't even make it up or down the front steps. Hell, he couldn't even put on his own shoes.

"Why did you decide to stay in Calgary?" Brett asked as they drove.

"Wow, okay, we're just getting right into it then."

Brett frowned. "How is that getting into it? Seems like a benign question."

Penny tightened her grip on the wheel. "Yeah, well, maybe for some people."

"You don't have to answer it, I was just trying to make conversation."

Penny sighed and ran her hands through her hair at the stoplight. It hung in loose waves over her shoulders. She pulled it together and twirled it before letting it fall down her back. Brett forced his eyes back out the windshield and focused on the license plate in front of them, then bit the inside of his cheek. HOT-869. *Thank you, Calgary.*

"I stayed because my parents didn't want me to move here in the first place, and I didn't want to admit that they were right. Is that a good enough answer?"

Definitely a strained relationship then. "Why didn't they want you to move here?"

"Because they didn't like the guy that I was with."

Brett's jaw tensed. "Did you like the guy you were with?"

"Obviously, otherwise I wouldn't have followed him here."

Brett shifted in his seat, trying to give his right leg a diagonal line under the glove compartment. "So you followed a guy here, it didn't work out, and now you're embarrassed to go back."

"That pretty much hits the nail on the head."

"Nice contractor metaphor."

Penny laughed. "I like to customize my speech to the interests of the people I'm spending time with."

"It's a very marketable skill."

She glanced over. "Is it making you feel more comfortable?"

Not in the least. Her snarky retorts were jacking his heart rate, not settling it. He loved that she told him the truth, which should have put him at ease, but it was difficult to relax when he could still see that soft color on her nails in his peripheral vision. "Yup."

Penny exhaled. "Is your work going well? Considering you have to be at home?" She turned onto Country Hills Boulevard.

"Going well might be an exaggeration. It's *going*."

"Well, that's something."

Brett rested his arm on the console. Penny was out of a job, so he couldn't complain. "It's something. I have good teams, and we've been getting plenty of bids, which isn't always a given. There are just some things that go smoother when the boss is around."

"So you're the boss?"

His pupils dilated at that phrase coming out of her mouth. "What do you think a general contractor is?"

"See, you didn't tell me that you were a *general* contractor. You only said 'contractor.'"

"And you know the difference between the two?" Shit. If she knew construction speak, he was in serious trouble. Hopefully she knew nothing about hockey.

"Absolutely. My dad does custom woodworking. He's planning to retire in the next couple of years."

Brett nodded, impressed. "That kind of work takes a toll on your body, for sure."

"Where did you start?" Penny asked

"I did construction, framing, drywalling, electrical."

"A jack of all trades."

Brett chuckled. "Not really. Good enough to get by. Then I went and got my MBA."

"Of course you did."

Brett turned to face her. "What is that supposed to mean?"

"Do contractors normally get an MBA?"

"If they want to run their own company, they do."

Penny sighed. "It's perfectly in line with what you told me about your family. You're ambitious."

"More like I didn't want to haul pipes or boards for the rest of my life," he commented. Penny pulled into the parking lot and took a spot marked staff only. "I don't think you can park here. You don't have a sticker."

She spun in her seat and tucked her hair behind her ear. "Do you really think someone will call me on it?" She motioned around the mostly empty lot.

"It feels like you have no experience with the RCMP."

Penny groaned. "Fine. I'll drop you at the front and then go park."

"I can just—"

"No way, I'm not going to make you walk all the way across the parking lot."

Brett motioned to the free spots. "Were you planning to park at the back? Need to get some steps in?"

"Ha. Hilarious coming from you." Penny was already heading toward the front. "Just get out, I'll be there in a second."

"Are we shopping together then? Having a little roommate grocery date?" As soon as the words left his lips and Penny's face shifted, Brett regretted it.

"No. Of course not." She stopped in front of the doors. "Just go get what you need and I'll meet you back at the front when you're done."

Brett opened his mouth to say something, but didn't know

how to respond to that. He hadn't meant to insinuate anything, but he'd obviously gotten too comfortable. He nodded once and got out, debating whether to grab his crutch from the back. He opted to take it since he'd forgotten to do any stretching on the drive.

He took his time walking inside, half hoping that Penny would catch up with him. She didn't, so he started through the produce section.

He couldn't control much in his life right now but he could control what he put in his body. Ever since he got sober, he'd admittedly been a bit obsessed with health. Ironic considering he'd spent so many years destroying his. *But that was an intrusive thought that didn't serve him.*

He could almost hear Tony in his head reminding him how capable bodies were of repairing themselves once you gave them the right fuel. Every time he heard Tony cough, he wondered how much he believed it.

This too would pass one step at a time, one day at a time. He began to rehearse his timeline as he bagged his fruits and vegetables. He would start his physical therapy. In a few weeks, after some hard work, his knee would become more flexible and he'd be able to walk and drive. Then he'd continue to work through that and be able to exercise again. Maybe even do a little stability work.

A few weeks after that, he'd feel mostly back to normal and be back on the jobsite full-time. A few more weeks and he'd be back on the ice. That was all he needed. He didn't even need to play in a game, he just needed to lace up and get out there with the guys at practice.

Then he could work on stabilizing everything else so he could *think* about working on his personal relationships. That was the order it had to happen because any other time he tried to mix and match he'd ended up slipping.

Which was fine when it was only himself. He knew how to drag himself back up out of the dirt. But women tended not to forget a thing like that, especially at this age. At twenty, maybe they had energy to forgive and deal with that crap, but at thirty plus, that trust was hard to build. There were too many guys like him who never recovered or never even tried to. He couldn't expect anyone to trust that somehow he'd be different. It wasn't pessimistic, just reality.

He laid his crutch in the cart and pushed it back through the aisles, picking up stuff for sandwiches and everything he needed to make tacos over the weekend. That had become more than a tradition at this point. Tacos on Sunday, leftovers the rest of the week. Part of the routine that worked for him.

"These tortillas are better."

Brett looked up to find Penny standing next to him. She held up a package.

"You're a tortilla expert as well as a physical therapist? I don't know why you're intimidated by my family."

Penny dropped them in her cart.

"I thought we were taking turns making dinner."

Penny pulled a bag of pita bread from the shelf. "We are."

Brett followed her down the aisle. "I'm already making tacos so you don't need those."

"What if I want to get my own tortillas?"

"Then that would be offensive because I already planned the meal."

"What other meals are you planning?"

"Haven't gotten that far yet." If it were just him, he would've settled on eggs and toast or a burger. Now that didn't seem quite good enough.

"I was going to do falafel—"

"Gesundheit."

Penny shot him a look. "If you tell me you've never had falafel—"

"I've had falafel. I've just never made it before."

Penny scooted down the next aisle and Brett followed. "It's easy. Just garbanzo beans and garlic."

"You lost me at garbanzo beans. Sounds like that guy from Sesame Street."

Penny laughed out loud. "Guy? You mean puppet?"

Brett feigned offense. "How dare you! They were real to me."

Penny pulled two cans of garbanzo beans off the shelf with a grin. "Falafel one night. Roasted chicken and vegetables, then maybe risotto on night three?"

"Damn, Penny, you keep stealing all my ideas."

She frowned. "You were going to make risotto?"

Brett laughed at the consternation on her face. "No, I wasn't going to make risotto. Who makes risotto?"

Penny threw up her hands. "You said you could cook!"

"No, I said I wasn't a *bad* cook. I can make pasta and tacos."

"Well, we're going to have to expand your repertoire then."

Brett shuffled along the main aisle next to her. "I'll make a red sauce on Wednesday—"

"Say bolognese. It sounds fancier."

"Do we need our food to sound fancy?"

Penny glanced up, and Brett's words echoed back to him. *We. Our.* "I didn't mean to make it sound like . . . I know we're just—"

"Housemates," Penny finished for him.

"Exactly."

They walked in silence for a moment. "Housemates can be 'we,' I think."

Brett exhaled. *Great.* He was overthinking this. Hypersensitive. Why was he overanalyzing? Probably because he had no idea what was going on inside her head. Not that it mattered. And yet he found himself thinking about it constantly.

He hadn't imagined her tensing up when he said the word "date" in the car, and he was dying to ask her why she had looked so upset this morning. He was dying to ask her about that email, about her ex. He wanted to know not just the details, but how she felt about it. *How she felt about everything.*

"Alright, is that it?" Penny appraised the items in her cart.

Brett's knuckles were turning white over the cart handle. "I just need to grab some ground beef and milk."

"Any particular kind?"

"Cow."

Penny's mouth turned up. "I meant the percentage of the milk."

"Two percent," Brett answered without hesitation. She balked. "Anything less than that is just tinted water."

Penny rolled her eyes. "That felt judgy, but I'll get the milk, you get the beef. Meet you at the front."

Brett nodded and tried not to stare at her backside as she walked away. He wasn't successful, and that's when he knew this was bad. He wanted her. Nevermind they barely knew each other and she happened to be sleeping in the room two feet from his. Even if it did take him twice as long to walk at the moment, that wasn't far enough.

Penny was adorable. She made him laugh. And if she kept wearing her hair down like that, one of these days he wasn't going to be able to keep his fingers out of it.

Penny was his housemate. She was going to be his physical therapist. And he was the lowest he'd been in two years.

He couldn't tangle his hands in her hair, in her life, in anything. No matter how badly he wanted to. Not yet, anyway. Maybe, if he could hold it together and heal, he could see where he was at the end of the summer.

He mentally added that to his timeline.

A few weeks until he could walk and drive normally.

A few weeks until he could properly work out.

A few weeks until he was back on the ice.

A few weeks until he could sort himself out and make a move on Penny.

CHAPTER
Six

PENNY SETTLED back into her room after unloading her groceries and saying an awkward goodbye to Brett. Their trip to the grocery store had been more than entertaining, and she didn't know how to feel about the fact that she wanted to pick up her computer and go out to work next to him at the table. Would that be appropriate? Probably not helpful for her productivity since she was still thinking about him even after the door was shut.

She hadn't meant to be a jerk when she walked out into the kitchen that morning and was grateful Brett hadn't held it against her. Penny opened her email and skimmed the words of the message again. It had Danny's name listed at the bottom, but she could have sworn his office manager Sheryl had written it. It was too kind. Too genial. Danny was a lot of things but diplomatic wasn't one of them.

Sheryl on the other hand was the one person Penny had been devastated to leave. She'd assumed that after years of working together they'd maintain their friendship even after she left the office, but she'd texted her a few times with zero response. She shouldn't have been surprised.

Danny was like that. Controlling and all-consuming, not

just with his girlfriend but with his staff. No doubt he'd tried to poison Sheryl against her or at least given specific instructions not to communicate with her. Even though she knew the power he wielded, it still stung that Sheryl would listen to him.

She focused on the last paragraph.

We hope you'll feel comfortable using us as a reference in your continued job search.

The last thing she wanted to do was list Danny's practice on her resume, but what choice did she have? The only other workplace she could include was back in BC and wasn't nearly as compelling in the industry. Plus, if that was all she listed, employers would definitely wonder what she'd been doing for the last two years. They'd probably assume she'd gotten pregnant or something.

Offices weren't allowed to discriminate, but everyone knew that women found it difficult enough to land a competitive job. The last thing she needed was a glaring red flag saying, "Hey I might be unreliable because of my uterus."

Penny flicked back to her resume and began to adjust the dates. She could put the office number that would go directly to Sheryl and not even mention Danny. Even though Sheryl wasn't responding to her personal messages, she would speak kindly of her if someone called to check, wouldn't she? Besides, who actually called references these days anyway? Did they always jump through those hoops?

Penny's mind drifted as she formatted. She and Brett had agreed to start physical therapy that night after dinner, which she was making since it was Tuesday. They'd grabbed lunch on the way home from the grocery store, so she wasn't planning on doing anything until about six o'clock.

Since Brett wasn't willing to take pain medication, she hoped that timing would work for him too. He was going to be in a lot of pain, but if he hopped into a hot bath and iced, hopefully the shock of working his knee would exhaust him to the point that he could sleep even if he ended up staying on the couch to prop his leg up again.

Penny mentally constructed their session. It would have to be basic since he hadn't done much work and his surgery was only a week and a half ago, but she wasn't going to go easy on him. Brett was motivated to improve, and she wasn't ever the one to hold a patient back.

This was good. Think about Brett as a patient. This was professional and nothing more.

Penny almost laughed out loud at herself. She could barely look at Brett without her ovaries twitching. But maybe that was also a blessing in disguise. Maybe what she needed was to be faced with temptation and still make the choice. She *would* figure out how to do what was best for her. Well first, she'd figure out how to *diagnose* what was best for her.

That was the end point most out of reach. It had always seemed so much easier to go along with everyone else. So much more peaceful when people liked her, when they thought she was pleasing.

But she was the one who always ended up with herself in the end, and there was nothing *pleasing* about sitting in this room with not one line on her life CV that looked the least bit impressive. By the time she went back to Vancouver, she had to have at least something to hang her hat on.

Penny worked through the afternoon submitting resumes and filling out application forms online. Only two jobs required a cover letter, and one of them was the job she was most excited about. A medical center focused on physical therapy and chiropractic, very similar to Danny's office but a few years ahead of him.

She was passionate about her work. She loved treating patients, and more than that, she loved building the business and finding ways to bring people that needed their services through the front doors. That had been a surprise to her and possibly one of the reasons why she'd stuck around longer than necessary. Hopefully she could find a new opportunity that checked all the boxes.

At a quarter to six she closed her laptop and walked out into the kitchen. Penny felt a pang of disappointment when Brett wasn't there sitting at the table. His laptop was gone, too.

She listened for the sound of water or any movement behind his closed bedroom door but didn't hear anything. Would he have gone out? Crutched his way to the gym? If he was stupid enough to do that before a PT session, she wouldn't feel the least bit bad about his discomfort later.

As she opened the fridge and started to pull out the ingredients she needed for a salad and tzatziki sauce to go with the falafel, the front door opened with a squeak. Penny turned and saw Brett hobble in holding the mail.

He smiled and gave a small wave before setting it on the table. He'd changed into athletic wear, and his shorts covered up most of the brace on his knee.

"How far is your mailbox?" Penny asked. An odd sense of protectiveness washed over her, but she tamped it down.

"Just at the end of the block." Brett stretched out his back, and she glanced over to find his crutch still leaning against the wall.

He followed her gaze. "I told you it gets better in the afternoon." She smiled and opened the cupboard, looking for a frying pan and a bowl. Brett made his way over and pointed. "Pans are in the cupboard next to the stove."

"I thought you said you didn't know how to make falafel."

"I don't know how to make them, but I know how they're cooked."

"Seems like a slippery slope."

Brett chuckled. "Do you mind if I watch?"

Warmth swirled in Penny's center. She'd made this a hundred times, but the idea of Brett paying attention to each movement made her nervous. "Only if I can put you to work."

"I wouldn't expect anything less."

"You have a food processor right?"

He pointed to the cupboard in the corner. "It's not great but it does the trick."

Penny assembled the rest of the ingredients and gave Brett the job of draining the beans he was such a fan of into the bowl with the blades. "Make sure you rinse them first," she instructed.

"Aye aye, Captain."

Penny rolled her eyes. Brett, it turned out, was an excellent sous chef. They worked in tandem until she had the sauce made and the falafel paste ready to go. She drizzled oil in the pan and twisted the knob on the stove to start heating it.

Brett rinsed his hands and dried them with the towel on the counter. "Want me to make the salad? That's definitely in my wheelhouse."

Penny nodded and tossed him the bag of salad mix. "I'm glad you're not one of those guys that just eats mac and cheese and cereal for dinner."

"Oh, I could definitely be one of those guys if I wanted to. You should've seen me in college."

"Where did you go for your MBA?"

"U of C. Stayed close to home. I was still working, so it made the most sense. You?"

Penny rolled the oil in the pan. "I went to UBC." She didn't elaborate since the reasons she'd stayed home were extremely different from his. Lucas had started to spiral the year she graduated high school.

At first, their whole family was convinced it was just a phase, a rebellious streak, after leaving the house and finding people who liked to party on campus. But when Penny hung out with his friends and said something about their wild weekends, Lucas's friend Sam had looked at her like she'd grown a second head.

Over the course of the night, she realized that Lucas seemed to be the only one getting smashed on the weekend. Alone. In his apartment. That was the first moment of many when she'd been scared for him.

She tried to talk to him about it, but he was convinced he didn't have a problem. He said it was normal to feel stressed and normal to try to take care of it himself. *I won't do it forever.* Those words echoed in her head like the peals of a gong.

At the time, he was maintaining good grades in school and nothing else seemed amiss, so she had no rebuttal as all the research she did defined addiction as behavior that negatively impacted everyday life. Lucas had seemed fine, even though the voice in her head was screaming that he was anything but.

"Penny?"

She looked up and saw Brett was watching her.

"Mm-hmm?"

"I think I lost you there for a second."

"Yeah, sorry, just thinking."

"About that email?" Brett's voice was low and gentle. Penny blinked. *Had she mentioned that to him?*

"Right, yeah." She paused, not sure what to say next, but grateful for anything that would steer her thoughts away from that night four years ago. "It was an email from my ex."

"The guy your parents hated but you liked and followed out to Calgary?"

Penny's eyes flicked to his. He'd been listening. She pulled a ball of falafel dough into her hands, patting it flat. "Yeah, I worked for him the last couple of years. This morning I got an email from the office manager."

"Are they refusing to pay you or something?"

Penny sighed. "No, nothing like that. It was very . . . congenial." Brett didn't respond, just watched her as he tossed the greens into the bowl. "I know it sounds ridiculous that I'm mad about a *nice* email, but when I told Danny I was leaving, it was like he didn't even care. We'd lived together for almost three years, and I helped him build that practice. All I got was a 'give me your two weeks notice and I'll make sure you get your paperwork.'"

"So you were kind of hoping for a bash fest?"

Penny dropped her hands into the bowl. "He could have at least called me a bitch. That would have been nice," she muttered.

Brett laughed out loud. "I'll file that away for future reference."

Penny grinned and popped the first falafel onto the pan. "It just would have felt good to know that any of it meant anything to him, you know? If he'd shown *some* emotion."

"I'm sure it did mean something. He was probably protecting himself."

She gave a sardonic laugh. "Well, you know Danny. He plays defence so hard, there is zero chance of getting a shot on net."

Brett opened his mouth as if he was going to say something, then closed it again.

"I thought you'd appreciate that. It was a hockey met—"

"Yeah, I got it." Brett's skin flushed a little, and Penny wondered if she'd gotten the metaphor wrong and said something stupid. She smashed the rest of the dough into patties and squished them in the oil next to each other.

"Smells amazing." Brett peeled the remaining cucumber they hadn't used in the tzatziki, chopped it, and added it to the salad.

"Thanks for your help."

"Thanks for showing me that garbanzo beans have nothing to do with Muppets."

Penny snorted and flipped the first falafels she'd put in the pan. "I got some pita. We can toast it if you want."

"Sure." Brett shuffled down the counter and reached past her for the bag of flatbread. His arm brushed hers, sending tingles across her skin, and she quickly took a step back.

"Sorry."

"No, you're fine."

Brett opened the bag and popped two pita into the toaster

oven while Penny worked to settle her pulse. Was it just her, or had the kitchen just shrunk three sizes? She was too warm. She stepped away from the stove and sucked in a lungful of air, then stepped back up to flip the rest of the patties.

When they were finished, she transferred them to a plate covered with a paper towel, then transferred the food to the table. Brett carried over the salad and dressing, and after Penny filled up two glasses with water, they sat.

Brett filled her in on the Snowballs while they ate dinner, and Penny was grateful for a fluffy topic of conversation. She doubted it was as mundane to Brett, though, by the way he'd clung to his hockey bag the other night. It was obvious how much he missed it.

"So you only practice once a week during the summer?" she asked.

Brett nodded. "Some of the other guys play summer sports."

"You don't?" She took a bite of salad with a new vinaigrette Brett had in the fridge. She liked it.

"Depends. Curtis has taken up Ultimate Frisbee, which I think looks fun. I probably would have signed up for the league with him if I hadn't wrecked my knee."

A wave of nausea rolled through her, and Penny clenched her fists. She drew a deep breath, then slowly released it. *Lucas had played Ultimate when he was in university.*

The fact that her body was still reacting this way any time something related to him came up probably meant that she needed more therapy. But since she hadn't vetted any therapists since moving to Calgary, she would have to wait until she had more mental energy to take that on.

"Hey—" Brett started, but her phone buzzed on the counter behind them. Penny hopped up to grab it.

Andrea. She debated making her leave a voicemail, but since her sister had also tried to call at the grocery store, Penny decided to pick up.

"Hey, what's up?"

"Oh, I don't know. The fact that you haven't texted me any updates and it's been two days already?"

"Dre, I've been kind of busy moving in."

"Well, I've been kind of busy waiting for you to send pictures of your roommate—"

"Housemate."

"Whatever. Why are you withholding this information?"

Penny's hands started to tingle. "I'm not withholding anything." She glanced over at Brett and noted the smirk on his lips. *"Fine."* She pulled the phone from her ear. "Brett, my sister Andrea is positive I'm keeping things from her. Do you mind if I take a quick picture?"

"Of me?" he asked, legitimately surprised.

"Oh, he sounds hot," Andrea said through the speaker, and Penny pushed her phone up against her chest.

"Yep, just a quick shot," she squeaked.

Brett leaned back in his chair and gave a cheesy grin. *Damn it.* This was going to be bad. Penny snapped a picture and texted it to Andrea. "There, you happy?"

"It hasn't come through yet, so no."

Penny tapped her fingers on the arm of the couch as she waited, then heard the audible gasp.

"What the hell, Penny? *You didn't tell me you were sleeping with the blonde version of Jason Momoa!"*

Penny's cheeks flushed an angry shade of red, and she stalked into the other room so her sister's shrill voice wouldn't carry through the kitchen.

She tried to keep her voice low as she hissed, "Housemates, Andrea! I'm not sleeping with anyone!"

Brett coughed behind her, and she squeezed her eyes shut. Apparently her strategy hadn't worked.

"Well, now I know exactly why you haven't sent me a picture. This guy is *exactly* your type. Did you notice that little detail before you signed on to live there?"

"No, Andrea. No, I did not. Because I'm a professional. Plus, I don't *have* a type or—"

"I give it two weeks."

Penny gritted her teeth. "Mmm, that's wonderful, Andrea. What *else* are you working on for that project you have going on for that thing? On that... day?"

Andrea snorted. "Wow, great cover. Sorry, am I embarrassing you in front of your new *housemate*?"

"Always. Was there anything else you wanted to talk about, or was this purely a reconnaissance call?"

"Nope, I am fully satisfied. I think *you* could also be fully sat—"

"Really? That's where you're going with this?"

Andrea laughed, and the sound of tinkling metal gave Penny a perfect mental image of her sister and the slim bracelets she always wore around her wrists. "Having any luck on the job front?"

"Working on it." Penny stalked back into the hall.

"Excellent. Tamara already sent me her portion."

"Of course she did."

"No competition, Pens. We understand you're in transition."

"Well, thank you for that."

"Ooh! I found a place for the party, the ballroom at Winnleton."

Penny grinned as she reentered the kitchen. "Oh, that'll be perfect. Mom loves that place. Do they have any idea?"

"No, they think Theo and I are taking them out for dinner. That's it."

Giddiness bubbled up Penny's throat. They'd never done anything like this, and her parents had no idea what was about to hit them. "Okay, love you, Andrea. Thanks for checking in."

"Thanks for the eye candy. I might have to pop that in the family chat."

Penny groaned. "Please don't."

Andrea laughed, and with a quick "I love you," she was gone.

Penny dropped her hand and drew a cleansing breath before turning to face Brett. "That was my sister."

"You mentioned that. Younger or older?" Brett looked way too pleased with himself as he slung an arm over the back of the chair.

Penny's eyes snapped to the ink curling under his bicep, and her mouth went dry. "Older."

"She seems fun."

Penny cleared her throat and walked back to sit down at her plate. "Well, she was certainly thrilled with the picture of you." She ignored the niggling thought that she was glad she had a picture of him, too. *She wasn't going to look at it.* Probably.

Penny finished the last of her falafel and took her dishes to the sink. "I figure we give it about an hour for your food to settle, then we can do our session."

Brett nodded. "I'll send a few more emails." He took a drink of water then glanced down at his phone, and his brow furrowed.

"Not looking forward to those?" Penny asked.

Brett sighed. "No, I just realized I forgot to text the guys about tomorrow."

"Practice?"

"No, that won't be 'till next Monday. I need a ride over to a job site."

Penny frowned. "Why are you texting the guys for that?" Brett looked up, his thumbs hovering over the screen of his phone. "I'm right here, and I have a car. I can take you wherever you need to go in the morning."

Brett set his phone back on the table. "I didn't want to assume."

"Assume away. All I'm doing is submitting job applications, and those are the definition of flexible."

"I have to be there at six in the morning."

Penny balked. "Well, that is unfortunate."

"Exactly, I know—"

"I'll still totally take you. It doesn't make any sense for one of the guys to have to drive over here."

Brett teased his teeth over his lower lip as he considered her point, and Penny looked for anything else in the room she could focus on. She grabbed the cloth sitting next to the sink and started to wipe down the counter.

"I can make you a shake. Or eggs or something," Brett offered.

"You don't need to repay me. I'm happy to help."

Brett nodded once and swiped his pita bread over the tzatziki that had escaped onto his plate. He chewed and swallowed, then pushed his chair back to stand and winced.

Penny rounded the counter and walked to the table. "It's the worst when you stay seated for a while, hey?"

"Penny . . ."

"Brett." She gave him a long look. "The sooner you accept that I want to do this, the less time we'll have to waste from here on out."

She scooped up his plate and cup and took them to the sink. Once they were loaded in the dishwasher and she didn't have anything else to do, she pushed her hands into her pockets and walked toward her room. "In an hour, then?"

"In an hour."

CHAPTER Seven

Tony 6:52pm

> Leah just got back from school and asked what icing was. I've never been so proud

Brett 6:59pm

> She was talking about cupcakes, wasn't she?

BRETT WAITED in the living room, his palms already sweating. He'd seen Penny out the window walking back to the garage behind the complex and wondered what torture device she'd be dragging with her into the living room.

It had been years since he'd done any physical therapy, but he remembered the hell on earth he experienced when he broke his ankle in high school. Though those sessions had been facilitated by an old Ukrainian woman. Penny wouldn't be that callous, hopefully. At least he'd be able to understand her.

He sat at attention when she entered through the front door.

"Ready to go?" she asked. It wasn't until that moment that Brett realized she was going to be touching him. *Of course she was going to be touching him.* That's how this worked. But the idea of physical therapy in his mind had never included *her*. Or her long wavy hair. Thankfully, she'd at least tied it up in a knot at the base of her neck. It didn't help as much as he'd hoped.

Brett swallowed hard. "As ready as I'll ever be."

Penny set her bag on the floor and worked at the zipper. "You know this first session is going to be the worst. Well, that's kind of a lie. They're all going to be brutal. But I like to say that to make people feel less existential."

"Does it work?"

"I don't know. I've never had to deal with the immediate aftermath of a session. They keep coming back, so that's something."

Brett laughed nervously. "Go easy on me."

"Is that actually what you want?" Penny gave him a pointed look. No, it wasn't what he wanted, and she already knew that. "I thought so." She rummaged around in the bag and pulled out a resistance band. "All right. I don't have my mats, but this rug seems plush enough to keep your tailbone from bruising at least." She lifted her head and sat back on her feet. "I could get my yoga mat if—"

"No, this is fine." Brett slid down from the couch and stretched out on the floor. *Did she want him to lie down now?* He stayed sitting until she instructed him otherwise. Anxiety gnawed at him as she pulled coloured bands from the bag along with a spiky foam roller that didn't look friendly.

"Okay." Penny scooted over and held out the band. "Go ahead and take off your brace."

Brett nodded, wanting to shrink the same way he had the first time he'd turned and coughed in the doctor's office. He clumsily removed the brace and wrap, then set them on the floor next to him.

Penny looped the band around his right ankle and stood. "You can lie back. I'm going to hold your foot a few inches off the floor. Your job is to flex and release your thigh muscles."

"That's it?"

"For now."

Brett laid flat and did as she asked, trying not to stare at her hovering above him. She'd changed into a white tank top and deep blue harem pants with some astrological pattern swirling through the fabric. Her golden skin seemed to glow in the light of the standing lamp. *Flex and release, damn it.* Here she was in her professional element while he clenched his muscles like a toddler and tried to keep his eyes off her breasts.

The slow burn in his leg made him feel impotent. How could something as simple as this be getting any kind of result?

"Feeling it now?" Penny glanced up at his face, and Brett tried to play off his discomfort. "One more minute of this, and then we'll move into leg raises and heel slides."

He nodded and continued flexing and releasing until she set his heel back on the floor. Before he could say anything, Penny was kneeling next to him with her hands on either side of his knee. Her fingers slipped under the fabric of his shorts as she massaged the muscle attachment points. "Does that hurt?"

Hurt was the wrong word. It made him nervous. "It's fine."

"I'm going to move your kneecap, it's called patellar mobilization. You should do this when you have a second during the day. Just to make sure it doesn't get stiff." Her fingers slipped over his skin, and he held his breath. *Shit.* He should not have worn fabric shorts.

He'd mentally prepared himself for pain, but not for this. Tendrils of hair escaped Penny's bun and brushed his skin as she manipulated his knee cap in slow circles. *His kneecap was the last thing he was worried about getting stiff.*

"Still fine?" she asked.

"Yep." He answered a little too quickly. *Please don't look up. Please for the love*—He gasped in pain.

"Mmhmm, there it is. Stiff on that side."

Not any longer. Penny sat up and brushed her hair back away from her face. "Leg raises. You ready?"

Brett nodded and sucked in a breath. "Just like it sounds?"

"Yep." She jumped up to her feet, oblivious to his few seconds of panic, and stepped over him in a standing straddle, facing his feet. "You're just going to lift your leg straight—"

"I can't straighten it all the way."

"That'll come later, just lift the leg and try to touch your toes to my hand, okay?" Penny shot a glance down over her shoulder.

At least now that she was facing away he didn't have to pretend he wasn't looking. He kicked his right leg up, leaving his left stretched out on the floor, but couldn't quite force his toes to hit Penny's hand.

"Pathetic. Try again."

Brett coughed a laugh. He kicked up again, and this time, Penny reached out, wrapping both hands around the back of his calf. She tugged gently, easing his leg toward her. He grunted.

"Don't hold your breath. Exhale. Deep breath in then deep breath out." Penny let go of his leg as he lowered it back to the floor, then bent over again and pulled as he stretched it back to the ceiling. Brett had a perfect view of her back end, and it was the only thing keeping him from swearing at the sting in his hamstring.

She's your physical therapist, douchebag. Brett forced his eyes to the underside of the couch and expelled the air from his lungs. *Housemates, Andrea. I'm not sleeping with anyone.* Brett grinned thinking about the conversation he'd very much enjoyed listening to with Penny and her sister earlier. *I don't have a type.* That comment was his favourite because she only would've said that if her sister thought he *was* Penny's type. He'd run that possibility through his head on repeat, secretly hoping her sister knew her better than she knew herself.

Not that he was going to do anything about it. Not yet.

"Good. Let's do a few more."

Brett's eyes glazed at that praise coming out of her mouth, and he clenched his fists. If they were going to do three sessions a week like this, he had to change his mindset. Take whatever was simmering in his midsection and shut it down cold. He gritted his teeth and started mentally repeating multiplication tables.

"Okay, get up and sit on the couch," Penny stepped back to his right side and waited for him to pull himself off the floor. Brett did as she asked. "Seated leg raises. We want to activate and strengthen those quads."

"Same thing?"

"Yep, lift the leg up past your other thigh." Penny leaned over and again helped him stretch the leg higher than he could get it on his own.

"I feel like an eighty-year-old man." Brett hissed air through his teeth as he worked to lift his leg higher.

"Well you don't look it." Penny winked. "Just enjoy this one. I saved the best for last."

"Fantastic." Sweat broke out on Brett's forehead, which made him question whether he'd ever worked out a day in his life. A few minutes later, when he wondered if his upper leg was going to spontaneously combust, Penny stopped him.

"Take a minute." She stood and walked into the kitchen, then returned with a clean towel. She rolled it up and set it on the floor then motioned for him to meet her on the rug. "Same thing as before. Lie down and place your knee over this towel."

"I don't like where this is heading."

Her lips drew into a line as he got into position. "You're going to flex your muscle again, but this time, push your knee to the floor."

Brett's heart kicked up a notch. "That's going to straighten the leg."

"Right."

"But it won't go straight right now."

"Right. I know." Penny patted his calf.

Brett laid back on the floor and froze when Penny threaded her fingers through his. "I'm right here with you, okay?" Adrenaline coursed through his veins at her touch, and right then, he felt like he could sprint a hundred meters if she asked him to. But all he did was press his knee into the towel.

Pain exploded up his thigh, and he clenched his teeth together to keep from crying out.

"You can scream." Penny's voice was soft, in complete juxtaposition to the movement she was forcing. She squeezed his hand as Brett released his leg.

"I don't want to scream."

"Yes, you do."

"Okay. I don't want to scream in your face."

Penny quirked an eyebrow. "It would be fun. I never get to experience that because we're usually in an office."

Brett pressed down again and gritted his teeth. "These walls are not that thick."

"I'll keep arguing with you if it helps."

Brett wheezed and tried to force his lungs to pull in air. He was a hockey player, for crying out loud. He'd taken elbows to the head, sticks to his thighs, and every part of himself to the boards. Now he wanted to cry like a baby because Penny was asking him to straighten his damn leg.

Penny's voice hummed. "This sucks. I know it sucks, but the faster we can safely get this mobility back, the faster you can build up your muscle again."

The pain clawed at his nerves so intently he barely heard her. Penny adjusted her grip, and Brett gasped, trying to keep tears from filling his eyes.

"You can stop if you want. We can—"

"No," Brett grunted.

Penny's hands landed on both sides of his face. Her touch was cool. Centering. She nodded once. "Okay. Breathe. Small break, and then we go again."

Brett was still shaking when Penny helped him to his room. She hadn't gone easy on him, and a part of her felt a little guilty. She never would have pushed the discomfort to that level with another patient. Not because it wasn't safe but because most people couldn't hack it. She hadn't been lying when she said she never had to deal with the aftermath. When people came in, they were usually accompanied by a loved one who helped them home.

She was helping, even if it looked like hurting at the moment, but she also had to witness Brett's expression as he shuffled into his bedroom alone. There was no loved one in there to help him into the tub, and while she'd retrieved the ice pack from the freezer for him, he dismissed the idea of her sitting at his bedside.

The pain he was experiencing was no joke, but what else could she do? Penny shut off the lights in the front room and locked the door, then retreated to her bedroom. She groaned when she remembered that Brett had to go in-person to work the next morning. Maybe they should have waited to have their first session until the following night.

Penny readied herself for bed and checked her email. There was nothing new besides a few confirmations that her job applications had been submitted. She didn't expect anyone to get back to her so soon, but she could always hope.

It was only nine-thirty, but their session had taken a lot out of her, too. She was exhausted. When she stared at her bed, she remembered the quilt situation and berated herself for not stopping over at Kelty's when they went grocery shopping that afternoon. It looked like it would be another night under a sheet wearing a hoodie. It was the least of her concerns, really. She set a reminder for herself to stop at

Kelty's the next day, then climbed into bed and went to sleep.

There was less crying than the night before but more tossing and turning. She didn't know if that was a step up. At least after sobbing for a while, she'd slept fairly peacefully. Instead, every time she woke that night, she thought about Brett and wondered if she should check on him. When she blurred between sleep and consciousness the last time, Penny checked her phone and saw it was just a few minutes before five-thirty, the time her alarm was set to go off.

She rolled out of bed and threw on her sweatshirt over her tank top and shorts. At least she'd already broken the morning face and breath barrier with Brett the day before. No need for pretense.

Brett was already in the kitchen with all the ingredients for his shake lined up on the counter.

"Do you want one?" he asked.

Penny nodded. Since arguing with him the other day had profited her nothing, she decided to give in and take what he offered. She yawned and leaned over the counter, pulling her sleeves over her hands. "How did you sleep?"

"Do you want the real answer?"

Penny grimaced. "That bad?"

"The hot water and ice helped."

"And hey, you didn't die in the tub." Penny yawned. "I'm so sorry, by the way. Are you sure you don't want to take anything?"

Brett shook his head, and now the assumptions she'd made before about why he wouldn't take medication didn't quite seem as plausible. He didn't seem like a guy who would suffer through pain unnecessarily to prove his manliness.

"Are you going to be okay at work today?" she asked. Brett gave a single nod and turned to start the blender. Penny's heart squeezed. That ice behind his eyes made her want to wrap her arms around him and hold him until he thawed.

She could do it. She thought he might let her if she tried. That gap inside her ached to be filled with adoration and gratitude. *If someone needed her, then she was valuable.* And there again was that beautiful toxic trait rearing its ugly head. When would she be enough for herself?

The blender stopped, and Brett poured their shakes, dropping a straw into her cup without Penny even having to ask.

"Thank you." She took it from him and drank. "Mmm. This one's different, it almost tastes like cinnamon."

"I used the vanilla protein powder today. You like it?"

Penny nodded. They stood there across the counter, both still a little bleary-eyed from sleep.

Brett finished his shake first. "I'm going to go brush my teeth."

"I'll take the rest of this in the car." Penny picked up her cup and walked to the door to get her shoes. When Brett shuffled out of his room, he was using his crutch. She nodded her approval. "That's a good idea."

Brett paused in the hall when he saw his shoes lined up in front of her. He frowned, and Penny didn't wait for him to make whatever argument he was already forming in his head.

"Please save us both the trouble and just come over here and put your feet in the shoes."

Brett's cheeks reddened, but he did as she asked. She was gentle with his right leg, but he still clenched a little harder on the crutch as she pushed the shoe into place.

"Are you sure you're going to be okay today?" she asked as she straightened.

"You're starting to sound like my mother."

Penny tensed. *There it was.* Even when she was hyperaware of it, she still slipped into that role. Brett was a grown man, and she was so desperate to kiss his boo-boos better she didn't trust that he knew what was best for himself.

Brett's expression sobered. "That's not a bad thing. My mom's awesome."

"Right." Penny dropped her eyes and walked out onto the porch. The crisp morning air caressed her cheeks, and she inhaled. It was fine. She could back off. It would just take a little practice to figure out what her role was in this new reality where the lines between work and home were smudged.

She hadn't even thought to ask Brett where the job site was. When they got into the car, she passed him her charging cord. "If you just plug this in and type in the directions, it should pop up on the screen."

Brett pulled up the address on the map. Penny briefly caught a glimpse of the words "Cove Park Dr." before it expanded into the street view. Something about that address rang a bell, but she didn't think too hard about it before pulling out onto the street.

"What contract is this for?" she asked, hoping they could move past her deer-in-headlights moment after his mom comment.

"It's a new build for a holistic medical center, not massive, but it has about twenty-two offices and an urgent care center."

Penny blinked. "That seems massive to me."

"Well, size isn't everything," he retorted. Penny shot him a look, and he gave a churlish grin. "Sorry. Working on that filter."

"Not hard enough." Penny held up a hand. "Don't even respond to that one."

Brett chuckled and leaned his seat back. "I prefer the smaller builds. Less . . . friction."

Penny ignored the low hanging fruit. "So who's doing this build?"

"I haven't met with him yet. It's David something."

Penny plucked her shake from the cupholder. She looked down and noticed Brett rubbing his knee. "Do you still think you're going to want to do three sessions a week?"

"I thought this was like labour. You're not allowed to talk about getting after it within twenty-four hours."

Penny laughed. "I don't even want to know how you're aware of that rule."

Brett tried to smile, but it looked more like a grimace. When he fixed his gaze out the windshield, Penny didn't interrupt with any more questions. Pain could be the most attentive companion, taking up all that brain space so there wasn't any room for anything or anybody else.

When they approached the building, Brett pulled his phone from his pocket and searched for something, then frowned. "Huh. I guess it wasn't David. It was Daniel."

Penny parked in front of the office building, and when she looked up, she nearly spit the rest of her protein shake all over the dashboard.

Standing inside the glass, directly in front of the car, was Danny.

CHAPTER
Eight

"GET OUT!" Penny barked, and Brett looked up from his phone, alarmed.

"What?"

"I said, *get out!*"

Brett shoved his phone in his pocket and reached for the door handle as Penny slunk down in her seat. He searched outside the windows trying to figure out what was making her act like they were mid-carjacking.

"Penny—"

"*Please, Brett.*" It was nearly a whimper. He did as she asked and pushed the door open, then reached into the back to retrieve his bag and crutch. He pulled everything out into the parking lot in one less-than-graceful maneuver, gripping the door for balance. He barely slammed it closed as Penny peeled out of the lot.

What the hell was that all about? Brett walked into the gutted office space and took a hard hat from Dominic, who was already inside waiting for him.

"Looks like you're in need of our services."

Brett turned to see a man dressed in a lavender shirt and

charcoal grey pants that looked tailored. His patent leather shoes definitely didn't belong in a construction zone.

Brett opened his mouth, but Dominic leaned in. "I already told him to wear a hard hat, but he refuses."

The man, who he assumed was Daniel from his email, took Brett's hand and shook it with a firm grip. "Nice to finally meet you in person. I stopped by last week and thought it was a bit strange you weren't on site."

Brett motioned at his knee. "I was most likely in the middle of surgery."

"Right, well, I assume you'll be present from here on out?"

Brett bristled. *Wasn't this guy a doctor?* He doubted he'd be keen on Brett telling him how often he needed to see patients. "I'll be here as often as needed." He glanced at Dominic, who dropped his eyes to his notebook.

Daniel continued. "This is the second build-out I've done, but admittedly it's bigger than the first. I just want to make sure everything runs smoothly."

Brett drew a calming breath and leaned on his crutch so he could pull his tablet from his bag. "We take pride in our team. We do good work."

Daniel barely acknowledged the comment. "I wanted to go over the timeline a bit and make a couple of adjustments to the back corner of the building. Specifically adding a second entrance..."

Brett had a moment to gather his thoughts as they walked to the back of the building. His mind swung like a pendulum back to the moment in the car with Penny. *What in the world could have set her off like that?*

He motioned for Dominic to pull out his notebook as Daniel explained the specifications. Normally, Brett would be happy to take the lead, but he was having a difficult time holding himself upright with his right leg throbbing and his underarm complaining each time he leaned on the crutch.

Dominic understood the assignment and jumped right in to

take measurements. The slight deprecating downward glance from Daniel did not escape Brett's notice. This guy was a piece of work. He corrected Dominic twice on how he should properly hold a tape measure, and Brett was about to jump in to take the heat when he heard the words *chiropractic office*. His ears started to ring as all the pieces snapped into place.

"You said this was your second build?" Brett asked, interrupting him.

"Right." Daniel launched back into his previous sentence, but Brett held up a hand.

"And your other office—where is it located?"

"Does it matter?"

Brett's shoulders tensed. "Just curious if I know the contractor."

Daniel looked annoyed but rattled off the name and the location down south. Brett flicked up the general sketch of the building on his tablet and reviewed the list of vendors already signed on for leases. Therapeutic massage, acupuncture, holistic medicine, naturopath, and bingo. Chiropractic and physical therapy: Dr. Daniel Ascott. Or, as Brett was now fairly certain: Danny.

Daniel prattled on about building flow, but Brett was fifteen kilometres away, back at his apartment. This was Penny's ex.

When Daniel was finally satisfied with the numbers Dominic was showing him, they made their way back to the front.

"Anything else I can help you with?" Brett asked. Daniel dipped his head and pulled him to the side, positioning himself between Brett and Dominic. Dominic ignored the rude bid for privacy and stepped back a few feet, writing a few more notes on the page.

Daniel lowered his voice. "I would really prefer that you're on site from here on out."

Brett narrowed his eyes. "I told you—"

"Listen, I'm a business owner. I understand how it is to hire a team. You expect great things, yada yada, but we all know that unless the man in charge is there, corners get cut."

Brett had said the same thing yesterday to Penny, but now the words felt sour. Especially when accompanied by the flicks of Daniel's eyes toward Dominic. His jaw tightened as he stepped back, gripping the handle of his crutch. "Dominic, would you come here for a second?"

Dominic stepped forward. He'd started out as a contractor working for Brett six years ago on a grocery store project downtown. Brett had been so impressed with his work that he'd helped him build his own team, and now he was a partial owner in Brett's company. Not a full half partner but close.

"I think with all the chaos when I walked in I forgot to introduce you two fully. Daniel, this is Dominic. He's not a contractor who works for me. He's my partner." Daniel's eyes widened slightly, and Brett doubled down.

There was no way in hell he was going to let this man talk down to one of the most honest, hard-working men he knew. Not because he was quiet and kept to himself and not because of the colour of his skin. "Dominic is one of the most thorough, detail-oriented men I know, but more than that, his team respects him. They do an excellent job, which is why I've worked with him for six years and invited him to partner with me. I assure you, no matter which of us is on site, the work is going to get done right, and if for some reason it's not, we will make it right."

Brett paused, waiting for Daniel to respond. When he didn't, Brett continued, "I recall we came highly recommended to you, correct Dr. Ascott?" *Daniel definitely didn't come highly recommended to him.*

Daniel's smile was all charm. "Of course, of course, I have no concerns whatsoever. I'm just always thorough whenever I'm not the only one with hands on the reins."

Brett forced a smile and squeezed Dominic's shoulder. He couldn't tell if the rage bubbling up inside him was only due to Daniel's rude behaviour that morning or if it was partially influenced by the knowledge that this dickhead had treated Penny poorly. He didn't want to know what he'd done to make her slink behind the steering wheel and pull out of the parking lot like she was in The Fast and Furious Part Five.

As soon as Daniel left the site, Brett pulled out his phone. He searched for Penny's number since he hadn't used it in a while, then typed out a text.

> Hey, are you okay? Seems like you might have some history with the client who hired me for this build. He's a twat, by the way.

Brett watched his phone, waiting for her to reply. After a few minutes, he turned it off and slipped it back into his pocket.

"All good, bro?" Dominic walked up next to him.

"Yeah." Brett rubbed his temple. "That guy was a piece of work, eh?"

Dominic made a face. "They don't make them the same out west."

Brett laughed. He'd met plenty of good people from Van City, but Daniel wasn't one of them. Dominic clapped him on the shoulder, and they went back to work.

Brett checked his phone four more times that morning, but there was nothing from Penny, and he was starting to get nervous. He had no reason to believe that Penny wasn't fine. Yes, she'd reacted strongly to seeing Daniel in person, but she'd probably gone home and gotten distracted with something. That was what normal people did.

But Brett had been surrounded by enough people who were abnormally adjusted he couldn't quite let it go. Once, he'd sponsored a kid through his AA group in university—about to graduate in engineering. He'd been sober for two and a half years when one of his ex-girlfriends blocked him on social media. One benign thing and he was back to the bottle.

To be fair, it wasn't *only* that thing. The kid hadn't been coming to meetings for a couple of weeks. Hadn't been doing his step work. It was too easy to get to a place where you thought you didn't need support anymore. Where you thought you could do it all on your own.

Brett needed to hit a meeting. He thought about stopping at the one in the plaza on the way home, then realized he didn't have a car. *Was Penny planning to pick him up?* They hadn't talked about anything before she turned into an ostrich and buried her head in the sand.

He typed out another quick text.

> Hey, would really love to know that you're alright. I should be done here around four. Since you told me to assume away, I wondered if you'd be able to pick me up. I don't mind catching a rideshare though so no pressure

He stared at the text and then deleted the whole thing.

> Hey, Penny. Let me know you're okay. I'll catch a rideshare after work. See you at home

He pressed send. This time, three dots appeared within seconds.

> Hey, sorry I didn't respond sooner. I went for a run when I got home, not to rub it in, and just barely got cleaned up. I was planning to pick you up, so don't you dare order a ride. See you at four

No mention of Danny and no response to his question about whether she was surviving. Either that meant that she'd already forgotten about the whole thing, or she was avoiding it. He knew plenty about that strategy.

Brett and Dominic got burgers and poutine at A&W next door for lunch, and then he put his head down and drowned himself in work for the rest of the afternoon. When he saw

Penny's car pull up through the window, his heart picked up speed.

Dominic followed his stare, then turned to look at him. "Who's that?"

Brett grabbed his crutch from against the wall. "A friend." Dominic raised an eyebrow, and Brett ignored it. "I'll be at home the remainder of this week, but I'm hoping next week I'll be able to drive again." Now that he was walking on his leg more consistently, he hoped it was only a matter of time.

"Got it, and hey, Brett?" Brett paused to look at his partner. "Thanks for earlier."

Brett nodded, gave a small wave, then pushed through the doors. It didn't take him as long to slip into the passenger seat as it had that morning. He still couldn't fully straighten his leg, and he had zero motivation to push it after the night before, but it was less stiff. *Penny had said to relax it, hadn't she?*

"So how was your day," Penny asked with a bright smile on her face.

Brett observed her warily. If she was trying to make him question his version of reality, it was working. His sister Cameron used to do it constantly. She thought it was funny to mess with him, but once he'd passed age ten, he refused to let her get in his head. He wouldn't let Penny do it either. "Is this your strategy?"

Penny blinked. "What are you talking about? That was a normal thing to ask somebody when you pick them up from work."

"Not when you drop them off by kicking them out of the car and acting like you had to hide from the paparazzi."

Penny grimaced and backed out of the parking spot.

"Did you get my text?" Brett asked.

"Yes." Her eyes flicked to his.

"Can you give me something here?"

She flexed her hands on the steering wheel. "What exactly?"

Brett's jaw worked. "Fine, you don't want to talk about it? I won't push." It felt like two stones were grinding against each other under his ribs. Why was she being so cagey? Possibilities began to swirl in his head, each option worse than the last. *Had Daniel hurt her? Threatened her?*

"Thank you." Penny pursed her lips and stared intently at the road. The minutes ticked by, and she didn't say another word.

The idea of Dr. Daniel Ascott lifting a hand against Penny made Brett's skin crawl. The fact that Penny was opting for radio silence and letting his worst imaginations swirl unchecked in his thoughts made him want to slam his working foot on the brakes. He'd answered all of her questions, hadn't he? Sure, they'd never gotten into the topic of dating, but if she'd asked, he would have told her.

Things had ended badly with her and her ex, but who didn't have a story like that? He could list at least three women that he wouldn't relish running into again. Though that had been years ago and Penny had just barely split from this turd bucket. Maybe he could cut her some slack.

They rode in silence the rest of the way home, and as she parked on the curb, Penny asked,

"How's your knee doing today?"

Brett pushed his door open. "Perfect." He hadn't meant it to come out snippy.

Penny's eyes flashed. "Perfect?"

"That's what I said." He stepped out onto the curb and turned his face so she wouldn't see him flinch.

"Huh. Well, I guess I didn't push you hard enough then."

"Guess not."

Penny slammed her door, and her flip-flops scuffed behind him on the sidewalk. He waited for her to pass, but she didn't. "I guess I was worried for nothing."

He hesitated as they reached the steps, barely remembering that he'd left his crutch in the car. He wasn't going to ask her for it now. "You were worried?"

A blush rose to her cheeks. "No. I mean, it's normal to check in with a patient after the first session of PT. I only meant . . . I wondered. Especially since you refused to take anything that would help with the inflammation."

Brett nodded and grabbed onto the railing as he took a step. "So you were worried about me not taking meds."

"No, not worried. I just wanted to make sure that I hadn't done anything to hurt you."

"Why didn't you text then?" Brett stopped on the landing, and Penny stomped past him and used her key to open the door.

"Never mind."

Brett followed her into the house, and his thoughts burst out of him. "Hey, I'm happy to talk about this with you, but I don't think it's fair that you aren't willing to answer my questions and yet you expect me to get all vulnerable."

"I'm not asking you to get all vulnerable, Brett," she murmured, not turning to face him. "I was only wondering if you were in pain."

"That's vulnerable!"

Penny huffed and slipped off her shoes, then stalked toward the hall.

"I'm making dinner tonight."

"I'm not hungry," Penny said as she opened the door to her bedroom, slipped in, and pushed it closed behind her.

CHAPTER
Nine

BRETT 12:07PM

> How's your week going?

CAMERON 1:42PM

> is this my brother reaching out for no reason whatsoever other than to say hello?

BRETT 1:51PM

> Let me know if you need me to call an ambulance

CAMERON 4:20PM

> i've got a big sales push this week. Little stressed

BRETT 5:05PM

> I'm sorry. Wish I could help

CAMERON 5:38PM

> you're terrible at sales

BRETT 5:39PM

> I meant with a foot massage or something

CAMERON 5:43PM

> zero percent chance I'm letting you touch my feet
>
> how are you?

BRETT 5:57PM

> Good

CAMERON 5:59PM

> really?

BRETT 6:00PM

> I don't understand women

CAMERON 6:00PM

> ok, yeah. you're fine. lol

BRETT MADE DINNER ANYWAY. Penny didn't come out of her room. He left a plate for her on the counter and found it gone the next morning. He hadn't slept well again, but he had succeeded in staying in his bed all night, which was an improvement.

It was becoming difficult to talk himself into a better mindset. *Accept the things you cannot change* . . . The problem was he didn't want to accept them. He'd be better off if he did—he had years of evidence to support that. But it was so tempting to wallow. To be angry.

He'd been sitting around on his ass for over a month, and he was sick of it. He was sick of his damn knee aching, sick of trying to force motivation at work when his mind felt foggy, sick of feeling useless. He wanted to run, to skate, to move his body again.

He wanted to take back the way he'd acted yesterday.

He wanted Penny to talk to him.

He should have given her time to process instead of pushing her yesterday. Their explosive interaction the night before made it that much more obvious that they didn't know each other very well. With the amount of time they'd spent together recently, he'd convinced himself that there was a level of understanding there that they hadn't earned.

Maybe there was a part of him that wanted to push forward too fast. Right now, he was missing all of his normal connections, and it was taking a toll. Still. He couldn't build a friendship on a house of cards just to fill the void.

Brett's phone buzzed on the table, and he picked it up. "Hey, Tony."

"Surprised you're up early."

"I'm always up early." He closed his eyes and drew in a deep breath, noting the tightness in his chest. The dull throb at the base of his neck. *He couldn't control this.*

"I just figured . . . you know."

Brett sighed. "No, I don't know, buddy." When he opened his

eyes, he froze. A pair of women's legs stood straight up outside the window, toes pointed toward the sky.

"That you and your physical therapist would be doing some late-night sessions."

Brett didn't answer, mesmerized by those legs splitting apart in a slow, graceful arc and stretching in opposite directions.

"Nothing?"

Brett blinked. "Sorry, Tony, what did you say?"

"I'm not going to repeat it. It's not funny if—"

"Late night sessions. Right. No, we mostly do PT after dinner."

Tony muttered something under his breath. "So, how's the knee?"

Brett's throat worked as Penny righted herself and dropped into a warrior pose, her hair pulled into a messy bun on top of her head. She wore a sports bra and, well, he couldn't see what was below her waist. He cursed the windowsill and pushed up in his seat. Boy shorts. *Holy hell.* Penny was doing yoga on the front landing in the morning sunshine with a bra and boy shorts on.

"Do you want me to call you back?" Tony sounded annoyed, and that was enough to snap Brett out of his momentary fantasy.

"No, sorry. I was just distracted by something." Brett's mouth felt like the Sahara. He stood and limped to the cupboard to grab a glass and fill it with water. "The knee is getting better. I'm hardly using a crutch." *This was fine.* She was just doing a workout, and he didn't need to watch.

"That's great to hear."

"How did the anniversary end up?"

Tony chuckled. "I bought her tickets to see Mother Mother."

"I think they're playing the Saddledome in a few weeks." Brett pulled the glass from the cupboard and turned.

"Exactly. That's what I wanted to talk to you about. Leanne and I are going to come out. Do you think we can crash?"

Through the glass, Penny threw her head back and stretched

her arm behind her, and as the sun hit her skin, Brett could've sworn it turned to pure gold. He coughed. "Yeah, of course. It'll be amazing to see you."

"We won't be putting you out?"

Brett grunted. "You're always welcome, buddy." Penny stretched tall then dropped to the ground and out of his sight.

"Excellent. I'll let you go. Date is June twenty-second."

"Mmhmm, see you then."

Tony ended the call, and Brett realized he was standing next to the sink still gripping an empty glass. What had they just talked about? Tony coming to visit . . . June something. Twenty-second. Brett set the glass on the counter and opened the calendar on his phone. *June twenty-second. Tony staying over.*

Tony staying over where? Penny was in the second bedroom now. He had the air mattress for camping, but he wasn't going to make his friends sleep on that. He exhaled and filled his glass with water, then took it back to the table and opened his project management dashboard.

When the front door opened, he leaned in closer to his screen. Watching her through the window had already sent his pulse skittering. He didn't need to see her two feet in front of his face.

He didn't say anything as she closed the door behind her, not sure whether she wanted him to or not. Penny set her rolled-up yoga mat next to the door and padded into the kitchen, then pulled a bag from the cupboard, scooped something into the coffee maker, and turned it on.

He'd seen that bag in her cart and thought it was coffee grounds, but it wasn't a brand he recognized. He'd meant to ask her about it.

Penny pulled an English muffin from the Lazy Susan, split it, and popped it in the toaster. Then she filled a glass with water, squeezed in lemon juice from slices she'd cut and stored in the fridge, and gulped it down.

Brett kept typing and watched all of this in his peripheral vision. She could pretend he wasn't there all she wanted. Fine by him. He felt her moving closer to the table before he saw her round the island. Her bare stomach flexed as she pulled out a chair and sat down.

She clasped her hands on the table and waited. Brett's pulse raced, but he didn't look up. If she was sitting there, she wanted to talk. While he wasn't angry about the night before, he was feeling a tad stubborn. Especially since he was still struggling to make his tongue work correctly.

"Am I interrupting?" Penny asked.

Brett drew a breath and glanced up. He hadn't decided whether he wanted to say yes or no, but when he looked at her face and saw those same puffy red-rimmed eyes from the first day she'd moved in, his heart dropped to the floor.

"Good morning."

"Good morning." Penny's lips twitched. "I just wanted to say I'm sorry."

With those words, Brett felt like he'd just scored on his own net. "No, I'm sorry."

Penny shook her head and flattened her hands on the table. "You have nothing to be sorry about. You asked a question, and my reaction was juvenile."

"I shouldn't have pushed you."

"You didn't push." Penny stared at her hands. "I didn't realize . . . I didn't expect to see him, and I think it's still so fresh. I'm not quite ready to talk about it."

Brett resisted the urge to reach out and hold her hand like she'd done for him during PT the other night. "I shouldn't have expected you to share something like that with a stranger."

Penny's brows pinched together. "You're not a stranger, Brett."

Brett locked onto her warm brown eyes. He thought back through the past forty-eight hours questioning why he'd ever thought he could ask Penny about Daniel in the first place. That answer was simple. Since getting sober, his whole life had to be built on openness and vulnerability. He walked into meetings all the time and told complete strangers intimate details about his life. That was the way he stayed healthy. That was how it worked.

But Penny wasn't used to that life. She didn't have the same demons, and she didn't have to break down those barriers to be safe. To survive. He didn't resent his experience—he was better for breaking down those walls. But not everybody was ready to do it, and he shouldn't have expected Penny to.

Penny dropped her eyes. "I'm sorry I reacted that way. It wasn't fair, and I appreciate you checking in on me." She tapped the tips of her beige fingernails on the tabletop. "The red sauce was delicious."

Brett breathed a laugh. "Isn't it bolognese?"

Penny shrugged, then walked back to the counter. The coffee maker was hissing now.

"I'm glad you liked it. What are you making, by the way?" That was a safe question, wasn't it?

"It's ground cocoa beans. Has a more sustainable form of energy than the caffeine in coffee. Do you want some?"

Brett's eyes trailed down the line of her back, resting briefly on the crease in her skin barely visible past the fabric of her shorts before he forced them back up. "Sure." Brett wasn't a huge coffee drinker, but he loved hot chocolate.

"It's nothing like hot chocolate if that's what you're thinking."

Brett laughed. "That's fine. I'm up for whatever."

―――

The next few days passed similarly. Pleasant conversation when they happened to be in the same room. Brett working from one of his three locations in the apartment while Penny mostly kept to herself, submitting applications and searching job boards.

On Thursday night, they worked through another PT session

—less painful than the first—and by Friday, Brett had not only managed to keep his attraction to Penny under wraps, but he was also starting the day without his crutch.

He made tacos Friday night, and Penny insisted he try one of the tortillas she'd bought. They were slightly better than his, and he made Penny beam by admitting it. She'd been particularly quiet that day, but he wasn't going to repeat his earlier mistake by pressing her for answers.

Which was why he was pleasantly surprised when she said, "I haven't received any offers."

Everything inside Brett stilled as he watched her from across the table. She was offering him a glimpse inside her head, and he didn't want to screw it up.

"Oh yeah?"

Penny nodded. "I've submitted over twenty applications, and the only responses have been 'wait-and-see.' Plenty of businesses haven't even gotten back to me. The one medical center I was really excited about asked for an interview and then cancelled it.

"They cancelled the interview?" That seemed unprofessional.

"I know. It was so weird. It was supposed to be this morning." She nudged a piece of lettuce back into her tortilla.

"I'm sorry. Did they give you a reason why?"

She slumped in her seat. "Nope, just said that they'd decided to go in a different direction. But I don't know why they would have offered me an interview if they weren't interested in hiring for the position." Penny shook her head. "I don't know. Maybe they got an applicant that was more impressive."

Brett reflected on the days when he'd done all the hiring at their company. He never would have asked for an interview and cancelled it, even if he had received a better applicant. It was just bad practice. "Frustrating."

"Yeah." Penny blew out a breath and stood to take her dishes to the sink.

Brett knew this routine by now. She would rinse them off,

load them in the dishwasher, and say something about how she needed to get a little work done before she went to bed. He wouldn't see her until the next morning.

But it was Friday night.

Tyler had texted that morning, reminding him that they were going to the Perch. Brett knew he'd mentioned it to Penny earlier in the week, but they hadn't talked about it since.

He picked up his phone and played it cool. "Did you have any interest in spending time with Kelty, Sean, Tyler and Emma tonight? I think they're still planning to go over to the Perch later."

"What exactly is the Perch?"

"An outdoor patio. People get drinks, listen to music, play some corn hole." It was their favourite summer hang besides the Stampede grounds in July, but Brett had only been there once since his injury.

"I'm terrible at corn hole."

"There's not a tryout."

Penny grinned and tucked her thumb in the pocket of her jeans. Brett wondered what his thumbs would look like in that same position. Pulling them off her. He shook his head and frowned.

"I don't know. It's not that I don't want to hang out with them. I think they're great, but I don't think I'm in the mood for noise or . . . anything that requires more energy than sitting down and staring at a wall."

Brett chuckled. "That was very specific. Is that what's pencilled into your calendar for this evening?"

"Oh, definitely. Every night this week. Gives me a lot of time to really steep in my current life situation."

"Sounds riveting." Brett's heartbeat sounded in his ears. "But we don't have to go out with them. We could do something else." *We.* He was making a bid—a small one—but by the way his hands started to tingle, it seemed his body knew better than he did.

Penny pursed her lips. "Like what?"

It wasn't a straight-up no. Brett shrugged as his pulse skated away from him. Did he want to spend time with Penny, or just another human in general? If he wanted to spend time with friends, wouldn't he have already planned to go to the Perch? "I don't know."

"What do normal people do when they're depressed because of a lack of job offers or a bum knee?" Penny smiled, and for the first time in days, it reached her eyes.

"I think it probably involves ice cream and either a really sad movie or a really stupid one."

She walked into the living room and opened the console underneath his flat-screen TV.

"I don't have any DVDs if that's what you're looking for. I mostly just stream—"

Penny gasped, and Brett startled so hard he banged his knee into the leg of the table. He grunted in pain, and Penny jumped to her feet. "Are you okay?"

"Yeah." Brett rubbed his knee as if that would stop the throbbing.

"I'm sorry. Was that my fault?

"No, I don't think it had anything to do with the fact that you just reacted like you were witnessing a murder."

Penny gave an apologetic smile. "I'm sorry, I just got excited."

Brett frowned. "About something in my TV cabinet?" He stood and hobbled over to where she was standing. Penny pointed to the shelf. "My old Xbox console from high school?"

"Yeah, you didn't tell me that you play."

"Because I don't. I haven't touched that thing in years."

"But you used to?"

Did her eyes look hopeful? Any girl he'd ever met only gave looks of disgust or annoyance when a guy brought video games into the conversation. "Of course, I used to. What guy didn't play video games in high school?"

"What did you play?"

Brett pointed to the drawer next to the cabinet door she'd opened. "All the games I played are in there. I don't think people even use physical games anymore. It's all downloaded."

Penny dropped to her knees, and Brett waited as she rifled through the games. She was going to be disappointed. Everything in there was either a sports or shooting game.

Before Brett could warn her, Penny gasped again and pulled one out, brandishing it in front of him.

"Halo?" He gave her a skeptical look.

"Umm, yeah. It's my favourite."

Brett's eyes narrowed. "Your favourite video game is Halo?"

Penny stood up. "Brothers, remember? We used to have tournaments with their friends in the basement."

"You played with them?"

"Oh, I didn't just play with them. I destroyed them. Want to have a go?"

CHAPTER
Ten

PENNY PICKED up the controller and smoothed her thumbs over the buttons, surprised at how familiar they still felt after all these years. She couldn't help but think of Lucas. As the brother closest in age to her, he was always the one most offended when she won.

She didn't win *every* time and may have exaggerated her skill just a little with her previous comment to Brett. But in her younger-sister mind, the goal was always to make her brothers rue the day they picked up those controllers, even if she pretended to be indifferent in the moment. Penny still hadn't admitted to her brothers how much she practiced when they were out of the house. Beating the bots never felt quite as satisfying, though.

Brett sat next to Penny on the couch, and she almost slid into him as the cushion compressed. She glanced down as she shifted to the side and noticed the rolled-up towel sitting on the floor. The one they'd used in their sessions. She distinctly remembered setting that on the counter the other night. *Someone had been practicing.*

Brett ran a hand over the back of his neck as the game loaded, and Penny grinned.

"Are you nervous?"

Brett frowned. "Not nervous. It's just been a long time since I played this."

"It's been a long time for me too."

"Yeah, but you just talked a big game. Now I feel all kinds of pressure not to lose. I'm a hockey player, Penny. I'm competitive."

"Well, then, I hope this doesn't ruin your night." She raised her eyebrow, and his jaw tensed. He wasn't kidding. A spark lit in her midsection. She liked that look on his face, especially since she'd put it there. Determination mixed with a bit of pride and annoyance. Now she wished both that he wasn't injured and it wasn't the off-season so she could see more of this fire in his belly on the ice.

"Let's make it interesting. Winner gets to pick the ice cream flavour." Penny watched Brett for a reaction. She hadn't wanted to go to a restaurant where she would feel pressured to waste money, but she'd gladly spend a few dollars on dessert.

Brett shrugged. "I hope you like peanut butter."

Damn it. She did, but she wasn't going to admit it. "I hope you like cookie dough."

He scoffed, and they delved into customizing their soldiers. Penny chose a sleek, agile build, her character's armour a vibrant shade of blue with a red visor. Brett went for bulk and strength, his soldier clad in intimidating black and looking like a walking fortress.

"Compensating for something?"

"Yeah. A working leg. The rest of me functions just fine."

Penny snorted. "I'm sure it does." She leaned forward and stared a little harder at the screen.

"What map do you want to play?" Brett asked, and she moved her arrow to the top right corner. "Ah, you're an Ice Age girl. You weren't traumatized as a child with Alberta winters."

"I don't think you can complain about it if you still choose to live here."

Brett chuckled. "No, it's fine now. I have a car with heat. I don't have to walk two kilometres to school in waist-deep snow."

"They didn't plow the sidewalks?"

"We didn't have sidewalks."

"Wait, where did you grow up?"

Brett tapped the settings on the screen. "Ever heard of Crossfield?" Penny shook her head. "It's just north of here. Small farming community."

"But everyone in your family . . . they seem like the antithesis of farmers."

"Are you saying farmers aren't smart?"

Penny scoffed. "No. But it just seems like your family would have lived in the city or something."

"My mom grew up on a farm in southern Alberta. Raising a family outside of the city made her feel close to her roots."

"So she liked growing up in the boonies?"

"I think she just wanted to inflict the same torture on her kids that she had to endure."

Penny laughed. She understood that sentiment. Her parents were always lamenting the fact that modern conveniences were making their children soft.

"Ready to get schooled?" Brett pursed his lips, and Penny worked not to bust out laughing. *Who said that?*

"Talk is cheap, babe. Let's see if you can back it up."

The map was mostly open spaces, which Penny loved because sniping had always been her strategy. *Find a high vantage point and scope him out.* She maneuvered her character with fluid grace, ducking behind cover so Brett hopefully wouldn't catch on to what she was up to.

Brett's approach was more direct, his character barreling through the map with the confidence of a tank. Penny tried to take him by surprise, but Brett was catching up too quickly. She hid and prepared to gun and run. When he approached, she ducked out and started shooting. Gunfire rattled through the speakers, but Penny's quicker reflexes won out, and Brett's character crumpled to the ground.

"First blood to me," Penny gloated, a triumphant smile on her lips.

"First blood?" Brett chortled, and Penny revelled in the surprised look on his face. *He had no idea who he was messing with.* "Enjoy that feeling. It's not going to last."

"Is that what you said on the ice before you got dropped?"

"Wow. Low blow."

Penny laughed with zero remorse as Brett stared more intently at the screen. Their soldiers were in a dance of cat and mouse. Penny's agility kept her one step ahead, but Brett wasn't easy to take down. They traded kills, and Penny started to get nervous.

With her health low, she darted around a corner only to be met by a well-timed grenade from Brett. With no time to react, the explosion engulfed her character, and she groaned, falling back on the couch while Brett did the most annoying victory dance in human history.

"You're not even standing. You're just scooting your butt across the couch cushion," Penny muttered.

"Jealous?"

"Of what? Your ass or the couch?" Penny pushed off his shoulder and moved further away from him. "Let's go. Round two."

By round six, they were tied at three wins each, but Penny had won the last two. With newfound confidence, she was relentless. She picked up a sniper rifle and found a vantage point with a clear view of the field. Brett's character appeared in her scope, unaware of the danger. She took a breath and hit the button to squeeze the trigger. The shot rang out, hitting him in the helmet.

Brett respawned while he cursed under his breath. He moved carefully, using the sparse cover to his advantage. She still had the upper hand, but Brett took her by surprise and charged her position, his character's heavy gun blazing. Penny's sniper was no match at close range. She scrambled to switch to a shotgun.

Their characters grappled, gunfire and melee attacks blurring into one chaotic clash. With a well-timed hit, Penny knocked Brett to the ground and finished him off. He threw up his hands, brandishing the controller over his head.

"You can't keep hiding out in the mountains!" he cried out.

"I'm sorry, isn't that the point of the game? To find an advantage?" Penny couldn't have quelled the giddiness in her gut if she'd tried.

"The point of the *game* is to battle, not squirrel yourself away and take cheap shots." Brett ran a hand through his hair. He was hot and bothered, and watching him all fired up pushed adrenaline through her veins.

"Come on, Brett, are you really going to pretend I'm not just better than you at this?"

He started another round. When her character appeared, she glanced over at Brett's map view.

"No screen peeking," he grumbled, and Penny laughed out loud.

"It's not screen peeking! It's the same TV—right there in front of me!"

"Still cheating."

"Says who?"

"My house, my rules."

"You sound exactly like my brother." Penny rounded a corner and ran down a hallway. Brett had wisely chosen a map with a labyrinth of corridors, so she couldn't employ her usual tactics. She switched out her weapon. He was still going down, and she wouldn't even *peek* to make it happen.

"Which brother?" Brett asked.

"Lucas." Penny surprisingly said his name without any hesitation. "He was the worst. Anything he could do to stack the deck in his favour, he was all in. One time, he even pretended that my boyfriend was on the phone to distract me."

"Did it work?"

"No, I didn't care about that boyfriend." Penny's chest warmed at the memory. So much of their time together was tainted with his alcohol abuse, it felt almost sacred to think of him as a carefree thirteen-year-old kid.

Brett glanced over, probably noticing that she'd clammed up, and she sent a shot into his soldier's turned back. When he looked back at the screen, his jaw went slack then clenched as he dropped his controller to the floor.

"Okay, that was definitely cheating."

Penny threw out her hands, feigning innocence. "I didn't do anything."

"You were—I thought something was wrong."

"I was just thinking!"

"It freaked me out."

Penny gaped at him. "So if I'm too silent, it disturbs your game? When ten minutes ago you said, 'You're talking so damn much, and I can't focus!'"

Penny was tempted to laugh at the look on his face, but she held it in. Brett practically had steam coming out of his ears, and as much as he touted being tough on the ice, she didn't know how much smack talk he could take without blowing a gasket. *Though she was tempted to find out . . .*

He turned toward her on the couch, then reached out and grabbed her wrist. Penny's heart rate spiked at his touch, and her skin burned under his fingers as he snatched the controller from her hand.

She scoffed. "Oh, because that's going to help?"

"This controller is giving you an advantage."

Her heart jumped in her chest like it had been shocked with defibrillator paddles as she stood and leaned over Brett to pick up his controller off the floor. Energy buzzed between them, and when his hand landed on her head and mussed her perfectly parted hair, Penny squealed. "Seriously? What are we, seven?"

She straightened and stared at him with a look of disbelief.

"You just got your *finger oils* all over my clean hair!" Brett pursed his lips, trying not to laugh. "Are you laughing at me?" Penny punched his shoulder and instantly regretted it. It felt like she'd knocked her fist against a brick wall.

Her eyes flashed as she smoothed her dark waves and tucked her hair behind her ears. She hovered over him, her knees almost touching his. "If we're switching players, we have to switch spots on the couch."

Brett frowned. "Why would we have to switch spots on the couch?"

"Because otherwise, I have to look diagonal to my screen."

"And you're not capable of looking diagonal? Seems like you've been doing that pretty well for the last six rounds."

"I *wasn't looking*, and it's more work for my eyes!"

Brett barked a laugh. "More work for your eyes? Are you serious?"

Penny stepped over his knees, then shoved him from his right side, careful not to accidentally hit his leg.

"You're going to have to push a lot harder than that if you want to move me from this spot."

Penny dug in and shoved as hard as she could, but Brett was like a boulder set in a field after a glacial melt. His blue eyes danced as he watched her pathetic efforts, and that only fueled the fire. All of her training with her brothers came back in full force at that moment, and she remembered the one secret weapon she'd always held against them no matter how much bulk they carried.

With one arm still pressed against his shoulder, she slipped her other hand under his arm and dug her fingers into his ribs.

Brett sucked in a breath, and with a reaction time his Halo soldier would've envied, he twirled his arm, grabbed onto hers above the elbow and yanked. Penny flew over the arm of the couch and landed sprawled over his lap. Before she could react, Brett's massive hands stretched over her entire rib cage, playing her ribs like a xylophone until she thought she was going to pee her pants laughing.

"Brett!" she gasped, her face on fire and her lungs tight and desperate for air. "*I can't breathe!*" she wheezed between staccato laughter.

Brett finally let up, and she scrambled to sit, sucking in air as soon as her diaphragm released.

She smacked his chest. "Not fair!"

"Now you know how I feel. But hey, don't dish it out if you can't take it." He was grinning from ear to ear, obviously pleased with himself.

Penny threw her hair away from her face and back over her shoulders, then closed her eyes and inhaled to calm her racing heart. When she lowered her head, she realized she was full-on straddling Brett with her legs folded against the outsides of his thighs. Their heaving chests were only centimetres apart, and her efforts to calm her nerves seemed suddenly futile.

Brett ran his tongue over his lower lip, and Penny's insides liquified. "You could have just asked nicely," he panted, his voice low and throaty.

Penny swallowed hard. "I thought I did."

"No, you demanded—"

"I did it in a *nice* way." She barely finished the last word as the citrusy scent her brain had already claimed as uniquely Brett overwhelmed her. *Had she just started a tickle fight with him? And why was she still planted in his lap?*

She couldn't make herself move. The feel of his strong legs beneath her and the warmth of his body sent a zing up her spine. Brett's hands twitched on top of her thighs, and every inch of her skin pricked up at attention, just waiting to see what he'd touch next.

It was stupid, right? Her rules? Her ideas about not getting with someone immediately after breaking up with Danny. Brett was nothing like him. Sure, she'd only known him for a week, but what did that have to do with anything?

Who cared if these were the exact same rationalizations she'd used every single time she'd gotten into a toxic relationship? Because right now, Brett's hair hung in dishevelled waves around his face, and he was watching her with those eyes that looked more like smouldering coals than deep blue wells.

All the frustration from that afternoon melted away as Penny dropped her hands, and her fingertips brushed over his.

Brett's fingers twitched. "Penny—"

The doorbell rang before he could whisper more than her name, and Penny jumped like a cat who just had its tail stepped on. She scrambled to the side and sat in her old position on the couch with her back ramrod straight like she was in third grade with Mr. Hall.

The doorbell rang again, and Penny jumped up. "I'll get it." She ran to the door and flung it open. "Oh. Hi." Penny stepped back to let Tyler, Emma, Kelty, and Sean enter the room. Kelty gave her a quizzical look, and Penny smoothed her shirt.

She knew exactly what she looked like right now. Flushed. Hair a mess. Brett sitting on the couch, casually holding a pillow on his lap. *He had a pillow on his lap.* That only made her cheeks burn deeper.

"It's a good thing you guys were here. Otherwise, we would have known you were ditching us for a better option." Tyler glanced over at Brett, then down at the pillow he was holding. His eyes narrowed. "Did you have a better option, Brett?"

Brett cleared his throat and leaned over to pick up Penny's controller off the floor. "Nope. Just a quiet night at home, buddy."

"Uh-huh. Were you playing video games?" Tyler asked.

Penny took a step toward the couch. "I was. Well, we both were. We were playing video games together."

"Is that what they're calling it these days?" Sean murmured, and Kelty pursed her lips to keep from laughing.

"It was my idea. I saw the console and thought it would be

fun." Penny stumbled over her words, and Sean raised an eyebrow.

Tyler slipped off his shoes and walked in to look at the screen. "I didn't know that thing still worked."

"That's what she said." Brett smirked, and Tyler laughed out loud.

"What is this, Halo?"

"My choice," Penny admitted. "I have three brothers."

Kelty flashed her a knowing look. They'd had this conversation before. She knew what that number meant. All her talk of Lucas during the game settled in her like a stone in a bucket of water.

"And here I thought I was the only one whose brother forced them to play first-person shooter games." Emma folded her arms in front of her.

Sean scoffed. "I never forced you."

Emma rolled her eyes. "I like you already, Penny."

Penny grinned and ran a hand through her hair. "It's just been a really long week. It was so nice of you guys to invite me out, but I didn't have it in me."

"What's your excuse?" Sean pointed at Brett, who gestured to his knee.

"Oh, I don't know. Attempting not to hate every aspect of my life while I try to heal before next season so you're not down a player."

"Which is exactly why we invited you out," Sean grumbled.

Brett's jaw worked. "I didn't—"

"Brett brought it up," Penny cut in. "He wanted to go to the Perch, and I told him I wasn't up for it. He was nice enough to chill here with me. We did talk about getting ice cream. Do you want to hang out, and I'll grab some? We can play cards or something?" *Did they even like cards?*

"That would be great, and no—" Emma gave Tyler a stern look. "Not strip poker."

Brett looked at Penny, his face unreadable. She needed to get some air. "Great, I'll run to the store. Anything else I can pick up? Beer? Something for mixed drinks?" As soon as she said it, she realized for the first time that she'd never seen any alcohol in Brett's cupboards. She'd sworn off alcohol as soon as Lucas went to rehab the first time, but she didn't mind if others drank with her there as long as it didn't get out of hand.

Tyler shook his head. "I don't drink."

Penny scanned the room. "Anyone else?"

They shook their heads, and Penny grabbed her purse hanging on the hooks next to the door. *Odd.* "Okay! I'll be back in a few minutes, and while I'm gone, Brett, why don't you explain to your friends why I'll be buying cookie dough."

CHAPTER
Eleven

PENNY 8:01PM

> Do you need anything at the store while I'm here?

BRETT 8:01PM

> I'm surprised you're asking

PENNY 8:01PM

> Why?

BRETT 8:02PM

> Because this is a victory trip

PENNY 8:02PM

> If it were a victory trip, you'd be buying

BRETT 8:02PM

> What's your PayPal?

PENNY 8:03PM

Stop. I was kidding

BRETT 8:03PM

> Let me buy your salmonella ice cream, Penny

PENNY 8:04PM

I regret my offer of kindness

BRETT 8:04PM

> A bag of rolled oats. And HP sauce

PENNY 8:05PM

You're a man of fine taste

PENNY SMIRKED as she watched Brett dig into the tub of cookie dough ice cream. "Looks good, don't you think?"

Brett shook his head. "You're worse than the guys on Pucks Deep."

"Is that supposed to mean something to me?"

"I like where this is going. Brett was telling us your trash talk is next level," Tyler called out behind them.

Emma exhaled. "Pucks Deep is our rival. The team they should've met in the finals last season."

Penny glanced at Brett. "Not the guys who jacked up your knee?"

"Not this time," Sean grunted.

"It was a head hunter on Stiff Sticks." Brett emptied the pint, making sure the six bowls were evenly filled. He turned and threw out the carton as Penny pulled six spoons from the drawer and picked up two bowls to take to the table.

"At least I didn't hurt more than your pride." She winked at Brett as she passed.

"My ribs beg to differ," he murmured, and his voice seemed to hum through her bones. *She'd been sitting on his lap*, and as brief as it had been, she'd reached for him. He knew it, and she knew it. *If they hadn't been interrupted, would she have done more than that?*

Penny set the first two bowls in front of Kelty and Emma, then went back for the others. Brett took dessert to Tyler and Sean, and she brought the last two bowls for them. They all sat around the table, and Brett dumped out a bag of Nestle Smarties.

"Will these work?"

"Little late now to ask that question, don't you think?" Kelty ran her hands through the chocolate morsels. "You are all going down."

Sean pulled the deck of cards from their carton and started dealing.

"I haven't played Texas Hold 'em in a long time," Penny admitted.

"Good. I don't think my ego can take another hit tonight." Brett picked up his cards, and Tyler quickly reminded her of the rules and gameplay while Emma divided the Smarties evenly among them.

Penny bowed out the first few hands, happy to give up her few buy-in candies. As the rounds progressed, everyone had their moments of glory. One hand, Kelty went all-in with her pocket queens only to be bested by Emma's straight. In another round, Tyler managed to bluff his way to victory with nothing more than a pair of twos.

"I don't think I can trust you anymore." Emma shook her head and scooped up the cards in a huff. "You're too convincing."

Tyler laughed. "You weren't complaining when I convinced our contractor to bring down the cost of installing the hardwood floors."

Brett reached out and stacked the empty ice cream bowls. "Wouldn't have worked on me, buddy. I know your tells."

"This pile of Smarties says otherwise," Tyler gloated. "By the way, we still want you for the build-out on Tepper Place."

Brett exhaled. "I told you, it's not a big enough project. We'd—"

"Dominic could spare his team for a weekend, don't you think? Just to get the framing done?"

Brett stood and carried the dishes to the sink. "You can take it up with him, bud. I'm staying out of this."

Emma leaned over as Tyler launched into another argument. "Kelty told me you're looking for a job in the northwest. Any luck?"

"I submitted a ton of applications. No bites so far." Penny played with the Smarties in front of her, organizing them by colour.

"It sucks. I remember that feeling. We were scrambling for contracts when our studio closed down at the beginning of the year."

"You're a designer, right?" Penny asked. Kelty had told her about Emma over the years, but she hadn't paid close attention before having a face to put with the name.

"Food stylist and now a project manager for these properties," Emma answered. "Remind me how you and Kelty met?"

"Kelty went to UBC. We met in anatomy our first semester."

"Wait, you took anatomy?" Emma spun toward Kelty.

Kelty grinned. "Undetermined major for a year and a half."

"And then you ended up doing business?"

Kelty sighed. "Goes to show how well anatomy went. If Penny hadn't been there to help me study, I would've failed that class."

She wasn't exaggerating. Kelty's parents had pushed her to go into a medical field, but all the memorization had given her heart palpitations. Kelty figured out she was a big-picture person. A strategist. She was good with numbers. Not so great with body systems.

"Good to know Brett's physical therapist isn't a hack," Tyler teased.

Penny pulled her hair back from her face and tied it into a low knot with the elastic on her wrist. "My test results speak for themselves."

"How about you let your dealing skills speak for themselves." Brett nudged her elbow, and her skin tingled.

"Is it my turn?"

He nodded, and Penny reached for the cards.

They played for another hour or so, and Penny won just enough to keep a few Smarties in reserve. She stayed in play until the last hand, where only Tyler and Emma were left standing. As Emma pushed all her candy into the middle, Tyler's eyebrows lifted.

"You sure about that?"

Emma's cheeks flushed. "Positive."

"You remember what's at stake?" Tyler's grin turned devilish.

Brett leaned back in his chair. "What's at stake, Ty? I'm sure Sean would love to hear about your secret sex bets with his sister."

Sean's face reddened. "Bowen, I swear to—"

"It's not a sex bet!" Tyler held up his hands, and Emma glared at Sean.

"Maybe it *is* a sex bet. A super hot, dirty sex bet—"

"I told her that whoever lost tonight had to get up tomorrow to meet the electrician at six thirty in the morning!"

Kelty laughed out loud. "The electrician that always hits on Emma?"

"He hits on Tyler, too!" Emma exclaimed. "But we can't find anyone else who's as good for the price, so . . ."

"Emma's going to have to deal with it tomorrow because I . . ." Tyler paused dramatically, then dropped his cards. "Have a full house."

Emma's eyes twinkled. "Or *am* I?" She dropped her hand to reveal four nines, the two in her hand and two from the flop and the turn. Tyler almost swallowed his tongue. Emma pushed back her chair and swung her arms over her head in a victory dance.

When she finished rubbing it in, she leaned over the table. "I can't tell you how good it feels to know you're going to be the one objectified tomorrow while I'll still be cozy in bed."

Tyler crossed his arms in front of him while she scooped all his Smarties to her side of the table. "It's fine. I'm getting breakfast at Noni's on the way."

"If you don't bring me a chorizo bowl we're through, Bowen."

Tyler grinned, and Penny decided Emma was her new favourite person.

"You all need to get out of my house. I'm turning into a pumpkin." Brett ran a hand over his face, and Penny glanced at the clock on the microwave. Almost midnight.

"When did you get old, bud?" Tyler clapped Brett on the shoulder as Kelty and Sean cleared their water cups and took them to the sink.

"Speaking of old, we need to plan something for Fly in the fall," Sean said.

Kelty frowned. "I can't believe it's his last season."

"Only with the Snowballs, right? He still has Masters," Emma said. Sean nodded.

Penny didn't know Fly personally since he hadn't been at the

Sunday supper she attended, but she'd heard his name mentioned enough to know he was important. "You could go skydiving," she offered. "It's good team building, plus his name."

Brett stood and scooted his chair in. "Have you gone skydiving?"

Penny nodded. "With my brother." Her chest squeezed. That had been one of her many attempts to help Lucas see there were better ways to get high.

"Do you think Fly would do it?" Kelty asked.

"Hell, yes. That's a great idea." Sean nodded approvingly. "Did you go with a company here?"

Penny shook her head. "No, it was back in Vancouver, but I'm sure there are plenty of places."

"I'll look into it. Thanks." Sean draped an arm around Kelty's shoulders and walked to the door. Emma and Tyler were already putting on their shoes.

"Thanks, bud." Tyler stood and pulled Brett into a hug. "Still on for AA on Sunday?"

Brett stepped back and nodded. "I might even be able to drive."

Penny rolled her eyes. "If he gets his leg straight tomorrow, I'll consider it."

Tyler winked at Brett. "Enjoy the rest of your *quiet night*."

They were all thinking it, weren't they? That she and Brett had been doing *something* when they showed up unannounced? The truth was, she wished they had been.

Brett pursed his lips. "I will. Thanks, buddy."

Brett closed the door and exhaled. He and Penny were alone again, and even with the cards and sugar as a distraction, he was still laser-focused on what had happened seconds before the doorbell rang.

As soon as Penny left to get the ice cream, Tyler and Sean had peppered him with questions about what exactly he'd been doing before they walked in. The girls were worse, accusing him of taking advantage of Penny when she was vulnerable. He'd barely succeeded in convincing them that nothing had happened before she'd returned from the store.

But he hadn't convinced himself.

"The dishwasher's dirty, right?" Penny asked.

"Yep." Brett walked to the table and began stacking the cards. "Do you want to keep these Smarties?"

Penny scoffed. "Gross, no. They were in all six of our hands."

"So . . . covered in finger oil?"

Penny gave him a look that said, *I'm both impressed that you remember that comment and annoyed that you're mocking me.*

Something had happened on that couch. The way Penny had looked at him—the way she'd put her hands on his. Was this attraction between them something that lived outside his own head?

All week, he'd worked to shut down the thoughts that cropped up anytime they were in the same room. Or when she was doing yoga on the front porch. Or really anytime he remembered she was in the same house. But what if he didn't have to? What if she felt the same way, even when she knew he wasn't at his best?

"So Tyler, he's in recovery?" Penny asked. Brett blinked. The question was so far out of left field that he couldn't form a response before Penny continued. "Good for Emma."

Brett put the cards into the box and scooped the Smarties off the table. "What do you mean 'good for Emma?'" The beat of his heart sounded like boots on the bleachers inside his head.

Penny rinsed out the bowls one by one. "I know how hard it is to support someone through that."

Brett worked to keep the strain out of his voice. "Someone

close to you is in recovery?" His knee ached, and he wanted to escape to his bedroom to lie down and suffer in solitude, but he couldn't tear himself away from this conversation.

Penny thought Tyler was the one in recovery. Brett thought back over the night and realized it made perfect sense. Tyler had been the one to say he didn't drink. Then Tyler had mentioned going to AA on Sunday. But Brett wasn't ready to admit that she'd misunderstood until he heard what was going to come out of her mouth next.

"Maybe for some people, it wouldn't be as big of a deal, but I could never do it again."

Brett walked over and sat down on a stool as Penny loaded the last few glasses into the dishwasher. "Did you date a guy in recovery?"

His thoughts immediately flew to Daniel. Nothing about the guy screamed recovery to him, but maybe that was because he wasn't working a program. Maybe Penny didn't understand the difference between white-knuckling it versus being in active recovery.

"No, I didn't date anyone in recovery." Penny paused as if considering her next words carefully. "It was my brother," she said finally.

"Lucas?" Brett asked. He was the brother that Penny talked about most. She nodded, and her shoulders visibly tensed. Penny pressed the button on the dishwasher to start it, then rinsed off her hands and dried them on the towel.

Brett's thoughts snapped back to all the conversations he'd had with his sister, Cameron, over the past few years. He remembered the disappointment on her face. How she'd refused to answer his calls for weeks and months at a time. How when they finally had talked in person, she'd looked like Penny in that moment. Tense. Wary.

He had a good idea as to why Penny would be averse to getting into a relationship with somebody who struggled with addiction after going through that once.

"Were you his person?" Brett asked.

Penny looked up. "His person?"

"Yeah, the one he would call when things were bad."

"Do addicts only have one person?"

Brett shrugged. "I don't think there's one formula, but the people that are available and try to be there for them typically get the most phone calls."

Penny considered this. "I don't know if he had other people besides me. But yeah, I was his person."

Cameron's voice echoed in his head. *"You sucked all the air out of my life, Brett. It's going to take some time before I can breathe again."*

She'd been his person, too. It had always felt easier to call her than to admit to his parents over and over again that he was in trouble. His friendships came and went over those eight years or so. Roommates, girlfriends, acquaintances. They were always willing to help to a point, and he didn't blame them for backing out when shit got deep. What person in their right mind would stick around with someone who had zero capacity to contribute anything to the relationship?

Addiction was selfish. Not that he was selfish to fall into it, but selfishness was the natural result. All he could think about was what he needed—what he wanted. Nothing was ever his fault until he got sober enough to realize that all of it was.

And that was too painful a truth to bear sober.

"I just don't think I could ever trust anyone with that history, you know?" Penny shook her head. "I know that sounds awful, but Lucas said so many things. He promised me so many things, and none of them were ever real. Sometimes he'd keep his commitments for a while, and those times were honestly the hardest. It gave me just enough time to feel safe before he tore the rug out from under me again."

"Did you ever go to any support groups?"

Penny shook her head. "I didn't know that was a thing."

That didn't surprise Brett. There weren't enough resources as it was, but the ones that existed were sometimes difficult to find. The best programs were run by people in recovery, but they didn't always have the best organizational skills. He'd found his program through word of mouth.

"How's he doing now?" Brett asked. Based on the fact that Penny said he hadn't kept any of his promises, Brett assumed the answer would be one of three things. Either he was still using, he was in rehab, or he was dead.

He hoped for one of the former two, but when Penny's eyes grew glassy, he knew.

"I'm so sorry, Penny."

She swiped at her eyes and drew a ragged breath, trying to swallow down her emotion. "It's been four years. You'd think I wouldn't get so emotional talking about it."

"Four years isn't very long." Brett stood and rounded the island, not thinking twice before pulling Penny into his chest. She stiffened at first, then relaxed into him and wrapped her arms around his waist. "I'm so sorry," he whispered into her hair as Penny rested her head against his chest and cried.

They stood there in silence. Long enough for every word that had left Penny's mouth to etch itself over the fears Brett already repeated to himself on a daily basis.

You're not strong enough.
You can't trust yourself.
You'll never be whole.

Wasn't that what Penny had just said? She couldn't ever trust anyone who had been an addict? He couldn't argue with her. He'd seen so many friends end up exactly like her brother or who ended up hovering between life and death, destroying anyone who got tangled up in their web.

He'd also seen people recover. People like Tony. People like him. But their stories weren't over yet. The way he'd been feeling the last month had zapped any confidence he'd previously held, and now every day felt like a battle with the voices in his head telling him that with one purchase, one drink, he could make all of this pain go away.

It hurt so damn much to feel everything. When he had hockey, when he had his morning workouts, when he had good food and music and conversations at work, it was manageable. But he didn't know if he would always have those things, and he didn't know if he could be successful without them.

He'd left every woman who had come into his life worse than when he'd found them. Even if the variables had changed, how could he, in good conscience, start a new relationship with someone he cared about when he wasn't sure if he was better? How could he tie himself to someone else when he couldn't be certain he was strong or stable? When that person's happiness depended on his ability to keep ahead of those demons?

He slowly rubbed his hand over Penny's back. *How could he ever do that to another woman again?* He couldn't, which was exactly why he'd kept to himself the past few years. Yes, he was sober. Yes, he was functional. Yes, he was beginning to believe he might be a good person.

But he didn't know if he'd ever be free.

Penny pulled back and gazed up at him with eyes that looked like melted chocolate. She dragged her hands over his waist and trailed her fingers over his wrists, then up his arms until she reached the edge of his shirt sleeves.

Brett's heart hammered against his ribs. It was late. Penny was vulnerable, and she didn't know the truth about him. He needed to tell her the truth, but the feel of her hands on his skin shorted the connection between his brain and his mouth.

"What is it?" she asked, and Brett followed her gaze to the underside of his bicep. She pulled up the fabric of his shirt to expose more of his ink. Brett lifted a hand from her waist and scrunched up his shirt sleeve so she could get a full view.

"It's a great day for hockey." Penny read the text, then traced her fingers over the sentence. Brett held his breath. "Why do you have a bird around it? Is that your favourite team or something?"

His skin buzzed under her touch. "It's a phoenix."

Penny rotated his arm like a spit so she could see the whole thing. "It's beautiful. Why a phoenix?"

Why a phoenix? Because it signified his rebirth when he got sober. It represented building a new life out of ashes, which was more than a generous description of what Brett's existence had felt like for those years.

"Penny, Tyler's not the one in recovery," he murmured.

Penny's brow furrowed. "He's going to that AA meeting for me."

CHAPTER
Twelve

PENNY 11:42PM

> Brett's in recovery

ANDREA 11:47PM

> Your roommate?

PENNY 11:47PM

> Housemate

ANDREA 11:47PM

> Whatever. Is it bad?

PENNY 11:48PM

> I don't think so? I only found out because he was going to an AA meeting

ANDREA 11:51PM

> Did Lucas ever go to those?

PENNY 11:52PM

> Only when he was forced to

PENNY WOKE Saturday morning feeling like she'd spent the night at fight club. Had she slept at all? She'd looked at the time on her phone at least four times that she could remember, and the rest of the night was a fever dream.

After Brett told her he was in recovery, Penny hadn't known what to say. Especially since she'd already spewed her internal thoughts when she thought he was supporting Tyler. *Such an idiot.* She replayed her words a thousand times, rewriting them endlessly in her head as regret ate at her insides.

The last thing in the world she'd meant to do was hurt Brett. There he was comforting her while she talked about Lucas when she'd just told him she would never consider being with someone in recovery. Not that she assumed Brett was considering her as an option, but she knew what kinds of thoughts were probably running through his head if he was anything like Lucas.

In his darkest moments, when he was a few weeks sober, Lucas would call her late at night and ask if she thought he'd ever be able to have a normal life. He was desperate for her to tell him that he could heal. That someone could love him. That it was possible to change and be happy.

She'd said it. Every time. She'd told Lucas that of course he could change. Of course he could find a partner who would love everything about him and accept him for who he was. *She was such a hypocrite.* Was it possible to believe something was true but only for somebody else?

Last night, she hadn't asked Brett for details. She'd left him standing there in the kitchen and escaped to her room, and that was what she regretted most. Her words had to have stung, and Brett had already alluded to how difficult things were with his life being out of sorts.

Penny gripped her sheets as emotion threatened to drown her. *What if she'd stripped his hope and motivation? What if he'd been working so hard and she'd ruined it? What if her words had been the final pin that pricked his sobriety bubble?*

What if he called and she wasn't there, so he gave in and went for a fix? What if she said the wrong thing, and he used? What if he found someone else? What if she said something that made him angry? What if, what if, *what if?*

She couldn't do it again. She couldn't be anyone else's person. She wasn't strong enough after Lucas. After Danny. She'd made herself so small and ground herself to dust trying to be exactly what they needed, and she *couldn't do it again.*

Penny threw herself out of bed and went straight into the bathroom for a hot shower. As water formed rivulets over her skin, she breathed and talked herself down. She hadn't meant to hurt Brett. He would understand why she felt the way she did. He seemed so obviously to be in a better place than Lucas ever had been those last couple of years.

Yet the pit inside her didn't want to fill. No matter how many ways she tried to comfort herself, she only succeeded in making it less deep. By the time she walked out into the kitchen with her hair hanging damp down her back, she felt confident she wouldn't break down in tears if Brett was out there making breakfast.

He wasn't. The door to his room was still shut, so Penny went to the cupboard and pulled out a packet of oatmeal. She put it in a bowl with water and heated it in the microwave, then added blueberries from the fridge.

Penny had barely sat down at the table when Brett walked in.

"Good morning."

Penny swallowed her bite. "Morning." Her heart rate spiked, making her hand tremble when she dropped the spoon back into the bowl. "I'm sorry, Brett." This was the second time she was apologizing to him first thing in the morning.

He frowned. "For what?"

"For disappearing last night. You told me something personal, and—"

"No, it's fine. It was late."

Penny nodded. She thought of the words on his arm ensconced in the wings of a phoenix. The way his skin had felt under her fingertips. She wanted to tell him that he could talk to her about it if he wanted. She wanted to know why Tyler came with him to meetings, how long he'd been sober, how it had impacted his life, and more than anything, whether he was okay.

But she knew that if she started, she wouldn't stop. It already felt like she'd known Brett far longer than a week, and the tug she felt toward him would only get stronger if she dug deeper into his life.

"Sunday Supper is at five tonight," Brett said.

Penny knew that. Kelty had created a group text between her and Emma last night on her drive home, and both of them had insisted she come again. She hadn't texted back yet. "Isn't it only supposed to be for the Snowballs? I don't want to keep crashing."

Brett gathered the ingredients for his shake. "People bring friends all the time. Emma's brought her photographer friends a ton."

"If you're just trying to score a ride, I can take you." Penny waited to see Brett's reaction to her attempt at a joke. Maybe they could go back to joking around and playing Halo and forget about last night?

"How do you always see straight through me?" Brett didn't look at her, but the corner of his mouth lifted. "Actually, I may just go over with Tyler. We're going to hit that meeting at three, and it's not too far from Sean's parents."

Penny nodded, grateful Brett wasn't making a big deal out of it. "Okay, sounds good. I might go with Kelty and Emma then." Brett looked up. "Any other plans for the day?"

Penny stretched her arms over her head. "Just submitting more applications."

"Right." Brett scooped protein powder into the blender. "I saw something this morning I wanted to talk to you about."

"Oh yeah?"

"I opened up the hockey boards—"

"Boards at the rink?"

Brett laughed. "No, we have a website with chat boards. A place where all the players in the league can ask questions or get in touch with other teams."

"Got it, sorry."

He put the lid on the blender but didn't start it. "There were a couple of guys on there from Calgary talking about how they were having trouble finding PT." Penny's ears perked up. "Made me think. Maybe you could work with people privately or something."

She considered this. "It sounds good in theory, but I don't know if other people would be excited to work out in their home where I don't have all my equipment set up."

"I thought about that, too. You have all your equipment, though, eh?"

Penny nodded. "It would be ridiculous to try and transport it all and set it up for one session."

"But what if you set it up in the garage?" Brett started the blender as if purposefully giving her time to ruminate on that idea.

When the motor stopped, Penny said, "You'd let me do that?"

"I'm not using that space for anything other than storage. We could move everything to one side or stack it against the back wall. I don't think it would take up more than a third of the space if we organized everything."

Penny took another bite of oatmeal. "Do you think they'd work with me? Take a chance like that?"

"I was willing to have you move in, so I'm guessing yes." Brett poured his shake into a tall cup. "Do you want any?"

"If there's extra, but don't—"

"There's extra." He pulled another cup from the shelf.

Penny took her bowl to the counter and sat on a stool, and Brett passed her the shake. "That would be amazing. Seriously. I could take care of everything in the garage. You wouldn't need to help."

Brett scoffed. "I need to go through my crap anyway. It'll be good."

"Okay. If you're sure." Something like hope bloomed in Penny's chest. She didn't have a job, but if she could see private clients? Even a couple of appointments a week would help toward the money she needed to come up with for her parents' surprise and fill the gap before she got a bite on her applications. "When would you want to do that?"

Brett took a drink of his shake. "Does now work?"

They cleaned up breakfast, and Penny put on some jeans and a T-shirt, then followed Brett out to the back of the house. He wore a hoodie and a pair of shorts with slip-ons. Penny found herself inspecting the musculature of his lower legs and the few inches of visible thigh—for purely professional assessment, of course. He opened the garage door, then limped toward the pile of boxes.

"Don't lift anything, Brett. Tell me what to move, and I'll move it."

Brett exhaled and nodded, then lifted the flaps of one of the boxes that sat on top of the stack. Penny stayed back, not wanting to intrude by peering into his personal stuff.

"Definitely don't need most of this." Brett reached into the box and pulled out a stack of old comics. "We could wait until Tyler gets here, and he could move—"

"Unless these boxes are full of dumbbells, I'm sure I can manage. Is this one ready?" Penny stepped up next to him. Brett nodded, so she picked it up and moved it out onto the driveway.

They continued through the stack, and Penny was impressed with how organized it was already. Brett had items from his old apartment that he'd held on to in case he had a use for them here. Since he didn't, Penny moved lamps, two end tables, a painting, an old coffee maker, and an iron to the driveway.

She insisted Brett allow her to look through an old photo album featuring a young Brett with braces and a mullet. On the last page, she found stubs from his first professional hockey game and a note written on pink stationery covered in hearts.

"Who's Anna?" Penny held up the note, and Brett's eyes lit up.

"Where did you find that?"

Penny grinned. "It was in the back of this album."

Brett hobbled over and opened the note. "Anna was the prettiest girl in grade five."

"She got ugly in grade six?"

Brett chuckled. "No, she moved." He showed her the note, and Penny read it out loud.

"Want to be partners for Mr. Allen's science project? Check yes or no. P.S. What shampoo do you use? I love your hair." Penny snorted. "Wow, Anna had gumption."

"She couldn't resist the half mullet." Brett preened, running his hand through his hair.

"Did you pass along your secrets?"

Brett folded the note and slipped it back in the album. "It was all about the Aussie."

"The shampoo in the purple bottle?"

"My sister told me I could only use it if I spoke with an accent the whole time."

Penny hoisted the box into her arms and moved it to the back of the garage. "I'm going to need to hear that."

"Nope. Only when in the act of shampooing."

"New plan. Sneak in while you're showering." Penny's cheeks warmed as she set the box down and realized what she'd said.

"I told you, you only have to ask nicely." Brett finished the sentence in an Australian accent, and Penny laughed out loud.

They worked in tandem until the boxes were sorted, then moved on to Brett's sports equipment.

"No skiing this year." Brett held out his skis for Penny to take to the back.

"What, you're saying skiing takes a toll on your knees?"

"Not if you're skiing powder."

Penny scoffed. "Not if you're skiing powder and you're good at it. I almost tore my leg off because I thought I had to carve."

Brett picked up his boots and helmet. "Gotta be gentle. Just give it a little nudge."

Penny propped up the skis in the corner, then moved two of her duffels out on the driveway. "Do you ski a lot?"

"As much as I can. It was easier when I was in school. Now I usually go up with guys from the team a few times each season, then make it up on my own at least once."

Penny hadn't skied once since moving to Alberta. There had always been something to do for the practice on the weekends. She rolled Brett's bike back and propped it against the far wall. "I figure I'll sweep this out, then set everything up."

"I can sweep." Brett headed toward the broom tucked into the front corner of the garage.

"False." Penny got there first. "You need to save your strength for our session. I'll be able to inflict all kinds of new torture once my equipment is set up."

Brett stopped and picked up a long bag. "I can at least move some of these lighter ones."

Penny didn't argue. She helped him move the rest of her

things out, then picked up the broom. Brett stood on the driveway while she swept. The floor was surprisingly clean already.

"Tyler's going to come a bit early for the meeting, and we'll take all this to the donation center," Brett called out.

"Perfect." She finished sweeping and surveyed the space. There was plenty of room for her set up.

"You can use those if you want." Brett motioned to the stack of black puzzle mats in the back corner.

"Are you sure?"

"Positive."

Penny glanced down at her watch. It was past noon. She set the broom back in the corner and started moving her equipment back in. "Can I make you lunch?"

Brett picked up a bag. "You don't owe me anything, Penny."

"I absolutely owe you." Penny felt a little like she had emotional whiplash. Things didn't feel as hopeless now as they'd seemed when she woke up this morning. Brett seemed completely fine after last night, and now she had a potential avenue to make a bit of cash on the side. This afternoon, she'd have to make up a document with her services and prices to pass on if any of these players actually booked.

"When I post on the boards, do you want me to give them your number?"

Penny nodded. "I think that makes the most sense, don't you?"

Brett shrugged. "I could field the calls if you want."

"No, you don't need to take that on. It's only guys in the league, right? They're normal?"

Brett laughed as he dropped the bag. "Normal is a strong word."

Penny walked with him back to the driveway and waited for Brett to close the garage. "Do you mind if I schedule appointments when you're home? Just so . . . you know. If something weird were to happen—"

"Absolutely. I can sit in a lawn chair with a shotgun."

Penny breathed a laugh as they started back toward the apartment. "Perfect. I'll add that to my disclaimer."

―――

Later that afternoon, Brett got in the car with Tyler, and they drove to the AA meeting on Sixteenth Street. They'd been to this one before. Tyler had only started coming with him after his injury, and Brett assumed he'd probably stop once he could drive on his own.

Tyler had been curious about his meetings when they were roommates, but he'd never offered to come with, and Brett had never invited him. He hoped he was getting something out of it because Tyler offering to come meant more to Brett than he would probably ever know.

The scent of stale coffee and the rustling of folding chairs echoed through the basement of St. Mary's Church as Brett and Tyler settled in. They waited for a few minutes while everyone filtered in. At three-thirty, they had seven people in the circle.

The discussion leader, a middle-aged woman with a warm smile, welcomed everybody then started the meeting. "Today, we'll be focusing on the fifth step: admitting to ourselves and others the nature of our wrongs," she began, then continued to read from the book. When she finished, she scanned the group. "What does this step mean to you? And how has it helped you in your recovery?"

A man in his fifties, wearing a worn-out baseball cap, raised his hand. "Hi, I'm Phil, and I'm an alcoholic." The group welcomed him. "For me, it was finally owning up to the pain I caused my family. My drinking cost me my marriage, but admitting that allowed me to start rebuilding my relationship with my kids."

The group nodded in understanding, and a young woman with tattoos covering her arms chimed in next. "Hi, I'm Mia, and I'm an alcoholic. It's about being honest with yourself, too. My boyfriend told me for three years that I had a problem, but I was always able to make things work, you know? Never lost a job or forgot to pay my bills. But the problem was, I wasn't living my life. I was floating through it, and that hurt a hell of a lot less, but it also meant I never touched my feet on the ground."

Brett knew that feeling well. It was terrifying when he'd woken up one morning and realized he hardly remembered anything from the past year. He'd been there, but he hadn't been there. Even worse, he didn't know how to be there anymore.

The man who spoke next sat with his arms clamped across his chest, his knee bouncing as he said, "Hi, I'm Jared, and I'm an alcoholic." The group greeted him, then waited for him to continue. He stared at a spot on the floor, his dark hair falling over his forehead. "I'm working my first step, and I'm going to be honest. This shit is painful." People nodded around the circle. "I can't even think about having to admit all this to anyone. Even opening my own eyes to the hole I'm in makes me want to chug a forty." He gave a sardonic laugh. "I know I shouldn't. I know it won't help anything. But I might do it."

The group leader nodded. "Thanks for sharing, Jared. Would anyone in the group like to respond to that?"

Brett drew a deep breath, then raised his hand. "Hi, I'm Brett. I'm an alcoholic." Everyone in the circle repeated, "Hi, Brett." "I know how you feel, bud. I've been sober a few years now, and even just this week I had those exact same thoughts." He motioned to his knee brace. "I injured myself and can't play hockey or stay active the way I normally do, and every day feels like I'm skating across a pond that just froze over for the winter."

Jared nodded. "So what do you do with that?"

Brett ran a hand through his hair. "I use every damn skill I learned here at these meetings. Do my step work. Talk to my sponsor to keep my head on straight. Remind myself why the pain is worth it. Give it up to my higher power and tell the truth so I don't drown in shame like I used to."

Brett thought of that moment in the kitchen last night with Penny. Sobriety was built on moments like that. Seconds where he chose to give it up instead of holding it tight and letting it fester. Penny knew the truth now, and that meant he didn't need to think about trying to make something happen. Even when he was feeling more stable. But he'd told her anyway, because hiding the truth wouldn't avoid that consequence. It never avoided any consequence. They always came sooner or later, and putting it off until later only meant more suffering.

"Thank you for sharing, Brett." The facilitator continued on down the circle, and eventually landed on Tyler. In the past, he'd stood and said his name and explained that he was there to support a friend and learn, but today, Tyler cleared his throat. "Hi, I'm Tyler." Everybody welcomed him the same way they had Brett, but Tyler didn't sit down. "While I'm not an alcoholic, I've realized over the past few weeks that you don't have to be an alcoholic to benefit from these steps. I think we all have negative behaviours in our lives that we wish we could fix. Being here has helped me start to figure that out, so thank you." Tyler dropped back into his seat, and the introductions continued around the circle.

Brett nudged Tyler's knee and whispered, "Thanks for coming, buddy."

Tyler nodded. "I meant what I said. This has been a good thing for me, so thanks for letting me tag along."

As the meeting came to a close, the attendees exchanged hugs and handshakes before filing out of the basement. Brett followed Tyler to his truck, the late afternoon air warm against his unshaven skin.

Tyler pulled the door to his truck open. "You're doing great, you know that? Impressive as hell."

Brett opened the passenger side and gripped the handle to pull himself up. "Thanks, bud." *Doing great.* Week after week, his parents had asked if he was doing well, clinging to those words like a prayer. Every time he'd tried to get sober, he'd wanted to make them proud, and every time, he'd failed. It still made him a little nauseous to think that someone cared enough about him to be invested in how he was doing. Because those threads hurt when they were clipped.

As they clicked in their seatbelts, Tyler asked, "So what exactly is step work?"

"It's journaling. There's a book called the Big Book—"

"Was that the one she was reading out of?"

"Yep. There are different sections that I work through and take notes, a lot of self-evaluation, goals, that kind of thing."

Tyler pulled out onto the road. "Why isn't everyone doing this?"

"What do you mean?"

"I mean that I've read enough business management books to know this is exactly what all the experts are trying to encourage people to do. Here there's this free program that's set up to walk you through it. So why isn't everyone going to AA meetings?"

Brett chuckled. "Only took three weeks for you to become an advocate, eh? This is like honey crullers all over again."

"That only took one time, and I will convert you." He flashed an arrogant smile. "Everyone needs to eat a honey cruller, and I think everyone needs to hear this."

"I agree, sans the geriatric donut," he quipped. Tyler laughed, and Brett leaned back against the seat. "I don't know why we all believed that we didn't need any help to become the best versions of ourselves."

"Yeah, I don't think we were ever meant to do this alone." Tyler's hands gripped tighter on the steering wheel, and a pang of understanding hit Brett's stomach. Tyler's dad had passed away at almost the same time that Brett got injured. His mom had passed away years before that.

Now he had Emma, but he didn't have any siblings or close family like Brett did. It seemed unfair. Here Brett sat with his immediate family still in his life when he'd been hell-bent on ruining those relationships for ten years. Tyler had made all the right choices and didn't get to enjoy the lasting relationships.

Brett cleared his throat. "You don't ever have to do this alone, bud. I'll always be here for you. The team will always be here for you."

Tyler nodded. "I know that."

They dropped the items at the donation center and headed over to Sean and Kelty's for Sunday Supper. Brett's phone buzzed in his pocket as they turned onto their block. He pulled it out and saw a notification from the hockey board he'd posted on earlier. "Huh."

"What is it?" Tyler asked.

"Looks like Penny has her first patient."

Tyler's eyes lit up. "Someone commented on your post?"

"Oh, someone commented all right," Brett muttered. Tyler put the car in park. "Guess who had the balls to pipe up that he needs PT for a rotator cuff tear?"

Tyler cursed under his breath. "Please tell me you didn't post Penny's number."

"I posted it like a slapshot in the dark, bud."

CHAPTER
Thirteen

BRETT 10:00PM

You feeling okay about tomorrow?

PENNY 10:05PM

Slightly bridge jumpy

BRETT 10:06PM

If you need help putting anything else up in the garage, let me know

PENNY 10:06PM

No, it's all good. Thank you, though

BRETT 10:07PM

I've got dinner tomorrow night

PENNY 10:10PM

> Better be something fancy

BRETT 10:12PM

> Chicken and rice

PENNY 10:12PM

> It's called pilaf

PENNY STOOD at the top of the driveway, waiting for her first appointment. She had three today back-to-back and was so nervous she wanted to throw up. This was like night and day from working in an office where all she had to do was the actual therapy work.

Earlier in the week, Brett had helped walk her through the business side of things. She'd never had to set up her own business entity, though she did at least still have active liability insurance. She'd gone to the bank and set up her business bank account, and she had a PayPal account linked. Before, everything like that had been handled through the offices she worked for. Now she wasn't just an employee. She was the owner, operator, and physical therapist. Thank the heavens for online submission forms.

A Land Rover turned onto the street, and Penny had a hunch it belonged to her first patient. Jordan Wheatfill. Brett hadn't said much about him besides reiterating the fact that hockey players had reputations, at which point she'd pointed out that he was a hockey player, and he'd said, "Not all of us have reputations, just most of us." When she'd asked for specific red flags to look for, he'd muttered something about *guys like Tyler* and then waved the whole conversation off. Which was unfortunate because she'd been loaded and ready to mention just how well Tyler and Emma were doing to clinch the win in the argument.

Penny had also been about to express that he had nothing to worry about because she always kept things professional, but then remembered the way their PT sessions had gone. Not that she'd done anything she shouldn't, but up until their conversation Sunday night, she'd been considering it. Even when she told herself not to. So he may have had a point in his admonishments.

Penny had treated young, attractive men plenty of times in her office, but there was a layer of protection there. She wasn't all alone with them. And she wasn't the only person they saw in the office. They weren't *her* patients. She was one of their wellness team members. That felt like a distinct difference.

Jordan stepped out of the Land Rover and walked toward her, and she immediately understood what Brett was trying to tell her. If Tyler had Playboy written all over him, this guy was twice as bad. He smiled like he knew it would get him somewhere.

"Are you Penny?" He slipped his keys into the pocket of his fitted jeans, noticeably avoiding his right arm.

"Hi, you must be Jordan. I'm sorry I don't have a fancy office to take you to." Penny motioned for him to follow her down the drive.

"Honestly, I prefer this. Those places make me nervous."

"Oh yeah? Had a bad experience there?"

"Don't *want* to have a bad experience there. I've had too many friends get bad news in those offices." Jordan walked next to her. He was taller than Brett, which meant he had to be at least six foot two or three. Penny was five foot nine, and Brett was about the same height as her brother Marco at six foot and some change. Not that she'd been paying attention.

It was easy to understand why athletes could hate medical

offices. They were young and healthy. Nothing good was going to spur that visit.

She walked Jordan past the house and pretended not to notice Brett standing in the window watching them.

"This is a nice place," Jordan said. Penny smiled wider than necessary and flipped her hair over her shoulder for her voyeur's benefit. "Did you just move to town?"

"I've been in Calgary for a while, just working down south."

"In Okotoks?"

"Not quite, but close."

"You left your job there?" He stood next to her as she reached for the garage pin pad.

"Yep. Just looking for something up here now."

"Shouldn't be hard to find. It's crazy how few appointments for PT are available right now."

"I know." Inside her head, Penny added, *but it might be harder than you think*. With high demand and low supply, it would be rational to think medical centers would be desperate to hire people.

It didn't always work out that way. People always assumed that a shortage within an industry meant there weren't enough people to work. Usually, it meant there wasn't enough money to pay the people who were willing to work.

Penny motioned for Jordan to stand on the mats. "Alright, so tell me what's going on with this." He'd sent her his MRI images, but she found that patient experience was just as important for informing her proposed recovery plan.

"Had a hard fall at practice. It wasn't because I slipped or anything."

Penny held back a grin. Heaven forbid you admit to slipping when you're skating at full speed over ice. "Right, so one of your teammates took you out at the knees."

Jordan chuckled. "Exactly."

"Did you give him hell?"

Jordan swept his dark hair from his forehead. He had a

messy faux hawk going on, and Penny was certain that would be on Brett's list of red flags. "Are you sure I'm not paying you for PR work?"

Penny grinned, then motioned for him to sit down on the chair she'd set up. "Is it okay if I feel things out?" Jordan nodded, so she put her hands on his shoulder and prodded.

Jordan winced. "It's not bad enough to need surgery, but they told me it'll be a few months before it's back to normal."

Penny groaned. "Are you telling me that you're another hockey player who wants to force his body to heal faster by pretending I have magical healing powers?"

"Wait, you don't have magical healing powers? Because that's the only reason I came today."

This time, Penny didn't hold back her smile. "Well, as long as we're on the same page."

The aroma of rosemary and lavender drifted through the space from the essential oil diffuser Penny had set up on a small side table. She'd left the door open, and all in all, it was homier than expected.

Her equipment was neatly organized along one wall: resistance bands, foam rollers, and yoga blocks. A therapy table, draped in crisp white linen, stood at the center of the space, flanked by a couple of potted plants she'd picked up yesterday that added a touch of life and colour to the otherwise industrial setting.

"Okay, Jordan, let's start with a few basics." Penny stepped back and pulled her long hair into a bun at the base of her neck then motioned for him to sit on the edge of the therapy table. "Have you done the pendulum before?"

"Only in bed."

Penny rolled her eyes. Apparently, it wasn't only Brett who leaned on innuendo for stellar first impressions. "Just lean forward slightly, support yourself with your left arm, and let your right arm hang down. Then, gently swing it back and forth."

Jordan did as she asked.

"How does it feel?"

"There's a twinge when I hit this angle." Jordan nodded when his arm lifted to the right.

"Yep, that's normal." Penny started her timer. They worked through a set of stretches and mobility tests, then moved on to a few preliminary strength-building exercises.

They were deep in external rotation movements with the resistance band when Jordan asked, "What's your ethnicity? Is that a rude question?"

Penny shook her head. "No, my grandmother is full Greek."

"Your mother's mother or father's mother?"

"Mother's." Penny adjusted the band. "What about you?" Jordan had dark features. She wouldn't have been surprised if he had a quarter of something in his blood.

"My great-grandfather was French."

"So you're more Canadian than all of us, is that what you're saying?"

Jordan laughed out loud. "It was a power play."

"That's your move, right? Ask women where they're from and then hope they—" Penny's head snapped up as movement caught her eye. She frowned as Brett appeared in the open garage doorway.

His eyes trailed over Penny, then landed on Jordan, shirtless on the table. Brett cleared his throat. "I hope I'm not interrupt—"

"You are." Jordan inspected him. "Bouchard, right? Snowballs?"

Brett nodded. He stalked along the far wall and opened one of the boxes then pulled out a power strip. "Sorry, just needed to grab this." He caught Penny's eye, and she quickly looked back to her hand holding the resistance band.

Brett had come into this garage exactly zero times since she'd moved in. What were the chances that he needed something so desperately that he had to come out and grab it right this second? "What's the power strip for?"

"New lamp," Brett answered without hesitation. He shot one last look at Jordan, then retreated down the drive.

"Sorry about that," Penny murmured.

"He's a neighbour?"

"Housemate, actually." There was no point in hiding it. Brett had been the one to post about her services in the first place. Gah. *That word.*

"That tracks."

Penny stepped back and slipped the band off his arm. She wasn't going to dig deeper into that comment. "Wasn't so bad, eh?"

"After our regular practice, that was downright balmy."

Penny looped the resistance band back over the hook she'd screwed into the garage wall. "You have one of those captains?"

"Worse, I am the captain."

Penny kept her back turned as Jordan reached for his shirt and pulled it over his head. "So you're a masochist. All of this is beginning to make more sense."

Jordan stood up and sauntered toward her with a grin on his perfectly symmetrical face. "It's hockey, babe." He pulled out his phone. "You said PayPal, right?"

"Yep, I think that's easiest for everyone."

Jordan nodded. "Can I get on your schedule again for next week?"

"Absolutely." Penny slipped her phone from her back pocket, and once they landed on a day and time, she put him on her calendar.

"I would ask if I could come again this week, but I'm headed out of town for the weekend."

"And why wouldn't you be? The weather is supposed to be gorgeous."

Jordan smirked. "Got to take advantage of those weekends. We only have ten good ones before we hit ski season again."

Penny laughed and moved toward the driveway. "So, which team do you captain?"

"Pucks Deep. Heard of it?"

The name immediately rang a bell. That was the team Brett had mentioned. Their rival in town. "Yeah, I actually heard—"

"From your housemate, eh?" Jordan cut in. Penny nodded. He exhaled and slung his left thumb through his belt loop as they approached the street. "Don't let him sway you. We're mostly good guys."

"Mostly?"

Jordan winked, and sunlight glinted off of his perfectly straight teeth. "See you next week, Copper."

"Ooh, very original. I've never heard that one before."

Jordan chuckled as he hopped into the driver's seat and waved before pulling away from the curb.

Penny jogged back up the steps and went inside for a quick drink of water before her next patient arrived. She'd scheduled a fifteen-minute break between patients, and present Penny owed past Penny a huge debt of gratitude for that.

"How'd it go?" Brett asked. He sat at the kitchen table with his computer, and Penny's hackles immediately went up.

"You got a front-row seat. How did you think it went?" She hadn't meant for it to come out so snippy, but there it was. Danny had regularly checked up on her during appointments, and it had always rankled. At first, she'd chalked it up to them newly working together. They had to build up trust. But after a year and a half, when he busted into her room, she felt like a child getting caught with her light on after bedtime.

Brett leaned closer to his screen. "I was there for less than thirty seconds."

"You should've been there for *less than* less than thirty seconds." Penny planted her hands on the table, and Brett blew out a breath before meeting her eyes. "Where's the damn lamp?"

"In my bedroom."

Penny pushed back. "I'd *love* to see it."

Before she'd fully turned to walk down the hall, Brett grumbled, "It's not set up yet."

She slowly spun on her heel to face him. "Not set up. Interesting. Considering you were so desperate to get a power strip, you interrupted my session with Jordan."

A muscle in Brett's jaw flexed. "I wanted to make sure you were okay."

"And there it is."

Brett held out his hands. "You asked if I could be around while you saw patients! How—"

"So that I could call if I needed to!"

"Well, if Wheatfill had you pinned to the ground, how exactly were you going to call?"

Penny pursed her lips. "You thought Jordan was going to walk into that garage and immediately force himself on me? After meeting me one time?"

Brett shrugged and ran his hands through his hair. Penny's eyes wandered to his tattoo before she caught herself. "I was checking. That's it."

"Did you think I was ruining your organization in there or something?"

The furrow in Brett's brow grew deeper. "Is it so hard to believe that someone—in this instance, me—would be concerned about your welfare?" He stood and limped to the counter. "I trust you, Penny. I don't trust that snake."

Penny wet her lips. "Why didn't you tell me Jordan was the captain of Pucks Deep?"

"I knew these sessions were important to you. I didn't want to put a bad taste in your mouth."

"You thought you'd just do it after?"

He flashed her a look. "I'm not the one who brought it up." *Fair.* He hadn't said anything about Jordan until she jumped down his throat for walking into the garage. "My opinion of Jordan has always been heavily swayed by Sean's opinion and my experience with him on the ice. He's an asshat."

"And how does one garner such a prestigious title?"

Brett leaned against the counter. "I don't know all the details, but Jordan slept with Sean's girlfriend years ago."

"That seems fairly detailed. How long is 'years ago?'"

He shrugged. "Twenty-ten?"

Penny rolled her eyes. "So Sean still hates the guy because thirteen years ago he stepped on his toes?"

"That's a little more than stepping on someone's toes. If you want to be *detailed* about it."

Penny folded her arms over her chest. "We were all idiots when we were twenty."

Brett mirrored her body language. "He's still a dick on the ice, and so are his teammates. Can't blame that on being young and stupid."

"And every Snowballs' player is chipper and considerate out there with the opposing team?"

"We're not like *that*."

Penny walked over and filled a glass with water, then took a drink. "Well, that's impressive." She took another gulp, then poured the rest of the water down the sink and set her cup on the counter before heading to the door.

"I guess you'll have to reserve judgment until you come to one of our games."

Penny hesitated. "Your season doesn't start until November."

"We have a few exhibition games at the end of October."

She twisted and pulled on the door handle. "I doubt I'll still be around by then." Brett didn't say anything as she stepped out onto the landing. She turned and poked her head back inside. "Thank you for checking in, but maybe don't do it again?"

———

By the end of the afternoon, Penny felt more at peace than she had in weeks. Every session had gone well, and she had four hundred and fifty dollars to add to her bank account. It had been a hassle to set up the business, and she did have to pay credit card processing fees, but she was taking home more than double what she made in a regular office with her contracted rate.

More than quadruple what she was making in Danny's office, though that had been because of the blinders she had on coupled with a healthy dose of stupidity. She was closing up the garage when she got a message on her text chain with Emma and Kelty.

Kelty 4:11pm

> Hey Penny, we're planning a camping trip for the weekend. Want to join?

Penny hadn't gone camping since moving to Calgary. Danny always said it would be disrespectful to their ancestors who paid such a heavy price to put roofs over their heads anytime friends invited them along. At the time, she'd thought it was clever.

Penny 4:20pm

> Give me the details

Based on how this week was going, if she scheduled the same three patients for the next six weeks before she needed to head home for the anniversary, she'd almost have enough to contribute her full share. If she could get two to three more patients a week or land a job . . . The idea of a job made her stomach twist. *Did she even want a full-time job?*

She'd thought she did. When she'd moved up here to stay with Kelty, she'd been sure she wanted to stay in the area and stabilize things before she went back home licking her wounds. But now the only thing she could think about was getting to Vancouver.

Andrea had texted yesterday and announced she was flying

through Calgary and had a twelve hour layover. Purposefully. The idea of seeing her sister had nearly made her burst into tears.

KELTY 4:24PM

> Just headed to a place past Canmore next to a lake. Beautiful site, great hiking. We'll leave Friday afternoon and come back Sunday night. Sean's got the van so we can all drive up together

Penny processed this. Of course Sean would be coming, probably Tyler too. *So were they really inviting her to be a fifth wheel?*

PENNY 4:32PM

> Who all is going?

KELTY 4:32PM

> We're texting some people from the team. Fly and his girlfriend are a maybe, and of course the four of us. And I think Tyler's texting Brett.

Okay, at least it wouldn't just be the five of them.

PENNY 4:36PM

> I would love to come, but I don't have any of my camping stuff. It's all back at my parents' house

EMMA 4:38PM

> No worries, my parents have plenty. They have a four-man tent you could borrow and a sleeping pad. They probably have a sleeping bag too, as long as you're not picky.

Penny wasn't picky. With six kids growing up, they were glad if they had anything to sleep on.

PENNY 4:40PM

> Sounds great. Do you want me to grab food, plan a meal or something?

EMMA 4:43PM

👪 👪 👪

KELTY 4:52PM

> I'll create a list once we know who all is in, and we can go from there. Is it OK if I text you Thursday night?

Penny gave her message a thumbs up. She was free as a bird until Tuesday morning. When she reentered the house, she found Brett still sitting at the same spot at the table.

"How's work going?" she asked.

"It's work."

"When you're finished, do you want to do a session out there with the equipment now that I've got everything set up?"

Brett nodded. "Sure."

"If we do one tonight and then maybe Friday, we could forego our Sunday session."

Brett glanced up. "You have big plans for the weekend?"

"Well, I got a text from Emma and Kelty. They invited me to go camping."

Brett rubbed the stubble on his chin. *Penny worked so hard not to notice everything about him, and then he did something like that.* "Oh yeah, Tyler texted me as well."

"It was nice of them to include me. I think it'll be fun."

"So you're going then?" Brett was still watching her.

"I think so. You?"

Brett blinked. "Yeah, of course."

CHAPTER
Fourteen

BRETT 5:02PM

> I'm in for camping

TYLER 5:15PM

> Yeah?

BRETT 5:16PM

> Got through work faster than expected

TYLER 5:16PM

> Fandabidozi

BRETT 5:17PM

> Not a word, bud

TYLER 5:18PM

> Did your sudden change of heart have anything to do with Penny deciding to come on the trip?

BRETT 5:18PM

> Nevermind. It's a great word

BRETT, Tyler, and Sean stood behind the van, waiting for Kelty to exit the house.

"She's making a point." Sean leaned against the open door.

"Did you tell her to hurry up?" Emma called from the back seat.

"I may have insinuated she was holding us up."

Emma groaned. "Sean, you're always the one—"

"I get it, Ems." Sean ground his teeth.

"Did you at least apologize?" she asked.

"She hasn't come outside yet or I would've."

Emma held up her phone and waved it at him. Sean grunted. Tyler clapped him on the shoulder then walked around to the side door and got in.

"Is there a reason you're in the backseat, buddy?" Brett asked as Tyler slid in next to Emma. "Plenty of space there in the middle."

"The middle makes me carsick." Tyler grinned, then did something to make Emma squeal.

Brett laughed at the expression on Sean's face. "Sorry. Couldn't help myself."

"Just get in. I'll—" Before Sean could finish his sentence,

Kelty strode out the door carrying her duffel, a flannel, and a hatchet.

"Good luck with that." Brett followed after Tyler and climbed into the van. He scanned the seats, noting that the middle bench was empty but hesitating since Penny was sitting alone next to the window in the front.

"Do you mind if I sit here?" he asked. "Purely to avoid hearing whatever is happening back there between Tyler and Emma."

Penny grinned. "Why do you think I chose this bench?"

Brett slid in next to her, making sure there was plenty of space between the two of them. "Who else is coming, do you know?"

Penny shook her head. "Kelty said she was texting Fly and his girlfriend and a couple other people from the team."

"Maybe they just haven't arrived yet?"

A few minutes later, that question was answered as Kelty and Sean got in the driver and passenger seat and motioned for them to shut the door.

"Is this all of us?" Brett asked.

Sean turned on the engine. "Yeah, turns out we didn't need a vehicle quite this large, but none of our cars hold six, so it's still a good thing I got it."

"What happened to the other people from the team?" Penny asked, her voice a little higher than usual.

"A couple of them said they were going to come and then ditched last night," Kelty answered.

Penny looked as if she was going to say something else but held her tongue. Brett had a good idea of what thoughts were tumbling around in her head. It was him and Penny and two couples who were disturbingly in love with one another. Mostly just Emma and Tyler. Not that Sean and Kelty weren't in love, but they were past the honeymoon stage.

"Well, this will be great." Penny exhaled and held her waist pack a little tighter.

As they drove out of the cul-de-sac, Brett lowered his voice. "A loonie says Sean throws a punch."

Penny turned with a grin. "Kelty told me he and Tyler already had it out during a game."

"It was epic. Tyler still hasn't given up on pushing Sean's buttons."

She shifted to lean in closer. "But they're friends, right?"

"Good friends." Tyler and Sean had gotten along swimmingly right up until Tyler showed interest in his younger sister Emma. Now that he'd proven he was in it for the long haul, Tyler and Sean spent more time together than most of the guys on the team. Though that probably had more to do with Kelty and Emma planning things than any motivation on their part.

"I've never understood that. Why are you all so aggressive?" Penny asked.

Brett feigned offense and held up his hands to make air quotes. "You all?"

"Yeah. Hockey players. It's like you're all auditioning for the role of 'Alpha Male' in a David Suzuki documentary."

"First of all, pretty sure that could describe all professional athletes."

"Fair."

"Second, hockey is too fast-paced to be low energy. It's like amped up chess with flying objects."

Penny's eyes danced with amusement. "Chess?"

"Absolutely. Always looking for an opening. Finding space." As a kid, Brett would replay sections of his PeeWee games on repeat, trying to find the patterns. *If he moves this way, I go here. If my teammate has the puck here, I bolt center.* "It's a dance. And a fight to the death."

Penny grinned. "So ballet plus Gladiator. Got it."

"No time to think, just act and react."

"Even when it means punching someone's teeth out?"

Brett fixed her with an intense stare. "Especially when it means punching someone's teeth out."

Penny's lips parted slightly. "Yours look intact."

"Because I'm a responsible adult. I wear a mouth guard."

"Testosterone fueled and pragmatic. How could any woman ask for more?"

"That's what I keep telling myself."

Two long beats passed before Penny dropped her eyes and Brett's heart decided to start pumping again. *What was this between them?* It was like every conversation was charged. Electric. Like Penny's voice was the only frequency his body was tuned in to anymore.

Brett hadn't realized how close together they'd moved, and he quickly shifted on his seat to give her more space. Sean reached up to adjust the rearview mirror in front of them.

Brett chuckled. "Trying to see the backseat a little better, Thompson?" Sean glowered at him.

Kelty busted up laughing. "Have you completely forgotten how we were when we got together? It was like you were a kid discovering candy for the first time."

Penny groaned. "I'm sorry, did you just compare your sex life to kids eating candy?" Brett put out his fist, and she bumped it. Having another girl around to call out Kelty was going to be a blast.

Kelty scoffed. "You know what I mean."

Penny sighed. "My brothers were the worst whenever I started dating someone. They were always making my boyfriends feel unwelcome."

"And they were justified, right?" Sean looked back through the mirror.

Penny opened her mouth, then closed it. "I mean, yeah. In my case they were. But Tyler seems like a nice guy."

"Thank you Penny!" Tyler called from the back seat, and Sean flipped him the bird.

Kelty turned in her seat. "Sean, you love Tyler—"

"I love Tyler when I don't have to watch him snogging my sister twenty-four seven."

"Which is why we're going camping together. Enjoying nature, hiking, sleeping in a tent on our own."

"Was there another option?" Brett laughed.

"Kelty wanted to bring the six man and have everyone dogpile into the same tent!" Sean threw out his hand for emphasis.

Brett smirked. "So romantic."

Kelty rolled her eyes. "Whatever. Camping isn't about romance. We sack out and wake up at first light. All we need is a place to crash."

Brett shook his head. "False. If camping isn't romantic, I don't know what is."

"How so?" Penny smiled and gave him a quizzical look.

"What's more romantic than staring up through Ponderosa Pines at the Milky Way?"

Penny's eyes sparkled with interest, and he wanted to find something else to surprise her so they'd never stop. "You're the expert on romance?"

"Obviously." He turned back to the front and leaned between the seats. "Luckily, you'll have plenty of romance because the three of us guys would barely fit in a six man tent, let alone adding the girls."

Sean nodded once. "Exactly. I don't know about the romance bit, but I do know I'm not sleeping next to anyone besides Kelty ever again."

Penny leaned forward, and her shoulder brushed Brett's. The smell of her shampoo wafted toward him, and his pulse quickened. "Then why doesn't she have a ring on her finger?"

"HA!" Brett clapped a hand on Penny's shoulder without thinking. She leaned into him as they both dissolved into laughter at the expression on Sean's face. Kelty turned around and gaped at Penny.

Brett hadn't heard anyone call out Sean like that on or off the ice, and he couldn't say a damn thing about it since Penny wasn't *his* close friend. Penny sighed and straightened, and Brett pulled his hand back to rest in his lap, immediately missing the feel of her soft cotton shirt and arch of her back under his fingers.

"What's so funny?" Emma called from the back.

"You'd know if you'd ever come up for air!" Sean barked.

Kelty sat smirking in the front seat, and though Sean tried to maintain a stormy expression, he couldn't keep the corner of his mouth from lifting. Penny wiped her eyes, then unzipped her waist bag and pulled out a stick of lip balm. She applied it to her lips, and Brett caught a whiff of cinnamon. "I'm glad I came."

Brett pulled his hair back from his face and secured it with an elastic. He lowered his voice just for her. "Because you need more romance in your life?"

She scoffed. "No, romance is the last thing I need."

Penny wadded up her hoodie and stuffed it between her head and the window, then settled in and closed her eyes. A tendril of hair had escaped her braid and framed her face. Brett tried to get comfortable while Tracy Chapman harmonized with blues guitar through the speakers, but his fingers still tingled, and he couldn't get that look on Penny's face out of his head.

By the time they pulled into the campground, it was just past noon—perfect timing to check in and load into their site. Penny had napped for much of the drive, then chatted with Kelty for the last forty minutes or so. From that conversation, Brett had learned that she loved Korean dramas, hated olives—even though they were the lifeblood of her people—and wanted to put the person responsible for the word 'murse' in an Albanian prison.

A deep ache had started just below Brett's ribs around the time Penny did her impression of Justin Trudeau, then spread through his midsection when she slipped her shoes off to "stretch her arches" and he saw her socks were mismatched.

Brett was smitten.

Which was quite inconvenient considering his and Penny's current life situations. They were housemates. She was his physical therapist. He was . . . useless. And Penny was planning to go back to Vancouver, possibly permanently, in six weeks. Add into the mix that even when he became fully functional, Penny had already made it perfectly clear she wouldn't ever be interested in *someone like him.*

Brett worked to release the tightness in his chest as Sean chatted with the ranger, then drove the loop and parked at their site. Brett scooted out onto the springy, pine-littered ground and started unloading their equipment. It wasn't difficult to find a place for each of their tents since Sean had booked a site large enough for a group twice their size.

Brett took his four-man tent a little further out from the site and cleared off a spot between two pines.

"Let's set up the tents a bit later so we can hike up to the overlook!" Kelty called out.

Brett re-zipped the tent bag and straightened. He wouldn't be going on more than a short jaunt to the Porta-Potties but didn't want to kill their mojo. "You guys go. I'll finish getting all this organized." He pointed at the cooler and bags of food. He could easily get everything in the bear bin and build a fire so they'd have good coals for the dinner Emma had prepped for the Dutch oven.

They'd assigned him breakfast the next morning. He wasn't sure if that was a compliment or sign of their lack of confidence in his cooking abilities.

"I'll stay," Sean offered.

"You don't need—" Brett stopped when Sean drew his hand across his neck.

"I can't leave you here alone. You couldn't outrun a beaver in your condition." Sean lifted the cooler onto the picnic table.

"What would I do without a big strong man like you around?" Brett pretended to swoon, and Kelty laughed as she lugged a duffel bag from the back and set it next to their bagged tent.

"We'll be back soon. Don't think I don't see what you're

doing, Sean." Kelty slapped his backside as she passed and motioned for the others to follow her to the trailhead. Penny set her borrowed tent on the ground between the fire pit and Brett's claimed spot, then jogged back to walk with the others. Brett's eyes lingered a bit too long on her retreating form before he grabbed some of the groceries and walked them over to the bear bin.

"You haven't told Kelty about your hamstring, have you?" Brett asked. At practice on Monday night, Sean had stopped mid-scrimmage and left the ice. Brett followed him to the dressing room before the rest of the guys ended practice and found him icing the underside of his leg.

Sean grunted. "No need. It'll heal up with a little rest."

"Do you need to get it looked at?" They were four days post practice. Not that he'd expect a muscle strain to solve itself that fast, but they were in their mid-thirties now. It wasn't like when they were college-aged and could sprain an ankle, tape it up, and skate the next day. "I bet Penny would give you her thoughts."

"I don't need anyone to weigh in. I pulled a muscle. It'll be fine by Monday."

Brett took the last load of bags to the bin. "Sorry you're dealing with that, buddy."

Sean unraveled the twine from around a bundle of firewood. "What about Penny?"

"What about her?"

Sean walked back to the van to get the hatchet Kelty had brought with her from the house. He didn't comment further, just let both of their questions hang in the air like a ping-pong ball drifting toward a racquet.

"She's a great physical therapist, if that's what you're asking."

Sean snagged two pieces of firewood from the table and walked them over to a stump. He set the first piece upright and started stripping off kindling with the hatchet. "You know that wasn't what I was asking."

Brett started pulling out the paper products and arranging them on the table next to the large orange water cooler. "She's a great housemate."

"Also not—"

"What do you want me to say? Are you hoping to hear we're sleeping together? Because we're not." *Unfortunately.* That pit in his stomach stretched wide as the image of Penny's legs stretching in front of the window blinked into his mind's eye.

Sean worked methodically with the hatchet, sending shavings and strips of wood onto the ground next to the stump. "It seems like you're keen. And it's been a while. That's all I was getting at."

"It's been a while for a reason." Brett moved on to setting up the camp chairs around the fire pit. Sean and most of the rest of the team had seen him at his worst before he started putting in the work to get sober. They experienced first-hand his erratic behavior and emotional instability. They had to deal with the aftermath of his toxic relationship with Amber, a waitress at One Place. He hadn't been able to go to the pub with them after games for almost a year before she quit.

"How long are you going to punish yourself?"

Brett exhaled. "It's not a punishment. I'm learning how to do it right."

Sean continued whittling away at the quarter log. "Kelty used to buy bags of All Dressed chips when they were on sale because she knew they were my favourite. Every time I saw them in the pantry, I'd grab a bag and snack while watching the game or something."

Brett slid another chair from the bag and pulled to open it up. He had no idea why Sean was telling him this.

"In the third period, I'd notice the bag was nearly empty. No matter how many times I tried not to eat most of the bag, I couldn't get it handled. So I told Kelty not to buy them anymore."

Brett slipped the strap of the carrying case over the back of the chair and moved on to the last two. "If this is leading to how you kicked a chip addiction—"

"Not an addiction. But I had no self-control. She stopped buying All Dressed, and problem solved." Sean tossed the now much thinner piece of wood into the fire pit and started on the second block. "I went six months thinking I'd figured out how to stop eating junk. Until Suraj brought me a bag for the tourney."

"I remember, you slammed that at One Place. Didn't order an app."

"Right. I realized that night I hadn't learned anything. I'd just avoided having chips in front of my face."

Brett set the last chair in the dirt and sat. "Spit it out, Cap."

Sean set the hatchet on the stump and started collecting the splinters he'd created. "You won't figure out portion control until you put a bag of chips back in the pantry."

"So . . . you think I need to get back on the horse?"

Sean carried the kindling to the fire pit and set the pile next to the metal ring. "You did say you needed more physical activity."

Brett picked up a pine cone and lobbed it at him.

It was three o'clock when Tyler and the girls got back from their hike. Brett and Sean had already set up their tents, and Brett had just started pumping up his air mattress when he saw Penny standing over her tent supplies with a frown.

Brett limped over. "You good?"

Penny motioned to the ground. "Tell me I'm not an idiot."

"You're not an idiot."

Penny rolled her eyes and bent down to pick up a still-folded pole. "I don't see how I can set up a full tent with this."

Brett leaned over and inspected the pockets on the tent. There were four for two poles, but Penny was only holding one. "This was all it came with?"

Penny nodded. "I unrolled it and this was the only pole in the bag."

Brett walked over to the picnic table where Kelty and Sean were putting out snacks. "Hey, do you have another bag of poles or something in the van?"

Kelty frowned. "For which tent?"

"Penny's. This was all there was in there." He held up the pole, and Kelty's frown deepened.

She walked to the van and searched in the back but came up empty. "Sean, did you open up that tent and check that all the pieces were there?"

Sean shook his head. "My dad handed it to me. It's the same tent we used growing up."

"Well, it looks like someone lost a pole."

Sean opened up a bag of trail mix. "Weird. Nobody would've used it for years."

Penny was now standing next to the table. "Do you think there's a way to rig it up with only one pole?"

Sean considered. "Could tie it to a tree."

Kelty laughed and handed the pole back to Brett as she called out to Penny. "You glad you came yet?"

Penny laughed and shoved her hands in her back pockets. Everything from her loose braid, golden skin, and mint T-shirt looked like it belonged here. "I can sleep in the van."

"Gross, no. We can figure something out. Have Sean sleep with Tyler or Brett and me or Emma could have you sleep in our tent."

Sean grunted. "You heard what I said in the van."

Kelty put her hands on her hips. "Sean, seriously? Penny doesn't have *a tent*."

"Brett does."

Kelty coughed. "I am *not* going to make her do that."

Sean scoffed. "Make her do what? They'd each be in their own sleeping bag."

Penny put up a hand. "We're standing right here."

Brett laughed. "No, let them continue discussing our sleeping arrangements as if we're toddlers and not grown-ass adults." Kelty planted her hands on her hips, and Brett continued. "I should have brought my hammock. I could've slept in there and Penny would have the tent."

"Hey, Bowen!" Sean called. Tyler looked up as he crouched over a stake next to the tent with a hammer in his hand. "Did you bring your hammock?"

Tyler shook his head. "No, we meant to but I left it in the closet."

"Do you want to sleep in the tent with Brett? Penny's tent is missing a pole."

Emma poked her head out of the tent. "What is your tent missing?"

"A pole," Penny answered.

Emma made a face. "I'm so sorry. Of course, you can sleep in here, and Tyler can—"

Penny waved her off when she saw Tyler's face fall. "It's fine. I can sleep in Brett's tent if he's okay with it." She looked over, and Brett's heart didn't get the memo that this was a sleepover of desperation. "Sean's right. We both have our own sleeping bags, and it won't be that different from being at home."

It was totally different. Penny was going to be inches from him. Lying down. And smelling like shampoo and cinnamon. "You sure?"

She nodded. "As long as you don't snore."

"I don't. At least I didn't use to."

Penny's face split into a nervous smile as she stared at the forlorn tent deflated on the ground. "I'll give you the verdict in the morning."

CHAPTER
Fifteen

ANDREA 6:32PM

> I can't wait to see you!!!

PENNY 7:15PM

> We only have six hours. How will it ever be enough!?

ANDREA 7:29PM

> It won't be. Just accept it now

PENNY 8:32PM

> When you get a sec, remind me of your flight time and airline. I'll be there with bells on!

ANDREA 8:34PM

> No bells. Or signs

Penny 8:34pm

> You know you just issued a challenge I can't back down from

THE SIX OF them sat around the campfire as dusk deepened into twilight, and Penny pulled on a sweatshirt. Smoke curled into the sky above the crackling fire Tyler had started for them.

She, Kelty, and Sean had just returned from washing the dishes, and her hands were still damp and a little chilled.

Accepting the tent situation had been easy after talking with Brett in the van. She'd been about ready to bow out and go home when she saw it was just going to be the six of them. Since she'd ridden over with Brett in his car, she didn't want to make things complicated and either ask him to drive her home or ask him for his keys. He probably would have given them to her no problem, but it still felt like just enough of a stretch that she stayed put.

Brett had driven for the first time that morning, and though he was in a little discomfort, it had gone just fine. That meant next week he'd be back to work on-site instead of sitting at the kitchen table.

Penny watched the flames dance in front of her and put her feet up on a log to warm her toes. She kept telling herself it was for the best, but the twist in her lower gut every time she thought about Brett being gone all day wasn't convinced.

Regardless, they wouldn't have to spend so much time together, which would make all of this less confusing. She wouldn't have to see the ink peeking out under his sleeve, see him twist his hair when he was concentrating, or feel warmth diffuse over her skin every time he looked up with those blue eyes when she entered the room.

Plus, now that she'd already met three of the players she'd be treating, she wasn't as worried about him being home when they came to their appointments. *Six weeks.* She only had to make it through six weeks. Get more clients, make the money, pay Andrea, and drive back to Vancouver. The rest she could figure out once she was back with family.

Andrea had a layover in Calgary on Monday, which was why she hadn't scheduled any appointments until Tuesday. She'd get to spend the day with her sister. Then she'd work, and that would be another week down.

The fact that she kept feeling a tug to stay in Calgary made her more sure she needed to leave. That was always how it went for her. She was like the needle of a compass always pointing to the path of least resistance. Wouldn't it be easier to stay in Calgary the rest of the summer? Wouldn't it be easier to be with someone than to be alone? Wouldn't it be easier to give in and cross boundaries with Brett?

All of it was a lie, because none of those things would be easier in the long run. Her track record had proven that unequivocally. The hard stuff always landed. Choosing the "easy" only delayed it, and she was sick of stagnating for years at a time waiting for the shoe to drop.

Penny needed to fill the hole in her heart with something other than a reflection. Brett only needed her for PT, and once he was healed, he wouldn't need her around for anything else. He needed to sort his own life out, and Penny was in the exact same boat. If it took writing on her bathroom mirror, she would force herself to remember it was possible to support each other without tangling their heads, emotions, or especially, their legs, and making everything more complicated.

"Did you guys see Country's latest video?" Kelty asked.

Sean looked skeptical. "He has another one? I thought he said his brother filmed him without his knowledge."

"I think he gave him permission at some point. They're hilarious," Emma said.

Penny had met Country at Sunday Supper but she had no idea what they were talking about. "Fill me in"

Brett leaned over. "Country has strong opinions about hockey like most of us, but he's a bit more colourful in his assessments."

Tyler snorted. "That's an understatement."

Brett grinned. "His brother caught it on tape while they were watching a Blizzard game. It went viral on TikTok, and now he's apparently posting more of them."

Kelty pulled out her phone. She stared at the screen for a few minutes before finally standing and stretching her legs. "I don't have enough service to get it to load, but you've got to check it out when you get home. His handle's @maplestickhandler."

Penny laughed. "Did he come up with that handle himself?"

Sean shook his head. "No, he had nothing to do with this."

"So he says." Kelty winked as she put another marshmallow on the end of her roasting stick.

"Is there an endgame here?" Brett asked.

Kelty shrugged. "I think his brother just finds it amusing."

"Sounds like the masses agree." Tyler pulled his marshmallow away from the coals. Penny was definitely going to have to watch that video. She wasn't a huge social media person, but every once in a while she loved a good rabbit hole.

"Now I regret not filming dad while he watches games," Sean said.

Emma breathed a laugh. "He doesn't really say much, though. Mostly just makes intense facial expressions and curses under his breath."

Tyler squished his marshmallow between two graham crackers with chocolate. "Still hilarious."

"Sports are so weird. We watch a game sitting in our living room and act like we're somehow a part of it." Penny reached for a roasting stick, inspired by Tyler's golden masterpiece.

"That's probably why Country's videos are so popular. He's a player. He does have insider information," Emma said.

"His videos are popular because he doesn't have a filter," Sean muttered.

Kelty sighed. "I love no-filter Country. He usually only comes out after ten o'clock." Penny grinned. She loved no-filter Kelty who tended to show up most strongly in the dark.

Sean broke off a piece of Cadbury and popped it in his mouth. "Only because you egg him on. Without fail, Kelty brings up Marchand or Evander Kane."

Kelty laughed. "What! Everyone needs a good Country rant to brighten their day."

Sean chuckled. "His hate list is longer than my arm."

"Well, your arms aren't *that* long."

"Oh, c'mon. Everyone needs a good hate list," Brett said.

Kelty turned. "Do you have a hate list?"

"Maybe."

Her jaw dropped. "You do not. You've never once roasted a player at One Place."

Brett took a drink of his Clearly Canadian. "Who said it was a player hate list?" Penny laughed at Kelty's widening eyes.

"Who do you hate, Brett Bouchard?" Kelty leaned forward in her chair. *There she was.* Impulsive and feisty, in all her nine fifteen p.m. glory.

"It's private." Brett grinned, crossing his left ankle over his healing right knee. Penny chortled as Kelty's face transformed from intrigued to hawk-like.

Kelty leaned forward. "Don't you dare. You can't bring something up like that and edge us."

Tyler's smile was smug. "I know what's on it."

Kelty whirled. "He trusted you with this information?"

Tyler lifted his hand and twined his pointer and middle finger together. "We're like this. I know all Brett's secrets."

Kelty's head swiveled between the two of them. "One of you better give me something."

Brett threw his arm over the back of Kelty's chair. "I'll tell you what. I'll give you one of the line items on my list if you sing the chorus of—"

"Don't you dare say it."

Brett could barely keep a straight face. "Of Photograph by Nickelback. It has to be done like the Chad himself." Penny clutched her midsection. Before she'd even known Kelty's last name, she knew about her hatred for that song. She was as curious as Kelty to know what was on Brett's list. She clapped her hands together and whooped, egging her friend on.

"You bastard." Kelty stood next to the fire, clearing her throat, and Sean's face reddened with silent laughter. She held up her roasting stick like a microphone and started in with impressive dedication to Kroeger's throaty rasp.

Penny just about died when a couple with a toddler walked by, and the kid tried to wander into their site to get a better look. When Kelty finished and sat back down, they applauded as she, Emma, and Sean wiped tears from their cheeks.

The fire glowed against Brett's face and made his eyes glisten as he reached for his phone in his pocket.

"This list is on your phone? What kind of psychopath are you?" Penny almost dropped into another bout of uncontrollable laughter.

Brett's laugh was a wheeze as he flipped to the right screen. "Kelty, that was an impressive performance, so I'm going to give you three."

Sean pulled Kelty's chair closer so he could lean over and kiss her cheek.

"Wow, enough with the PDA, Thompson!" Tyler scolded, and Sean gave him the finger for the second time that day.

Brett cleared his throat. "Kelty, here you go. Three entries on my hate list: Nellie Olson from the *Little House on the Prairie* television production that ran from 1974 to 1983, Muffy from the children's cartoon *Arthur*, and Triumph the insult comic dog on CFCN."

Kelty gaped at him, then started laughing so hard Sean had to slap her back to get her to breathe normally. Penny's abs screamed, and her face felt like it might split at the seams. Brett nearly dropped his phone in the dirt as his shoulders shook.

"How long have you been keeping this list?" Emma finally squeaked out.

"And how long is it?" Penny wheezed. "I have so many questions."

Brett untied his hair and teased it out. "Grade four, and I have fifty two entries."

"My favourite is 'The Todd' from Scrubs." Tyler ran a hand over his face.

"What the hell, buddy! That wasn't approved discussion of the hate list."

Tyler shook his head as he tried to compose himself. "You're right, I'm sorry. I couldn't help myself."

Penny stretched her arms over her head. "I'm going to pee my pants." She couldn't remember the last time she'd laughed this hard, and it was a good reminder to do Kegel exercises more consistently.

"Grab your toothbrush. I'll walk with you down to the flush toilets." Emma jumped up only to have Tyler pull her into his lap. He wrapped his arms around her and rubbed his scruff against her neck until she squirmed then let her go. Sean didn't even complain.

Kelty got up and went to the van then reappeared with her toiletry kit. They walked down the gravel road in the dark with Emma's headlamp to guide them.

"That was an impressive rendition of Photograph, Kelt." Emma nudged her with her hip.

"Desperate times." Kelty coughed a laugh, her voice raw.

In the bathroom, Penny used warm water to wash her face and brush her teeth. When they'd left that morning, she wondered if she'd regret being here, but now she couldn't imagine being anywhere else. All week after Andrea told her about her layover she'd been missing her family, and the last hour had buoyed her spirits in ways she hadn't known were possible.

Was this how it worked? She'd never had a friend group, only instant couple friends that came bundled with whoever she was dating at the time. Because she always poured all her energy into her relationships, most of her friendships had fizzled out after her time at UBC. All except for Kelty and her old roommate, Fiona. Friendships were magic, and she'd been missing out on it all this time.

Penny packed up her toiletries and used the flush toilet so she wouldn't have to go into the Porta-Potti in the middle of the night. Hopefully. When Kelty and Emma finished, they made their way back to camp and saw Tyler and Sean had already disappeared into their tents. Everything was put away and only Brett remained next to the fire, poking the dying coals with a long stick.

Penny put her toiletries in the bear bin and strode over to sit in the chair next to him.

Brett looked up, his face shadowed in the dim glow. "I told Sean and Tyler I'd take care of putting out the fire whenever we went to bed."

We. There was that word again that, when he spoke it, made her stomach flip.

She breathed in the scent of cool pine and campfire, then yawned. "I think I'll head in now. It's getting a little chilly out here and I forgot my hottie."

Brett's brow furrowed. "Hottie?"

"Hot water bottle."

The corner of his mouth quirked. "You use one of those?"

"Not in the summer. That's why I didn't think about it."

"But in the winter you do?"

She nodded. "Our family has notoriously bad circulation in our hands and feet. See?" Without thinking, Penny pressed her cold fingers against Brett's cheek. His warmth seeped into her skin, and she yanked her hand back.

Brett wet his lips. "Definitely cold." He resumed his coal poking. "I'll drench this and be in in a second."

Penny nodded, then stood and walked toward Brett's tent nestled between the pines. What had she been thinking, touching him like that? She didn't need to prove anything about her circulatory system. Saying the words was plenty.

She knelt and unzipped the tent, then took off her shoes and crawled in. Penny slipped off her bra as fast as she could so Brett wouldn't walk in on her, then pulled it out the bottom of her sweatshirt and tucked it into the tent pocket.

Penny snuggled down into her sleeping bag, and as her head hit the pillow, she looked up, and her breath caught. Brett had left the rainfly off of the tent, and she was staring straight up into a star studded inky sky.

She gaped, hardly moving until scuffling outside the tent broke her trance. The zipper engaged, and then Brett pushed inside and sat down on the air mattress, making Penny's body lift a few inches. He turned and took off his shoes, then crawled inside and zipped the tent back up.

"Sorry," he murmured as he made his way to his sleeping bag and jostled the mattress. Finally he lay still, and both of them stared out through the top of the tent.

"How did you know this would be the perfect spot?" Penny asked.

"Perfect?"

"Yeah."

Brett chuckled. "I've been camping enough to know what my priorities are."

Penny thought back to his words in the van. *There's nothing more romantic than staring out between two Ponderosa pines at the Milky Way.* "You look for romance even when you're on your own?"

"I look for romance everywhere." His voice was low and soft, and Penny's whole body stilled.

"What do you mean by that?" she asked, suddenly desperate to hear every thought rolling through his head. At this point, she'd gathered that Brett hadn't been in a serious relationship for a long time, and she was insatiably curious as to why.

Brett exhaled. "I guess I spent a lot of years of my life just trying to survive from one day to the next. Sometimes not even wanting to survive from one day to the next. And now I realize there's so damn much to fall in love with."

Penny's heart thumped against her ribs as his words sank in. A slow ache sank through her middle as she thought back to Lucas and how many conversations they'd had about all the good he was missing.

"How long?" she asked.

Brett didn't make her repeat the question. She'd told him about Lucas, and he'd told her he was in recovery. He knew exactly what she was asking. "Two years and ten months."

She drew a breath and held it, then let it release when her lungs burned. "How?"

Brett paused, considering. "I don't know, exactly. I know a big part of it had to do with the team. I didn't want to lose my spot on the Snowballs."

"You almost did?"

"Yeah. A couple different times. First with Fly and then with Sean when he first became captain."

"You've been playing with them for bit, then."

"They're like my second family."

Penny stared up at the swathe of glittering points. If she was being honest, they were starting to feel like her family, too.

"I was lucky. Lucky that something clicked in my head, and lucky to have the support that I did."

A lump formed in Penny's throat. She'd tried to give Lucas all the support he could possibly need—their whole family had. Why did some people find a way through it and so many others couldn't? What made the difference, and why hadn't she been able to find it?

That question gripped her with sharpened claws. "I tried so hard," she whispered. "I did everything for him. I was available anytime he called. I gave him money. I gave him all the time he asked for. I gave him everything—"

Her voice caught, and she worked to swallow back her tears.

Brett didn't try to shush her or tell her she'd done everything right. Instead, he tucked his arm under his head and said, "My sister did the same thing for me. I think I ruined her life for a long time."

The words tugged on the end of a string and loosened a knot she'd held in her chest for almost a decade. Penny turned in her sleeping bag to look at his moonlit profile.

"Eventually it got to be too much and we didn't talk for a long time," he continued. *Yes,* Penny thought. She'd hated Lucas. Wanted to never talk to him again. Hoped he'd do something permanent so he couldn't hurt her anymore, and those were the thoughts that made her want to shrivel up and die whenever she remembered them. How could she love him and think those things? *How could she want to abandon him when he was so desperate for help?*

Because it hurt. Because each time he fell back into using, a thread inside of her snapped, and she didn't know what would happen when the entire rope frayed to nothing.

"Do you talk to your sister now?" she asked.

Brett nodded. "We're working on it."

Penny rubbed her feet together under her sleeping bag trying to get friction to work its magic and warm her up.

"Here." Brett propped his head up, then reached over and found the zipper on her sleeping bag. "Is this okay?"

Blood rushed in Penny's ears. She nodded because she couldn't think straight enough to ask him what he was planning to do. Brett unzipped her sleeping bag, allowing a cool rush of air in next to her. She shivered.

"Give me your feet," he said. Penny balked, and Brett breathed a laugh. "I'm serious."

With trepidation, she unfurled her legs and pointed them toward his sleeping bag. He caught her ankles and slipped off her socks, then pressed her icy soles against both sides of his right knee and clamped his other leg over her toes. She nearly sighed at the sudden burst of heat.

"My knee is aching, so I figured you could ice it for me."

Penny laughed and shifted so her hip wasn't rotated at an odd angle. Brett looked down at her legs that were only covered in her joggers. He reached out and grabbed on to her sleeping bag, tugging her closer, then pulled the top of his sleeping bag over her knees. "Better?"

Penny nodded. This was better. So much better she was having a difficult time convincing her lungs to fill with air. Especially since Brett's face was barely six inches in front of her face, and even in the dim light, they reflected blue.

"Thank you," she whispered.

"You're doing my knee a favour, remember?" The corner of his mouth lifted, and Penny had never wanted to kiss something so badly in her entire life. Maybe it was the laughter, or the cozy feet, or the vast night sky over their heads, but Penny suddenly couldn't remember why she'd ever thought kissing Brett was a bad idea.

"I'm sorry your tent only had one pole," he murmured, and Penny shivered as his voice vibrated through her.

"Very inconvenient."

Brett's lip twitched. "Good night, Penny."

"Mmhmm." She didn't trust herself to form any more words because every sentence rolling through her head started with "kiss" and ended with "me, please."

Penny didn't remember falling asleep. She only remembered warmth. Peace. The hush of pine branches. And staring into deep blue.

CHAPTER
Sixteen

AS BRETT'S CONSCIOUSNESS ROSE, he became aware of three things at once. First, there was light streaming in through the thin tent walls. Second, he was sleeping on his back, which he never did. From the time he was able to roll over as a baby, he was a stomach sleeper through and through. Third, his arms were wrapped around something soft and warm . . . and breathing.

Brett tried to look down, but couldn't because a part of the something he was holding was buried between his neck and shoulder. Adrenaline shot through his veins as the night before slammed back into his brain. *Penny.* This was Penny in his arms. No longer in her own sleeping bag with her feet cooling his knee, but fully pressed up against him, at least one of her legs draped over his, both of them under his sleeping bag, and . . . *was her hand inside his shirt?*

Her palm was definitely flat against his stomach. His skin prickled and warmth spread through his thighs. Each time she exhaled, Penny's breath whispered against his Adam's apple. There would be no getting out of this gracefully.

A gentle breeze rustled through the trees above their tent, and he stared up at the swaying branches, working to calm his breathing. His cognitive functioning was a bit off first thing in the morning under normal circumstances, and this was testing his self control.

Penny doesn't want more than a friendship, he reminded himself, but that didn't stop his nerve endings from standing on point or the tips of his fingers from burning. Was there anything he could do to move without waking her up? As he calculated his options, Penny stirred against his chest.

Brett held his breath as Penny's fingers twitched against his bare stomach. He was going to explode. His chest felt like a shaken up keg, and the soft sigh that slipped through Penny's lips was about to pop his cork.

He knew the second she realized where she was and what her hands were touching because Penny's whole body stiffened. She pulled her hand from under his shirt with a mumbled apology and attempted to roll back to her side of the air mattress, but landed right back on top of him. He grunted as her knee landed dangerously close to his groin.

"I'm sorry!" she squeaked, pushing up against his shoulders. Her braid was disheveled and tendrils of hair fell around her face as she hovered over him. "I think the mattress lost air."

Brett breathed a laugh. "The rock under my left thigh concurs with your assessment."

Penny wobbled, trying to maintain her balance while she lifted to her knees and attempted once more to remove herself from his personal space. She laughed as the sleeping bag slipped under her, then flopped backward, pushing a little more air under his backside.

"Well. I'm so sorry for—"

"For what?" Brett sat up, pushing his hair away from his face.

Penny's eyes dropped briefly, then shot back up. "For—there was—I—" She stopped and drew a deep breath as her cheeks flushed. "For using you as my own personal heating blanket."

He chuckled and gestured at himself. "What else is all this good for?" Penny's lips parted, but she didn't say anything, just pulled out her elastic and started re-braiding her hair. "You don't need to apologize. I didn't realize this air mattress had a slow leak."

"Or it's not used to holding two people." Penny glanced up. "Not that—I mean, I'm sure you've taken other people camping, I just—"

"It hasn't held two people in a long time." Brett pulled his legs from his sleeping bag, then searched for the air pump along the side. "I'll fill it back up and see if I can figure out where we're losing air." His heart jolted at the thought of them sleeping here a second night. *Did he want to fix the leak?*

"I can help you with that, but I need to pee first." Penny pulled on a sweatshirt.

"Not a bad idea." Brett found the pump and set it above his pillow, then pulled his sleeping bag up. With the grace of two baby deer learning to walk, Brett and Penny managed to slip on their shoes and climb out of the tent. They walked to the bear bin and pulled out their toiletries then started on the path down to the plumbed bathrooms.

"How is nobody else awake yet?" Penny peered through the trees at the other two tents.

"It's only eight o'clock."

"Exactly. I'm surprised I slept so late."

Brett grinned. "You were cozy."

Penny rolled her eyes and nudged him with her elbow. "That's all I need to sleep well? A man-sized heater in my bed?"

"I'm available anytime." He laughed, then caught the blush on her cheeks. *Too far?* He always joked like this with friends, but he was pretty sure they were both very well aware of the tension between them. *Less funny when it was true.*

They went to their respective bathrooms, and when Brett walked back outside, Penny was nowhere to be found. Since he wasn't sure if she was still in there or if she'd already walked back, he decided not to wait.

When he returned to the site, he set to work preparing breakfast, reveling in the fresh morning air laced with the scent of fresh pine. He grabbed the cast iron skillet from his camping gear, a hand-me-down from his mom. His sister Cameron inherited the Dutch oven from their trips growing up, which was okay by him since he preferred to cook fast and furious.

Thankfully the backdoor of the van was unlocked since Sean was still MIA. He pulled out the cooler and fold-out camping stove and set up his workstation on the picnic table. Penny walked back into camp and joined him. They cooked the bacon first, and Penny used tongs to pull out the finished strips, setting them to cool on a plate with paper towels while Brett cracked eggs into a bowl.

"Morning!" Emma emerged from her tent, stretching her arms above her head and looking like she came straight out of an ad for rugged mountain gear. Tyler followed, and moments later Sean and Kelty dragged themselves into the morning sunlight.

"The gang's all here," Brett murmured. He whisked the eggs with a plastic fork until they were light and frothy then lowered the heat on the stove and poured them into the heated skillet. They sizzled as he sprinkled in salt and pepper and scraped the edges of the pan with a wooden spoon.

"Smells amazing, bud." Tyler rubbed his eyes as he took a seat near the makeshift kitchen. "You two make a good team."

Brett shot him a look. The last thing he needed was for these four to start making comments. He had no idea what was going through Penny's head right now, but making her feel cornered was going to take his already slim chances with her and drop them to zero.

She'd been through hell and back with her brother, from what she'd described and what he knew from personal experience. Maybe if he could prove to her that he was serious—that he was willing to do the work and she could trust him—she'd reconsider. Because the more time he spent with her, the more he couldn't imagine her walking out in six weeks and moving back to Vancouver.

When the eggs were done, he set the skillet on the table next to the bacon and encouraged everyone to dish up. Penny sat across from Brett, and her eyes flitted to his before dropping to her plate.

"Did Brett keep you up with his snoring?" Emma asked.

Penny laughed and took a bite of eggs. "No snoring. Not that I heard anyway."

"Snoring is better than laughing." Sean took a piece of bacon, and Emma scoffed.

"What, we're supposed to be grumpy like you when we go to bed at night?"

The furrow in Sean's brow deepened. "I'm not grumpy at night."

"Well you're not happy," Emma muttered.

Kelty leaned over and planted a kiss on Sean's temple. "You're intense. It's not a bad thing. Plus, it makes me feel more special that I know exactly what makes you *less grumpy*."

Emma pretended to gag.

Sean grinned smugly. "Not so fun when you're on the receiving end, is it?"

"That's what she said," Tyler murmured, and the whole group busted up laughing. Brett couldn't have been more grateful for the spotlight to be pointed away from him and Penny.

They finished their breakfast while Kelty suggested plans for the day, and Penny was the first to stand and pick up her plate.

"I can help you clean up."

Brett nodded, and together they gathered the dishes they'd used to cook and set them in a small tub, then carried them to the dishwashing station with the small bottle of biodegradable soap from Kelty's camping bin.

"I'll wash, you dry?" Penny suggested. She jumped in and scrubbed while Brett rinsed out the tub then dried the clean dishes and stacked them.

"Have you ever tried washing dishes in a stream?" Penny

asked. Brett shook his head. "I did it once when I was a kid. It was freezing, but the whole time I imagined I was a pioneer or something."

A smile tugged at the corners of his mouth as he imagined Penny as a little girl standing next to a gurgling stream. "That's adorable."

"I think I lost three plates and my mom's measuring cups."

Brett chuckled. "You don't need measuring cups anyway. Just eyeball it."

Penny grinned. "I would love to see you express that opinion in front of my mom."

Brett's throat constricted at the thought of meeting Penny's parents. He couldn't help it. Without his permission, his imagination was already working double time behind the scenes, building out possibilities brick by brick with Penny front and center. But she wasn't in his life, not permanently. Which was exactly why he'd avoided relationships for so long. He was efficient at managing his life with all the variables he knew to expect. If he kept the inputs the same, he knew the output. Even if it was a less than satisfactory one.

This injury was an unknown. Penny . . . she wasn't just an unknown variable. She was the forward that skated onto the ice and flipped the entire game on its head. He couldn't use the same strategies here, and that left him standing on thin ice. Worse. He could hear it cracking, and he was still begging to skate across.

Once the dishes were clean and stacked in the bin, they walked back to their site. He asked Penny more questions about her camping trips growing up, which was a mistake. Every detail he learned about her only fractured into a hundred more details he was desperate for. He felt like a kid on Christmas morning using every fiber of self control to keep from tearing off the wrapping paper and looking at the box.

Brett's neck flushed. That metaphor was disturbingly appropriate.

Penny retreated back into their tent to change out of her pajamas. He needed to change too, since they'd all agreed to take a trip into town, but he was happy to give her dibs. He needed time to clear his head. To focus on something other than unwrapping . . . things.

Penny emerged from the tent a few moments later wearing jeans and a loose tank top, her dark hair now pulled back into a ponytail. *That wasn't enough time.*

Brett grunted a hello as he passed and ducked into the tent. He changed and met the others by the van, then sat up by Sean before Kelty could claim the passenger seat. She may have thought him rude, but it was self preservation.

The six of them spent the rest of the morning exploring the nearby town, then drove to a gorgeous waterfall after lunch. Brett sat on a boulder larger than his apartment, soaking in the roar of water and the fine mist hitting his skin, and closed his eyes.

These were the moments. This was why working his steps was worth every second of discomfort. Why he went to bed feeling antsy or sat in his pain instead of numbing it. Being alive and present in these moments was a rivet in his soul.

He breathed in the spray, then opened his eyes and blinked. Penny sat next to him, her eyes closed and her face pointed toward the water. Brett clamped his eyes shut again, wondering how long she'd been there, and unable to see anything in his mind's eye other than her dewy skin and flushed cheeks.

"I'm really glad I came." Penny's voice floated over the rush of water.

Brett blinked. "I think you already said that once." He probably should've shown some surprise at hearing her voice if he wanted to pretend he hadn't noticed her already.

She laughed and leaned back on the rock, her eyes glittering in the sunlight. "Maybe I did need a little romance in my life after all."

"Everybody does." Brett watched for her reaction. Penny

grinned and when she dropped her eyes, she looked almost bashful.

"You coming, Penny?" Sean called out from the path. Brett exhaled, grabbed his backpack, then stood and slung it over his shoulder. He was about to offer Penny a hand when she jumped up next to him.

She took one last look at the waterfall, and her eyes crinkled with her smile. "Moments don't get much more perfect than that."

———

Penny sat with Emma and Kelty on the front bench in the van as they drove down the mountain toward their campsite later that afternoon. The five of them had continued on to a high mountain lake after the falls without Brett. She felt bad leaving him, but he'd insisted he was content with his nature therapy and didn't mind waiting while they hiked.

When they arrived back at the trailhead, Brett was leaning against a tree with his backpack next to him, writing in a notebook. *Was it a journal? A place where he jotted down inspiration?* What she wouldn't give to see what he wrote on those pages.

As soon as they got back within the city limits, Penny's phone caught service and buzzed in her bag. She pulled it out and saw fifteen messages on their family chat. That she'd check later. She opened a message from Andrea, and her heart flipped in her chest as she read through her sister's text.

> So excited to see you tomorrow! I think I already told you, but my flight is on Flair and I'm getting in at 7:55!

"Is everything okay?" Emma asked.

Penny looked up as dread settled in her gut. "I think I screwed up."

Brett turned in the passenger seat. "Screwed up what?"

Penny scrolled through their messages, scouring the ones sent by her sister. The words started to blur and she squeezed her eyes shut. "Andrea's flight time. Turns out, she's coming in tomorrow morning. Not Monday like I thought."

CHAPTER
Seventeen

PENNY 5:42PM

> YOU SAID MONDAY!

ANDREA 5:46PM

> Why would I be flying home on a Monday? I have a job, remember?

PENNY 5:46PM

> People take time off all the time! I'm looking through our old chats.

ANDREA 5:46PM

> That won't help you because I said Sunday

PENNY 5:48PM

> HA! You said the 16th! That's Monday!

ANDREA 5:48PM

> I said SUNDAY the 16th. I just read through the messages too

PENNY 5:49PM

> So we're both right. Kind of

ANDREA 5:49PM

> I'm sorry I messed up the date. And your camping trip

PENNY 5:49PM

> I'm sorry my brain skipped over the Sunday part. It's fine, Dre. I'll see you tomorrow morning

"IT'S NO PROBLEM. I can drive you back down and then come back up for the evening," Kelty offered as Sean parked the van.

Penny checked the time on her phone. "It's already four. You wouldn't get back up here until eight thirty."

Kelty waved her off as they piled out. "It's seriously not a big deal. Still plenty of time to enjoy the fire."

"Are you sure?" Penny bit her lip. She felt like a doofus. Even if Andrea had messed up her text message, she should've noticed the discrepancy and clarified. Or she should've driven up herself so she had a vehicle. *So many shoulds so little time.*

"I'm sure. Let me just change out of this." Kelty beelined for her tent, and Penny jogged to hers. She unzipped the tent and hurriedly stuffed her clothes into her duffel bag, then packed up her sleeping bag and grabbed her pillow.

As her knees scraped the ground, she remembered the air pump and reached for it. She couldn't wait around to help Brett find the leak, but she could at least pump the mattress up for him. Penny felt for the valve and attached the pump, then crouched up against the wall with her knees on the tent floor.

"Are you filling the mattress right now?" Brett called from outside the tent.

"Maybe?" Penny pumped the handle faster.

He sighed, and she could almost see him with his hands on his hips, giving her a look that said, *seriously?* "I can do that after you go."

"I know. I'm sorry. I just didn't want to—"

The tent opened with a zip. "Seriously. Stop." Brett noticed her sleeping bag and pillow and grabbed them. "Just bring your bag."

"I wanted to help."

He nodded. "I know." Brett took her things and pulled back. He was obviously annoyed, and why shouldn't he be? Here they'd invited her on their trip, driven her up, packed and prepared all the food besides the snacks she'd been assigned, and now she was ruining everything.

Penny scrambled after him, grabbing her duffel and shoving her feet into her shoes. Her ribs felt like they'd shrunk in the wash. "I'm sorry I can't—"

"Penny." Brett turned and fixed her with a serious stare. "Stop apologizing."

She pursed her lips. "But I'm wrecking your weekend."

"You're not wrecking anything."

She switched the duffel into her other hand. "I'm just sorry I didn't check the date."

Brett shook his head. "We all make mistakes, and I already told you to stop apologizing."

Penny's face pinched. "But I'm Canadian."

Brett's lips twitched, and his arm tightened, choking her pillow. "Will you just get in the damn van?"

Penny didn't want to get in the damn van. She did, and she didn't. Until this second, she hadn't realized that she'd been looking forward to tonight. To crawling into the tent and looking up through the pine trees at the night sky. She had a list of topics she wanted to discuss with Brett, but not out in the sunshine. Not when the others were around. Not even back at their apartment. The dark, quiet woods felt right.

"I second that!" Kelty stalked past Brett and motioned for Penny to follow her. Brett obeyed first, tossing her things onto the bench through the open side door. He stepped to the side for Penny to slide her duffel onto the floor.

"What'll I do without my heater?" she teased, but Brett didn't laugh. Her heart jumped into her throat when she realized she may have given too much away, so she didn't look at him. Penny reached past him and slammed the side door closed, then grabbed the passenger door handle and climbed in. "Thank you!" she called out to the others before closing herself in and buckling her seatbelt.

Kelty wasted no time in starting the engine and pulling out onto the road. If Penny had felt like an idiot before, she'd doubled down in the last thirty seconds. *What'll I do without my heater?* She slumped into her seat and pressed her fingers against her temples.

"Is that—?" Kelty peered into her rearview mirror, then hit the brakes. Penny sat up, whipping her head around to see why Kelty had stopped.

"What?" Penny murmured as Sean caught up to the van and slowed next to Kelty's now open window.

"What the hell, Sean? You couldn't text?"

Sean held up a finger as he caught his breath. "Can you come back to the site?"

"Did I forget something?" Kelty asked.

Sean nodded, then opened the side door and hopped in. Kelty pulled into the empty site on their left and turned around, then drove back to the campsite. She put the van in park then hopped out with Sean.

Penny watched, trying to decipher through terrible lip reading what was happening outside the glass. A few short moments later, Brett walked toward the van carrying his bag, and Penny's brow furrowed just as her stomach swooped. Was he—?

Brett pulled the side door open and shoved her things further down the bench, then climbed in.

Penny whirled around. "You're coming back, too?"

Brett nodded. "I mentioned to Sean I need to do a work thing. He said he'd bring the tent and mattress back."

Penny nodded as Kelty jumped back in, and her pulse quickened. Why did "I need to do a work thing" sound a lot like "I need to get a power strip?" She was about to ask him what *kind* of work thing when he said, "Plus we have that PT session Sunday."

Her heart plummeted. *Right.* Brett was focused on playing next season, and he needed her to keep to the schedule so he could have any chance of getting there. "Of course. That makes sense." She turned back around, and Kelty pulled out of their campsite a second time.

"So it's actually a good thing you mixed up the date," Brett added.

A good thing. Penny swallowed hard. "Glad it worked out."

"Me too, actually. I have something I wanted to show you, Brett." Kelty blasted the new Nickelback single three times in a row before Brett finally gave up three more people on his hate list: Shredder from the *Teenage Mutant Ninja Turtles*, ALF acting as himself in Season Ten Episode Four of the Simpsons, and Xander from *Buffy the Vampire Slayer*.

By the time they got home, Penny had heard a full-on debate about two out of the three, and her stomach had gone from aching out of regret and guilt to aching from laughter.

Kelty pulled into the driveway, and Brett and Penny got out and grabbed their things. They thanked Kelty for the ride and Penny made her promise she'd text and let them know she got back up to the campsite safely. That and allow her to pay for gas money. Penny knew she wouldn't agree, so she'd already stuffed a twenty into the cupholder.

As they walked up the front steps, Brett spotted a package sitting on the front porch. "Did you order something?"

Penny shook her head. The porch light wasn't on, so Brett pushed it out of the way to open the door, then flicked the switch. When she saw her name scribbled on the cardboard, the blood drained from her face.

She knew that handwriting.

Brett held the door open for her, so she dropped her things inside on the floor, then picked up the box and stepped over the threshold. "Do you know what it is?" he asked.

Penny shook her head. She could barely wrap her head around how Danny would've gotten this to her. How did he know where she was living? She mentally flipped through every person she'd told about her situation here with Brett, and couldn't think of—

Her veins iced over. *Sheryl*. She'd emailed and asked if she could mail her last check, and Penny had given her Brett's address. She hadn't received the check yet, but this?

"Are you going to open it?" Brett closed the door behind her and flicked off the light.

"I don't think I want to."

Brett took a step back and stared at the box. "From your ex?"

She nodded. "Do you want me to—"

Penny kicked off her shoes and took the box to the counter,

then unfolded the flaps. She reached inside and started pulling things out. The yoga blanket she'd given him on his birthday. A set of bluetooth headphones. The smart wallet she'd purchased for Danny before they traveled to France last summer. And, the pièce de résistance at the bottom, Danny's Butchart Gardens sweatshirt she'd always stolen on the weekends.

"What a dick," she muttered, anger reaching a low boil in her midsection.

"Are those your things?" Brett walked up to stand next to her.

Penny whirled. "Nope. They're *his*. They're things I gave him—no, not even that." Penny snatched the sweatshirt off the counter. "This was *his*, his. I love oversized shirts, and I used to wear it on Saturdays instead of a robe, so the asshole sent it to me in this—" Her voice caught as something fluttered out of the sweatshirt and landed on her toes.

She leaned over and picked it up. Her check. Not even in an envelope. Two-hundred dollars and sixty-three cents. Penny laughed out loud and dropped it on the counter next to the rest of Danny's things.

That's what she was. His *thing*. A tool. One he'd gotten great use out of until he'd used her up. "I spent years helping Danny build his patient base. I gave up my own salary so that he could wrap profits back into the practice." She bit the inside of her cheek. "I'm sorry," she whispered, then pushed past Brett and stalked down the hall.

Penny slipped into her room and closed the door, leaning against it as tears pricked her eyes. She wrapped her arms around herself, wishing she could block all the nooks and crannies where loneliness and hurt seeped into her. The tasks of washing her face or brushing her teeth felt insurmountable, but she forced herself to go to the bathroom, then turned off her light and climbed into bed, grabbing her decorative pillow since she'd left her real one in the entryway. She tucked the blanket around herself and curled into a ball, trying to warm her feet.

The sun hovered well over the horizon as Penny dragged herself to the car at seven in the morning. She opened the door to find her camping things sitting just outside in the hall. After cleaning herself up, she marched out into the kitchen to find the box and all of Danny's crap gone besides her check. She hoped Brett had smashed or burned them. Preferably both.

The drive to the airport was quiet and uneventful, giving Penny time to calm her thoughts and prepare for the whirlwind that was her sister. She stopped and grabbed a coffee and donut at Tim's. She would need high energy today, and since her tank was currently at "E", that was going to take a miracle. Timmie's was at least a good start.

As she pulled up to the arrivals curb, she spotted Andrea wearing a bright red sweater and waving with the exuberance of a golden retriever, probably pissing off every person standing next to her who, like Penny, believed no day should start before eight.

"Hey, Pens!" Andrea rounded the hood and pulled her into a tight hug as soon as Penny parked and stepped out of the car. "Let our best six hours commence!"

"Love you too," Penny laughed. "How was your flight?"

"Ugh, you know me and flying," Andrea rolled her eyes. "I spent the whole time praying we wouldn't hit turbulence."

Penny reached inside the car to pop the trunk, and Andrea rolled her carry-on back and hoisted it in. When they were both back in their seats, Penny asked, "Where to first? Breakfast?"

Andrea shook her head. "Your place. I'll eat whatever you have, but I refuse to let you get out of not showing me your apartment. Or your room—"

"*Housemate*, and I'm not trying to get out of it. There's just no rush. Are you sure you don't want to hit breakfast first?" Penny asked, praying that Brett's "work thing" would take him out of the apartment most of the day. Andrea typically had a content filter like a colander, but with a limited timeline, Penny was worried it would be more of a cheese grater today.

"To the apartment!" Andrea pointed to the end of the covered pick-up zone like the captain of a ship.

Penny tapped out a text to Brett while she waited to merge.

> My sister wants to see the apartment. I recommend pretending you're still asleep

"Who are you texting?" Andrea asked, leaning over in her seat.

"Just bringing up the map." Penny swiped back to the directions and put both hands on the wheel. As they made their way back to Northwest Calgary, they chatted about everything from Andrea's latest romantic escapades—most notably a heliski instructor who she ran into buying groceries for a guided backcountry tour who she then went out to dinner with—to their favourite family recipes they wanted to make together the second she got home.

As it always seemed to do with Andrea nowadays, the conversation eventually circled back to Brett.

"So he plays hockey. What else?" Andrea asked.

"I guess you can ask him yourself."

"You two don't talk?"

Penny drew a deep breath. "We talk, but I don't know why you're so interested in him." She knew exactly why Andrea was so interested. Her sister wasn't stupid, and try as she might to lead her off the scent, she couldn't seem to give normal responses when Andrea brought him up. This was her attempt at nonchalance, and she hoped it was working.

"Okay, that's fine. I can interrogate him when I get there. But just for the record, I'm *interested* because this is the first time you've had a roommate." Andrea put her feet up on the dash.

Penny didn't bother to correct her. "After Danny, I want to make sure this guy understands the situation."

Penny focused in hard on the signs for the highway exits. "And what exactly *is* the situation?"

"You need someone who's going to look out for you, who's not a selfish prick."

Was that even possible? Penny thought about Brett carrying her pillow and sleeping bag to the van, and her heart picked up speed. "Dre, I don't need someone, period. I think I need time to figure myself out."

Andrea sighed and ran a hand through her hair. "Pens, I've already figured you out. You're always going to be that person who takes care of other people."

"You don't think I could be happy on my own?"

Andrea made a face. "I'm not saying you couldn't do it, but happy?"

Penny blew out a breath. "Well that's good to know. My own sister doesn't think I'm capable of flying solo."

Andrea put a hand on her arm. "I wish I was more like you. Honestly."

Penny scoffed. "No, trust me. You don't. How's work?"

Andrea filled her in on the new project management system they were transitioning to in her department, and Penny told her about the email she'd received the night before about signing on with a local lacrosse team. They'd seen a post she'd made on a job board. It was only a few nights a week, but that was another drop in the bucket.

When they arrived at the house, Penny's stomach fluttered. She pulled her phone from the mount and swiped to her messages. There was one from Brett.

> Why would I pretend to be asleep?

Penny replied as Andrea debated whether to leave her bag in the trunk.

> Because you're not ready for this kind of energy at the butt-crack of dawn

Three dots appeared before she could push her door open.

> I made eggs

Penny groaned as she got out of the car, and Andrea followed her to the step.

"This complex is great. I love how small it is. In my head I was envisioning one of those massive apartment complexes that . . ." Andrea prattled on, but Penny wasn't listening. All she could think about was whether Brett would be wearing one of his white T-shirts and if his hair would be wild like it was in the tent or if he'd pull it back into a low bun. Either one was equally devastating.

". . .I bet there isn't a lot of that, since you only have one neighbor on—" Andrea stopped mid-sentence as she stepped into the apartment and spotted Brett serving up scrambled eggs onto three plates lined up on the counter. "*Shit, Pens.* That picture did not do him justice."

It was a grey T-shirt and bun day. Penny exhaled. "Andrea, this is my housemate, Brett."

CHAPTER
Eighteen

BRETT WAITED as Andrea looked him up and down. He wasn't completely unused to this type of treatment, but women didn't normally undress him with their eyes first thing in the morning, while standing in his own kitchen. He could think of worse problems.

"Hungry?" he asked, and Andrea bobbed her head. She slipped off her sandals and walked with Penny to the counter. He tried to avoid openly inspecting Penny for any signs of distress after last night, but when he snuck a glance, her eyes weren't nearly as puffy and red as he'd expected.

"This was so thoughtful," Andrea purred, and Brett could've sworn he caught an eye roll from Penny. If Andrea was drinking him in, Penny was the complete opposite. She hadn't looked at him once, only zeroing in on the eggs on her plate.

"Thank you," she murmured as he handed them both a fork. It was obvious the two of them were sisters. They both had the same olive skin and jet-black hair, though Andrea's was cut into a wavy bob that hit just below her jawline. Her nose was thinner than Penny's and her cheekbones a bit more prominent.

Andrea sat down at the stool and took a bite. "So, I feel like I have to apologize for ruining your camping weekend."

Brett looked over at Penny. "I see it runs in the family."

Penny gave him a look, and a thrill zipped down his spine. *All attention was good attention.* "She's allowed to apologize because it was technically her fault." Andrea smacked Penny's arm, and Brett laughed.

"I had something I needed to take care of anyway. It worked out," he said, and Andrea took another forkful of eggs. "What do you two have on the docket?"

Andrea chewed and swallowed. "I have to be back at the airport around two thirty, so I thought we'd start here, then Penny mentioned the African festival in the park and a favourite lunch place."

Brett turned to Penny. Her having a favourite restaurant was news to him. "What is it?"

"Jackie's Thai. Just in Eau Claire Market."

Brett tucked that tidbit away. Penny liked Thai food. "Are you heading home to Vancouver?"

Andrea nodded. "Just on my way back from a client meeting in Denver."

"I don't think Penny told me what you do."

Andrea tucked her hair behind her ear. "I'm a corporate trainer for Cascadia Crest hotels and properties. We're expanding into the States, so I'm traveling more than usual right now."

Brett's eyes widened. "Wow. Impressive."

Penny's fork scraped on her plate. "Well, I'm finished. Should we head over, Dre?"

Andrea nodded. "These were delicious, Brett. Did you put something in them besides salt and pepper?"

Brett grinned. "Just salt and pepper, but I do use a pepper blend." He picked up the jar from the counter, and Penny slumped over the table. *Why did he love that she was annoyed at her sister's praise?* "Uses three different peppercorns. I think it adds a bit more flavour."

Andrea took it from his outstretched hand. "I agree." She

inspected it, then set it back on the counter. "I think Penny scored with you as a housemate."

Brett had to admit, hearing her praise fluffed his proverbial feathers.

Penny clenched her jaw. "Right, well, we should get going. So much to do, so little time."

Couldn't she admit that he was a pretty great housemate? He'd woken up early to try and cross paths with Penny before she left, and when that attempt had failed, he'd jumped at the chance to impress her after finding out she and Andrea were stopping by. Now she was acting like she'd done him some kind of favour.

"You said you had something to take care of today?" Andrea asked as she set her plate in the sink.

Brett turned to pull the pan from the stove to start it soaking. "Yeah, I needed internet to submit a contract. No service up at the site. I took care of it when I woke up this morning."

Andrea beamed at him. "So you're free today?"

Brett looked between her and Penny, not sure what his answer should be. "Yes?"

———

Five minutes later, all three of them piled into Penny's car. Brett offered to drive, but Penny insisted. If she had no control over this situation beyond how fast they went, she was going to snag it.

"So tell me more about this injury." Andrea started in on him as soon as they pulled away from the curb. Penny's thoughts raced as Brett filled her sister in on all the details Penny already knew. Andrea had given an excuse as to why she was so interested in all things Brett, but Penny was beginning to wonder if she had extra motivation. *Was she interested in him?*

She'd told Andrea plenty of times that she wasn't trying to

get involved with Brett, which meant her sister probably thought he was fair game. *Which he wasn't.* Penny's heart raced as that thought slammed down like a cage. The idea of Brett going out with Andrea or texting her like he texted Penny made her want to pull the car over and throw up.

But what was she supposed to do? She couldn't claim him for herself. Couldn't stick a flag in him that read "reserved." *On layaway for when I finally figure out how to be enough of myself to love somebody else.*

She thought back to Andrea's words on their way back from the airport. *I've already figured you out.* Penny just needed to rid herself of whatever insecurities were driving her to want to be right for everyone else. She needed to embrace more of her own opinions in relationships and stand up for what she wanted. She needed to want more and feel worthy of it in the first place.

"...our mother finally realized we hadn't seen Penny in ages, so she sent me to look for her. I found her in the boys' bedroom drawing an almost-to-scale portrait of our family. In Sharpie," Andrea finished.

Brett laughed from the backseat, and Penny met his eyes through the rearview mirror. "They had the boldest colour."

"You never told me you were an artist," Brett said, still grinning.

"Because I'm not. There's a reason that was my first and last wall mural."

Andrea turned in her seat. "Penny had to repaint the wall."

"By yourself?" Brett asked.

Penny's smile grew tight. "Lucas helped me."

Andrea sobered, and they drove in silence a few moments before she said, "So this African festival. Tell me about it."

They spent the morning enjoying live music, sampling food from street vendors, and strolling through the artisan market. They then made their way to Eau Claire for Thai food. Andrea and Brett got along so well, it was tiresome. Penny stopped trying to fight it because there was no way to slow the trains on the tracks.

By the time they all finished lunch, the two of them had a handshake and inside jokes. Penny excused herself to the bathroom and tried to convince herself she was glad they'd gotten along. *Had she wanted them to hate each other?* No, she'd wanted them not to know each other. There was a difference.

When she walked back out, Andrea and Brett both had their phones out, and the slow burn inside her received another log on the fire.

"Oh, hey! Ready to go?" Andrea asked with a look of complete innocence. They'd just exchanged phone numbers. Her sister had asked for Brett's number.

Penny nodded once, not trusting herself to speak. They walked to the car, and Andrea suggested they should drop Brett off at home since they had time and then he wouldn't have to drive all the way over to the airport with them. That was fine by Penny. She had some words for Andrea that weren't appropriate for mixed company.

When they got to the apartment, Brett thanked them both for the fun and exited the car. Penny waited until he climbed the first step to the apartment before taking off down the road. "What the hell was that, Dre?"

Andrea's eyes widened. "What are you—"

"Is that why you chose a flight with a layover? So you could meet him and shoot your shot?"

Andrea scoffed. "I wasn't shooting *anything*, I—"

"You were practically presenting yourself on a platter with an apple in your mouth."

"I'm sorry, are you comparing me to a *roasted pig?*"

"I mean, if the cloven hoof fits!" Penny's foot was heavy on the gas, and she forced herself to ease up even though all she wanted to do was plow through the next intersection.

To her surprise, Andrea started laughing next to her. Penny's eyes flashed. "What?" Andrea held up a finger. "What is so funny?"

"Thank you for this," Andrea wheezed. "I wasn't sure on the phone, so thank you."

Penny merged onto the Ring Road. "If you don't start talking, I swear—"

"*You're into him!*"

Penny's face flushed. "I'm not—"

"You're a goner, Pens! I have *never in my life* seen you so angry about someone flirting with a guy. Even when that business executive or whatever showed up for lunch to talk to you and Danny about partnering with them—remember? She had that maroon collared shirt with the buttons undone down to her navel?"

Penny snorted in spite of herself. That day, she'd been worried they were going to get dinner and a show. And, yeah. Andrea was right. She hadn't cared one bit. Mostly because she knew anything Danny said was only to get what he wanted and . . . *holy shit*.

She knew that about him.

Way back then, she knew that he was a manipulating skeeve, and she'd still stayed with him for another year and a half. *Had she actually believed she was the exception to his narcissistic rule?*

Andrea wiped her eyes. "Ugh. That was a gift, babe, and can I just give you a smidgen of advice?" Penny waited, knowing it was going to come whether she wanted it or not. "Lock that down because Brett is a triple shot espresso in a world full of decaf."

Brett went to work Monday still thinking about the messages he'd exchanged with Penny over the rest of the weekend. Since

Kelty and Emma weren't going to be at Sunday Supper, she'd decided not to come along and had spent all of Saturday night and most of Sunday out.

Saturday she'd worked a lacrosse game and he'd waited up. She greeted him pleasantly, but all the walls that he'd thought had come down between them seemed to be ramped back up. Penny was quiet. Standoffish. She blamed it on being tired, but Brett started to worry he'd done something to upset her.

Even when they did their PT session Sunday morning, something had been off. By Sunday afternoon, he'd broken down and sent her a text.

> Hey. You okay? Intense weekend. I'm making a baked potato if you want one

He'd waited for her to respond with some fancy word for that, but all he'd gotten was:

> I'm good. Went to an art show with a friend from yoga

That had been a punch to the gut. He knew Penny went to the yoga studio in the plaza a few blocks from them, but she'd never mentioned a *friend*. His mind immediately jumped to some guy obsessed with calisthenics wearing short shorts and a tank top ruminating on impressionism with Penny while he stroked his ironic moustache.

He had a hard enough time with Jordan and other players having one-on-one time with her in the garage with the door open, and they were dirt bags. Was this *friend* smart? Accomplished? Not in recovery with a limp? Those questions sent his nervous system into a tailspin, and even after a good night's sleep, he still felt like a charged up air compressor tank.

Brett's knee twinged when he got out of the car, and it was then that he realized how rarely he'd thought about his injury over the course of the week. Not only his knee, he hadn't felt as exhausted or depressed as he had for the past month. It may have had something to do with the fact that he wasn't using his crutch anymore, or the fact that he'd gotten his autonomy back with driving privileges, but that wasn't the whole story.

Brett wasn't thinking about his knee because he was thinking about Penny. Constantly. He wasn't feeling down or useless because Penny was there in the apartment making him laugh or sitting with him at the dinner table. He was making good progress in PT because of her, and that gave him some modicum of control and goals to shoot for.

All it took was one day of her not being there, and that cloud was already beginning to roll back over his life. *Was he getting better or was he just inserting another way to numb?* It terrified him. Not only because he hadn't appreciated how big of an impact she'd had in such a short time, but because he needed to keep those clouds at bay. If Penny pulled back, where did that leave him?

He wasn't proud of the thought, but he let it sit for a minute before he strode through the doors and inspected the job site. The smell of sawdust and sound of clomping boots were like balm for his senses. It was a much-needed break to drop into analysis mode and troubleshoot with his team. They'd made good progress on the electrical and on the added entrance Daniel had requested but were waiting on a pallet of brackets to complete the framing on the upper floor.

Brett was nearly ready to head home for the day when Dominic called for him at the front. He caught sight of blond hair and aviators, and his stomach clenched. *Take your damn sunglasses off when you enter a building, dickhead.* "Hey, Daniel. Wasn't expecting you today."

"Hey there, looks like that knee is doing better." Daniel pulled off his glasses and looped them in the pocket of his crisp button-up.

"I have an excellent physical therapist."

Daniel blinked, then moved on. "I was passing through to meet a client of mine and thought I'd stop by for a looksie."

Brett gritted his teeth and forced a smile. "Excellent. I can take you through." Brett led him to the back and gave him a quick walking tour of the changes they'd made since he'd seen the site last. They were making their way back to the front when Daniel's phone rang. He looked at the screen, then held up a finger to Brett as he answered it.

Instead of taking the call outside, his voice boomed even louder than before. "Hey, yes, this is Dr. Ascott. Thanks for making the extra call, I just felt it wasn't appropriate for my office manager to be answering those questions since I'm the one who works so intimately with my physical therapists."

Brett swallowed the bile that rose in his throat at the word "intimately." *And physical therapists, plural?* Was this dude pulling in other young women and treating them the same way he had Penny? He pulled out his phone, searching for something to serve as a distraction and lower his blood pressure.

Daniel sighed. "Right, we had to part ways, unfortunately. If I'm being honest, the main reason was because she couldn't handle the patient load."

Brett's ears perked up. How big was Daniel's office? Had he "parted ways" with other staff recently, or just her?

Daniel ran a hand through his hair, pressing his ear to the phone to keep the sound of hammers and drills away from the speaker. "She's a nice girl, but in that kind of environment, I don't think she'll be a strong enough team player. She'd do great in a stand-alone physical therapy office, but she's not a collaborator. At least in my experience."

Daniel looked back at Brett and gave an apologetic smile, then turned and finished the call. By the time he spun and slid his phone back into his pocket, Brett was seething. He'd been talking about Penny—he had to be—and everything out of his mouth was complete and utter horse shit. *Penny not a team player? Penny not a collaborator?* Sure, he'd never worked with her in a professional setting, but she was the least prideful person he'd met in ages. He couldn't imagine her not being an excellent addition to any team.

All the moments that Penny had mentioned not getting interviews or in one instance, having her interview canceled, flooded into Brett's head. Daniel Ascott was actively sabotaging her job prospects.

"Sorry about that. I've been getting calls to be a reference for a previous employee."

Brett bit the inside of his lip so hard he drew blood. "Seems like a time commitment."

"Well, you know. It's my duty to give my honest opinion. Make sure other offices don't make the same mistake I did."

Brett clenched his hands and nearly snapped his pen in half. He turned and continued on toward the front door. "Sounded like this was a physical therapist you had to let go?"

Daniel nodded, falling into step next to him. "Frustrating situation. I brought her in, gave her an incredible opportunity, and she showed zero gratitude for any of it. She was critical, tried to monopolize my time, and was impossible to manage. At a certain point, I had to wash my hands of her."

This time Brett did snap the pen, and ink splattered over his fingers.

"Whoa!" Daniel laughed. "Don't know your own strength there, eh?"

Brett nodded. "Dominic, can you walk Dr. Ascott out?" He held up his hand, and Dominic dropped the nail gun he was holding. Brett escaped into the office where they had a working sink, pumped soap into his palm, then held his hands under the warm water and scrubbed.

I had to wash my hands of her. Daniel Ascott would either be gone from the site by the time he walked out of the office, or Brett was going to lose his contract because there was no way he'd be able to stop himself from planting his un-mitted fist into the side of that smug bastard's face.

CHAPTER
Nineteen

Mom 3:03pm

> You're coming back to have dinner with us for our anniversary, yes?

Penny 3:24pm

> I wouldn't miss it!

Mom 3:25pm

> How long will you stay?

Penny 3:27pm

> I'm not sure yet. I was planning to come out Wednesday. See the nieces

Mom 3:28pm

> Maybe you could come at the beginning of the week? Stay until after the weekend?

PENNY 3:28PM

> Zero pressure?

MOM 3:28PM

> Not trying to pressure you, love. We just miss you.

PENNY 3:29PM

> I know. I miss you too. I'll look at it and let you know 🖤

PENNY WAS in the middle of deboning a chicken when Brett walked in through the front door. She glanced at the clock. Three forty-two. He'd told her he wouldn't be home until five. "Hey." She pushed a stray tendril of hair back from her face with her wrist.

Brett grunted and tossed his keys on the table by the door.

"That good, hey?"

He stopped and looked up, and Penny froze with her hand wrapped around a thigh bone. The fire blazing behind his eyes made Penny's insides trade positions. "I'm going to the gym."

She nodded. "Dinner will be ready in—"

"I want to kill your ex, you know that?" He stopped next to the counter, and Penny swallowed hard, looking up at his stony expression. "I've never wanted to beat someone to a pulp so bad—"

"Never?" Penny's heart galloped in her chest as she tore the bone out and set it on the plate.

"Only on the ice."

Penny's curiosity ran wild. *He'd seen Danny at work?* "What did he do?"

Brett's jaw worked, and she could've sworn he inched closer to her before saying, "You weren't the problem in that relationship. You know that, right?"

Penny's mouth opened and closed like a guppy. "I don't think you have enough information to—"

Brett put a hand on her cheek, and her skin prickled. "You weren't the problem, Penny."

She stared into his blue eyes, momentarily forgetting the chicken on her hands or what part of the house she was standing in.

As quickly as his touch came, he pulled away and stalked into the living room, growling under his breath. "I need to sweat. I need to run or sprint on skates, I need to—" He ran his hands through his hair, and Penny quickly scrubbed her hands with soap and dried them on a towel.

"Brett, I'm so sorry. I don't know what happened, but I one hundred percent know this feeling. I think the gym's a good idea."

Brett gave a sardonic laugh. "It's not enough. I need to sweat. I need to run myself ragged after the filth I heard spewing from that asshole's mouth, and there's nothing I can do! I can't run with this knee! I can't get on the ice! I've been taking it easy for weeks, trying to accept that I have to give my body time, but I don't do well with *time*."

Brett's chest rose and fell in quick bursts as explosive energy rolled off him in waves. Red flags went up inside Penny's head screaming *Danger!* but she knew better. This was Brett. True, she'd never seen him this riled up, but somehow, she knew instinctively that he'd never do anything to hurt her. *He* was hurting. That's what this was about, and if there was anything she was good at, it was helping people work through pain.

"Do you have a swimsuit?" she asked.

Brett frowned. "Yeah."

"Go put it on."

"I hate swimming."

"You said you wanted to sweat, right? You want to run yourself ragged?"

Brett stared at her, his chest still heaving. "I'm not a swimmer, Penny."

"I didn't ask if you were a swimmer. I asked if you had a swimsuit. Are we going to stand here and argue about it?"

Brett's throat worked, but he nodded once, then retreated to his room. Penny strode back into the kitchen, covered the pan still holding the half-finished chicken, and slid it back into the fridge. It was early enough, she could roast it up when they got home. She rushed to her room and changed into running shorts and a tank top so she wouldn't roast next to the pool, then put on her flip flops and grabbed her waist bag.

Brett emerged from his room wearing board shorts and a faded T-shirt and holding a towel under his arm. Penny nodded approvingly, then walked out the door. She drove them the few blocks to the community center, then checked in and pushed through the doors to the indoor pool.

It wasn't huge. Three lap lanes, a hot tub, a wading pool with a small slide for toddlers, and a steam room next to the bathrooms. Perfect. Brett set his towel on a chair, and took off his sandals. Penny did the same and dropped her bag on the chair next to his.

A woman who looked to be seventy plus was swimming in the far lane, so Penny motioned for Brett to take the closest one.

He peeled off his shirt, then hesitated. "You're not getting in?"

"Why would I get in?" Penny worked to keep her expression even as she took in his broad chest with her peripheral vision.

Brett's eyes wandered over her athletic wear, and Penny shivered. "I thought we were swimming."

"No, *you're* swimming. I'm going to coach you."

Brett's nostrils flared. "I don't know what I'm doing. I doubt this will be—"

"Can you just get in the damn pool?" Penny planted a hand on her hip to emphasize her point, and Brett stalked to the edge of the water. He dipped his toe in like a gazelle testing for crocodiles, but before she could give him a hard time, he took the plunge and dropped into the shallow end. The water barely came up to his hips.

Penny stood by the edge of the pool, her dark hair still pulled up into a messy bun from when she'd started prepping dinner. She crouched down in front of Brett, trying not to notice that his skin grew tight and prickled in the cool water.

"I probably should've recommended we try this earlier in the week, so I'm sorry about that. This is one of the best ways to get your muscles back into action without straining anything," Penny explained. Brett nodded once and folded his arms over his chest. "I'm going to teach you how to flutter kick the right way."

"I know how to flutter kick."

Penny rolled her eyes. "You just told me you aren't a swimmer."

"But I've gone swimming before."

"Fine. Show me a flutter kick." Brett turned to go down the lane, but Penny stopped him. "Right here. Just hold onto the wall."

Brett's lips were tight as he gripped the tiled edge of the pool and stretched his legs out behind him. He started to kick, and Penny got down on her knees. "You need to engage your core and keep your legs straight. Don't bend your knees much. Instead, focus on kicking from your hips while keeping your ankles relaxed." Brett nodded and made the adjustments. "Better."

"Just better?" His blue eyes rose to her in challenge.

"Right. *Better.*" Penny stood. "Do you know a proper front crawl?" Brett dropped from the wall and showed her the arm motions. She nodded. "Get on your knees and drop your top half into the water. Show me how you breathe."

Again, Brett did as she asked. When he pulled his face out of the water, Penny said, "Keep that right shoulder fully rotating. Don't let it get away with less motion. And you need to exhale fully. Don't hold anything back before your next breath."

Brett nodded and pushed his hair away from his face. He had it in a hair tie, but she should've thought to bring him a swim cap. Penny stood. "Okay. Let's go. Give me a lap." When he got to the other end of the pool, she told him to work on even kicks, then set him loose for lap two.

When he stood in the shallow end, he sucked in a breath. Penny crouched in front of him and grinned. "Tired?"

Brett wiped the water from his face. "I'm just getting started." He turned and did another two laps while Penny walked along with him on the pool deck. His form was still jerky, but it was improving. This time when he stood, he struggled to catch his breath.

"Lungs burning yet?"

Brett nodded. "Feels good."

"You're welcome."

He dove back in and did another two, and when he paused at th e wall the third time, Penny suggested they end there. Brett shook his head and pushed off the wall again. The water churned around him as he swam, and this time, he paused at the deep end. His breaths were shallow and rapid, his chest heaving as he clung to the edge of the pool.

"Let's stop and tread water. Get different mobility in the leg."

Brett nodded. Once his breathing slowed, he pushed off the wall and started to spin his legs beneath the surface. Penny laughed. "You're flailing like a drowning cat."

"I'm treading water."

She shook her head. "That's not treading water. You need to do this—" Penny stood on one foot and tried to demonstrate the motion. "Your legs should be two beaters on a hand mixer, you know?" Brett flailed harder, and Penny showed him a second time. "It needs to be smooth, not erratic."

Brett reached for the wall and looked up at her, sucking in air. "I can't hear you."

"What?"

He pointed to the toddler who'd arrived a few moments before and was laughing maniacally in the pool next to them. He curled his finger and motioned for her to come closer. Penny crouched down and began to repeat what she'd called out from the pool deck when Brett's hand circled around her wrist and yanked.

Penny plunged into the water, then flailed and spluttered as she grabbed onto Brett's shoulder and thrust her head above the surface. "Are you serious? What are we, twelve?"

Brett's laugh echoed off the tiled walls. "I just thought it might be easier for you to show—"

"I'm not even in a swimsuit!"

"Whose fault was that?"

Penny smacked him, then realized she was still clinging to him like a baby opossum and transferred to the wall next to him. She glowered at him, and Brett tried and failed to look repentant.

"My underwear is wet."

"I do tend to have that effect." He raised an eyebrow, and Penny groaned.

"I walked into that one."

"You did."

She shivered, then pushed off the wall and treaded water while she fixed her hair. "This is how you do it. Like a duck. Smooth on the surface and busy underneath, and do not make a comment about getting busy."

Brett smirked, then pushed off the wall and tried to mimic her motions. "So much easier when I can see it demonstrated."

Penny's lips drew into a thin line. "I bet it is."

"How long do we go for?"

Penny lowered her voice. "As long as you can, I guess."

Brett's lip twitched. "I'm known for my stamina."

Penny arched a brow. "I'm going to need references." She expected Brett to laugh, but instead, his expression clouded over. "I was *kidding*."

He shook his head as he started to grow short of breath. "That was what Daniel did at work." Penny frowned, not following. "He was acting as your reference."

"What?"

Brett kicked harder, and his shoulders rose in the water. "He got a phone call. Said he'd asked for his office manager to forward those kinds of calls, then proceeded to trash you on the phone to someone interested in hiring you." Penny's blood turned to ice. "Did it right there in front of me."

Penny didn't know how to respond to that. *Danny had trashed her on the phone? Sheryl was forwarding the calls?* She saw the last two weeks like a flip book. Her throwing out bids and Danny slapping each one off the ice. "I'm an idiot."

Brett frowned. "How did anything I just told you lead to that conclusion?"

"Because I trusted Sheryl. She's the office manager." Penny's eyes filled with tears, and she reached for the edge of the pool. She couldn't blame her though, when she thought about it. Danny had everyone on his staff pinned under his thumb. If he told his office manager to jump, she'd have to ask "how high?" or risk the same treatment Penny had endured.

Brett followed her to the wall as she hoisted herself out of the pool, trying to catch her breath. He pushed himself up to sit next to her, both of them dripping water onto the deck. She tried to hide her tears, but when they blended into the water on her face anyway, she gave up. Penny wrapped her arms around herself and shivered.

"Let's go to the steam room," Brett suggested, and Penny

nodded. He stood and reached out a hand, lifting her up from the deck. As she straightened, he didn't let go, instead gripping on tighter and leading her to the door in the wall across from them.

Water trailed down her legs in rivulets from her drenched clothes, and the fabric stuck to her skin, but Penny didn't care. She didn't even care that she hadn't gotten a job now that she had money coming in. It very well could've been that Danny had done her a favour, but at that moment, she couldn't see past the box of shit on her step and the words she imagined him saying in front of Brett.

What *had* he said? They walked into the steam room, and Penny sat on the wooden bench next to Brett. He didn't let go of her hand, instead placing it along with his on his damp thigh.

"What did Danny say about me?"

Brett shook his head. "I'm not going to tell you that."

"I need to know." Penny sniffed.

"None of it was true."

She looked up at him, tears still welling in her eyes. "How do you know that? You've only known me for a few weeks, Brett. Danny knew me for *years*. He was my boss. Maybe everything he said was—"

Brett's lips crushed against hers, his free hand cupping her jaw as he slid his fingers into her wet hair. Penny reeled as every thought in her mind evaporated. *What had she been saying?* She closed her eyes and tipped her head back, allowing his palm to cradle her as she parted her lips and tasted him.

Steam hissed from a valve on the opposite wall and billowed around them, layering over their skin like a blanket. Brett was kissing her. *Brett was kissing her.* Her body whistled like a tea kettle as Brett's fingertips urged her closer, and she happily acquiesced. Penny pulled her hand from his and reached for his shoulders, dragging herself onto his lap without allowing their lips to part.

This was heaven. Pure, unadulterated bliss. He tasted warm

and sweet, and the eucalyptus swirling in the cloud around them made her heady. The heat dilated every blood vessel, making every nerve ending a live wire, and Brett put them to good use. He skimmed his hands over every inch of bare skin, pressing and tugging when he found spots he liked.

Penny sighed against his lips as Brett slipped his hands under her damp tank top and explored new frontiers of slick skin.

"Is this okay?" Brett asked, his voice husky against the hiss of steam.

It was the same question he'd asked in the tent, and she had the same answer. Penny nodded, pulling out the elastic in his hair and running her fingers over his scalp. She'd wanted to do that since the first day they'd met in his living room. Now, her hands were unstoppable as they dragged through his locks, then ran over his neck, his bare shoulders and back and catalogued every contour of the parts of him she'd visually learned by heart.

Brett's hands dove past the waistband of her shorts and cupped her butt, pulling her flush against him with such force she gasped. "*Penny.*" He whispered her name as she dragged her teeth over his lower lip. "Penny, I'm going to—"

The door to the steam room sighed open, and Penny jumped like she'd just stepped on a snake, landing hard on the bench.

"Clouds, mommy!" A shrill voice echoed off the walls as the steam sucked through the open door. Penny gripped the edge of the bench, her lips flushed and swollen as she worked to catch her breath.

The toddler's mother pulled him back, but Penny and Brett sat frozen. What had just happened? *Did it have to stop?* She didn't want it to, but that interruption had brought the fact that they were in a public place back to the forefront of her very compromised frontal lobe.

"We should go," Brett murmured, his voice so husky, it made her thighs clench.

"Mmhmm." Penny's heart was going to pound out of her

chest. She couldn't remember why they'd come here in the first place or why she'd been upset in the pool. *Had she been crying?* Every thought in her head was now singularly fixated on Brett. On his tangled hair and rough chin. On his hands, *holy hell, his hands.*

Penny stood, and her legs wobbled like she was a newborn foal.

Brett cleared his throat. "Can you hand me my towel?"

She nodded. It was still outside on the chair. "I didn't bring one. Do you mind if I—"

"You can use it. I only need it to make myself...decent."

Penny's eyes dropped to his suit, and she breathed a laugh. "You're saying that paper thin fabric doesn't give good coverage?" Brett found his elastic on the bench and quickly tied his hair back with a grimace. "I'll be just a second."

She pushed through the glass door and gulped down a breath of fresh air. She was going to pass out. Penny strode to the water fountain and drank like a camel in the desert, then pulled the towel off the chair and hastily ran it over herself. She walked back to the steam room and handed it to Brett who dried his chest and arms, then wrapped it around his waist before stepping out onto the pool deck.

His pupils were dilated to the size of marbles and they were drinking her in. "Home?"

Penny nodded, her hands trembling as she gathered her things and slipped on her sandals.

CHAPTER Twenty

PENNY COULDN'T THINK STRAIGHT AS they walked to the car. Any executive functioning was hijacked by the trails of liquid fire still smouldering in the top layers of her skin. She tried to access all the reasons why she shouldn't be planning to go home and pick up right where she left off with Brett in the steam room, but couldn't. Kissing Brett had felt like the most natural thing in the world—the hottest, most exciting thing in her world—and she desperately wanted more.

They dropped into their seats, and it took Penny three tries to start the car properly. Then she put it in neutral and revved the engine twice before realizing her error and finally knocked it into reverse.

"Do you need me to drive?" Brett smirked.

"*No.*" Penny bit her lip to force herself to focus on the road. *Three blocks.* She could drive three blocks without pulling over, couldn't she? Gooseflesh rose on her skin as she hit the second stop sign, and she rubbed her hands over her arms.

"Your lips are turning blue."

"Probably because all the blood in my body is being directed *elsewhere.*"

Brett laughed. "Or because you're cold?"

"Probably a lesser factor." Penny leaned over the steering wheel like Cruella DeVille, willing the car to get up to speed faster. Finally, she parked against the curb and flung her door open.

"Penny." The tone of Brett's voice made her freeze. *Oh shit, did he regret this?* Was he about to tell her he wasn't interested, and— "I need to know what to expect when we walk through that door."

"What do you mean?" She swallowed hard and turned with one foot still on the asphalt.

"I mean, I've got a hundred things running through my head right now, and all of them stipulate that you accompany me to my bedroom and don't leave until morning." Blood rushed in Penny's ears, and she could barely see straight. *Praise the heavens.* "You told me you couldn't—that you didn't want something like this with anyone in recovery, and I promise I heard you. But—"

"That's fine."

Brett's eyes snapped up. "Which part, Penny?"

"The first part. About your plans. For tonight." Penny's mouth was so dry she grabbed the water bottle in the cup holder and took a swig.

"It's fine," Brett repeated, motioning for her to pass the water to him. Penny watched as he tipped it to his lips. *Ugh, he was even sexy when he swallowed.* She handed him the cap, and he took his time screwing it on and setting the bottle back in the cupholder.

Penny waited for him to open his door, then stepped out onto the street. Realizing she forgot her waist bag in the car, she leaned back in and grabbed it, then hit the lock button twice and slammed the door shut.

She followed Brett to the steps, then waited, shivering, while he opened the door. Her stomach swooped as she followed him into the house. Brett pushed the door closed, then caged her in with his arms as he slid the deadbolt into place. Penny wrapped her arms around his waist, feeling his muscles flex as he lowered his head and caught her lips between his.

"Your hands are freezing." He hissed air through his teeth.

"I'm sorry," she murmured, beginning to pull back before Brett grabbed onto her wrists and held them in place. His skin prickled under her touch. Brett pulled her back from the door and scooped her up from the floor. Penny wrapped her legs and arms around him, but as he took a step back, she stopped him.

"This isn't a good idea." Brett's expression darkened, and Penny breathed a laugh. "To *carry me*. With your knee."

Brett's hands pressed into her thighs. "What if I don't care about my knee right now?"

"You don't get to not care about your knee because I've put in way too much work for you to blow it out showing off."

Brett's throat worked. "But you see that I *could* carry you back there, right? So I still get to add that to my man card?"

Penny laughed as Brett buried his face in her neck and nipped at her skin. She dropped her legs and slid down the front of him then hooked her thumb in his board shorts as he turned. The towel fell from his waist.

This was happening. She'd spent weeks trying to fortify herself against the attraction she felt for Brett, but that had only left her vulnerable to who he was behind the mussed hair, thick build, and inked bicep. She loved talking to him more than she loved inspecting his ass in those faded jeans, and that was saying something.

"Do you have condoms?" she asked, and Brett quickened his pace.

"As long as they aren't expired."

"Do they expire?"

"I think they're probably fine."

Penny swatted his left cheek. "'Probably fine.' Exactly what every woman wants to hear."

"I'm kidding. I'll check. And if they're expired, I'll go get new ones."

"I have some in my room."

Brett laughed out loud. "Well shit, Penny. Lead with that."

As soon as she walked through the door, Brett turned and pulled her tank top over her head. "I've wanted to do this every single time you've walked into the kitchen wearing your yoga clothes."

"You barely looked at me when I walked through the kitchen in my yoga clothes." Penny's pulse quickened as she crossed her arms and pulled her sports bra off, lifting her arms as Brett assisted in slipping the fabric over her hands and dropped it on the floor.

"Self-preservation." Brett drank her in, his fingers trembling as he skimmed them over her skin, taking his sweet time. She closed her eyes and leaned her back against the wall as her breath quickened and her heart thundered in her chest. *Pure bliss.*

Brett leaned in and tugged on the waistband of her shorts. His breath was hot against her skin. "You weren't kidding. These are *soaked*."

Penny laughed against his lips and ran her fingernails over his back. "I can't believe you pulled me into the pool."

"I can't believe you didn't get in in the first place instead of just standing up there barking orders like you owned me." He pulled her damp underwear over her hips, and she stepped out of them. His breath caught as she pulled the bow loose on his swim shorts, and his hands gripped her hips. "Shower with me?"

Penny nodded, and Brett led her into the bathroom. Her shower was nice, newly renovated in stone with a rain shower head, but Brett's? He had a double head and wall sprayers. "How did I not know this existed?"

"Would it have changed anything?"

"Absolutely. I would've used this every day while you were at work."

Brett groaned. "That would've killed me. Knowing you were here naked while I was talking to Dr. Asshat on the job site."

"I wouldn't have told you." Penny drew lazy circles over his lower back as he checked the water temperature.

"I would've sensed it."

She snorted. "Because you can tell when a naked woman's been in your shower?"

"Since it happens literally never, I guess I can't speak to that." Brett stepped into the hot spray and pulled her with him, snaking his arms around her waist and cinching until their bodies fit together like puzzle pieces. "No, I was wrong. I can tell."

Penny grinned. "You're *sure* a naked girl's in your shower right now?"

"Positive." Brett lowered his lips to hers, and warmth seeped into her as her entire world shrank down to where their bodies blurred together. Hot water cascaded over her chilled skin, blending with Brett's fingertips, sending ripples of pleasure through her from the crown of her head to the tips of her toes.

She felt the stone under her feet. The sigh of his breath against her lips. The tense and release of his hands as he explored every inch of her.

This wasn't anything like Danny or Jeremy. Physical intimacy with every guy she'd been with had been about doing things *right*. They directed the show, and she did her best to follow the play-by-play. Not that she hadn't enjoyed some parts of it, but it had never been like this. It had never felt like they wanted *her*. Not her body or the things she could do for them, but her.

Brett touched her like he wanted to make each second last. Like *this* was the end goal, not where he hoped it led. Which of course, made her want to lead him there so bad, she ached. Each time Penny reached for him, he redirected her and whispered, "*I want to touch you a little longer.*"

In the last fifteen years of her life, Penny had never once reached the point where she couldn't wait another second, but she was standing on the precipice. Brett grinned against her lips as she very clearly communicated this fact, then finally dropped his hand.

Penny arched against him as her whole world exploded in a symphony of colour and light. She clung to him like he was the only thing keeping her from free falling, and maybe he was. She was butter on a cast-iron pan. Ice cream on a hot summer day. Wax under a flame. "Brett, you don't—"

"The sooner you accept that I want to do this, the less time we'll have to waste from here on out." His voice was rough in her ear.

Penny would've laughed at her own words being repeated back to her in that moment if she could've done anything but suck in a ragged breath. She thought of crouching down and helping him put on his shoes. Of wiping the sweat from his brow as he worked to straighten his knee against the towel.

He'd trusted her in his most vulnerable moments, and the least she could do was do the same. Penny forced her mind to take a back seat as she folded against him and left everything safe, everything sure, everything she thought she knew in the rearview mirror.

———

Brett surfaced to the sensation of breath and skin and warmth. He grinned as he realized Penny was draped over him exactly as she had been in the tent the other night, except this time he wasn't worried about her waking up and realizing where her hands were.

Last night had been the best night of his life, hands down. Hands everywhere, really. He and Penny hadn't come up for air until midnight, when both of them realized they hadn't eaten since lunch and were in danger of collapsing from a calorie deficit. Which was how they ended up roasting a spatchcocked chicken at one o'clock in the morning, then staying up until two thirty with renewed vigor after refuelling.

Penny stirred, her fingers brushing over his navel. He drew a deep breath and spread lazy fingers through her hair.

"Morning," she hummed. Brett kissed her forehead as she lifted her chin.

"Morning." He smiled down at her as she pushed herself higher in the bed and rested her head on his shoulder. The sheets were soft against his bare skin, but Penny's body was straight velvet. She glanced at the clock, and her eyes widened. "Don't you have work?"

Brett smoothed her dark hair from her forehead. "I let Dominic know I'd be working from home today. The first time this surgery has proven convenient."

Penny grinned. "So I get you all to myself today?"

"Well, you have to share with my computer." She scoffed and pinched his waist. Brett caught her hand before she could get any other ideas. Penny already knew he was ticklish. "Do you have appointments today?"

She freed her hand and ran her nails over his stubble. "I cleared my schedule because I thought Andrea was going to be here, remember?"

Brett chuckled. "Right. When you ruined my camping trip." Penny's eyes widened, and he laughed, hugging her into his chest. "Kidding."

"Rude!" she mumbled against his shoulder. She pushed back, and they settled in next to each other, their legs intertwined. Brett rolled to his side so he could see her better.

He ran a hand over her shoulder and rested it on her ribs under the sheets. "We should've been doing this from the day you moved in. No, sooner. The second you showed up at the door."

Penny laughed. "I don't think either of us wanted that."

"I did. I definitely did." That wasn't a lie. He'd thought about her every day since the moment he'd caught a glimpse of her through the broken blinds not knocking on his door. But then he'd been so worried about the consequences—worried about his own capacities—he hadn't let himself move.

As if reading his thoughts, Penny's expression sobered. She ran her fingers over his clavicle.

Brett exhaled. "What is this for you, Penny?"

She met his gaze, her eyes dark chocolate pools. "I don't know." Her teeth teased over her lower lip, and Brett's stomach twisted. "It's not that I don't know about you, Brett. You're . . ." she trailed off and rolled to her back, lifting her arm over her head as she stared up at the ceiling. "Incredible. Kind. Funny."

"Amazing in bed."

Penny rolled her eyes. "Definitely that."

"I don't even care if you're padding my ego."

She laughed, but her smile didn't last long enough. "Every second I'm not with you, I'm trying to find a way to remedy that." Brett twirled his fingers in circles over her soft stomach. "But I've never been on my own. For the last few weeks, I tried so hard to fight this. To try and be my own person because I don't know how to do that. I feel so lost that I glom onto the first guy who wants me and end up changing my shape to fit into whatever mould they build for me."

"I don't have a mould for you, Penny."

She nodded but didn't drop her eyes. "I know. I think I know that."

"Are you still thinking you'll move back to Vancouver in five weeks?" he asked. Penny turned her head, and she didn't need to answer for him to know what her answer was. He exhaled, trying to hide the panic creeping up his spine.

"What about you?" she asked.

"What about me?"

"You flirted with my sister more than you flirted with me."

Brett's eyes widened. "Again, self-preservation."

"Did you get her number?"

Brett laughed out loud. "Andrea gave me her number for emergencies. She didn't think you'd given me any contact information for members of your family, which you hadn't, by the way. She also gave me Theo's number just in case."

Penny grinned. "You have Kelty's number, and she's connected with Andrea on social media."

"Perfect. If you get in a car accident, I'll text Kelty, who'll send a message that will sit in Andrea's unchecked inbox for two weeks. Maybe while I'm at it, I'll call the RCMP and they can send up a smoke signal and hope your family sees it."

Penny pushed against his shoulder, but Brett pulled her against him. She searched his eyes. "So you wanted this. This whole time?"

"Hell, yes. But with everything going on . . . with my history. Then, with what you told me about your brother . . ."

"You didn't think you were ready. Didn't want to stretch yourself too thin." Penny filled in the blanks, and Brett nodded. She reached up and twisted his hair around her fingers. "Did we push it? Is this going to be too hard?"

"Penny, I haven't thought about my knee or my life being out of control for weeks. I know I still have a long road ahead of me, but you've made this easier, not more difficult."

Something flickered over Penny's face, but a smile replaced it so fast he wondered if he imagined it. "So we make things easy. Even if it's only for five weeks."

Brett felt a twinge in his midsection. *Five weeks*. He'd take five weeks over nothing, but he already knew he was never going to be satisfied with that. Five weeks was just enough time for his heart to fuse with hers. Hell, it already had. If and when she left for Vancouver, they'd both be left bleeding.

That meant he had five weeks to convince her this was nothing like the relationships she'd had in the past. Five weeks to prove he wouldn't require her to be a chameleon. Five weeks to convince Penny to stay.

CHAPTER
Twenty-One

MONDAY NIGHT, Penny sat in the stands at the rink, watching with fascination as the Snowballs glided across the smooth, glassy surface. The chill in the air was a welcome contrast to the heat of the day, but because she'd forgotten the inside of a hockey rink wasn't comparable to the blazing Calgary sun, she'd failed to dress appropriately.

"Here, take my jacket," Brett offered, draping it over her shoulders.

"You won't need it?"

He shook his head. "I work out while the guys are on the ice."

"Hence the reason you didn't go to the gym this morning?"

Brett's face broke into a devilish grin. "I still got my cardio."

Penny laughed then pulled his jacket around her knees as Sean barked out drills. This was Brett's world, and while she'd watched plenty of hockey, she didn't know how it felt to play. To be a part of a team. "Have you always played?"

Brett grunted as he held his plank. "Always. From the time I was six. Except for those years when I was out of my head."

Penny swallowed hard. She'd never asked him about those

years. She wanted to, but didn't know if she was ready to hear the details. "You never considered hanging up the skates?"

"I considered it every season for years. Hockey chews you up and spits you out. Then you come back and ask for more."

Penny laughed. "Gluttons for punishment?"

"The worst. But that's why it's so important." He dropped to his forearms, then pushed back up. "If I can be uncomfortable there, I can be uncomfortable anywhere and not give in."

It clicked then, why Brett was so desperate to get back. Desperate enough that he invited a stranger to move into his house so he could receive treatment. Lucas never figured out how to take charge. Every time he tried, he was dragged back under. Maybe if he could've forced himself past his physical limits for a game, he could've done it for his life.

"I'm glad you have this," she whispered.

Brett looked up, and that sadness she'd glimpsed the first time they met flickered behind his eyes. "I'm sorry he didn't."

———

On Tuesday, Penny woke in Brett's arms for the second time. Technically third if she counted camping. Now that she knew he'd wanted her there all along, it felt like it counted. Brett kissed her temple and pulled himself out from under her.

"I was trying to escape without waking you up. Looks like I failed."

"I'm glad you failed. I wouldn't have wanted to wake up and find you gone." She propped her head up on the pillow as Brett sat on the edge of the bed and stretched his legs. "Still sore?"

"Swimming's a bitch."

Penny laughed. "And you only swam, what, eight laps?"

"I'm going again tomorrow. Wanted to give my body enough time to rest."

Penny rolled to her back and stretched her arms over her head. "I think that's a wise choice."

Brett rounded the bed and hovered over her, running his hands over her skin from her wrists to her shoulders, then kissing her before walking to his dresser. "I'm going to go down to the gym and lift. I would invite you to come, but I know how you feel about *those people*."

"They're the worst." She grinned as he turned and shot her a look. "I'll probably doze a bit longer, then do some yoga."

Brett looked at his phone. "With your friend?"

"Who, Chastity? The one I went to the art show with?"

Brett snorted. "That's her name?"

Penny nodded. "Don't you dare make fun of it, and I wasn't planning to go to the studio, easier to just do it here on the porch."

"Perfect. Start that around seven if you can."

Penny frowned and pushed up on her elbows. "Why?"

"So I can watch you through the window while I eat breakfast." He smirked as he pulled on his gym shorts, and Penny fell back on the pillow.

"Your wish is my command."

Brett pulled on a T-shirt and returned to her side of the bed. His expression was serious when he said, "You know I'm kidding right? Do yoga whenever you want."

She reached up and ran a hand over his hip. "I know. I'll see you when you get back."

He gave her hand a squeeze. "You have patients today?"

Penny yawned. "Same guys I saw last week plus this guy Beckett who's a friend of Jordan's. Then I have the lacrosse games this week."

"What nights?"

"Thursday and Saturday. Team practice on Friday, though. They want me there for that, too."

Brett exhaled. "I got a message from my mom last night. They went hiking with Cameron two weeks ago and since I couldn't come, they wanted to do something together this weekend. Kind of last minute, but my dad ended up having Saturday off."

"Oh that's great. What do they want to do?"

"Go up to Sylvan Lake Friday night, come back Sunday. I was going to see if you wanted to come, but it sounds like you're booked."

Penny grimaced. "I wish I could. I've never been up there, and I miss my lake time."

"You're one of those people?" Brett brushed her hair behind her ear.

"Oh definitely. If you mean bumming along with my cousins and camping on Lake Okanagan so we could use my uncle's boat."

Brett smirked. "That's the only way to do it. My dad is meeting up with a colleague so we can use his boat this weekend."

She smirked. "You either pay money or time investing in a friendship you don't want."

"Good thing I don't have a boat or I'd be questioning your motives."

Penny snatched Brett's hand and brushed her lips over his knuckles. "So I won't see you this weekend?"

He shook his head. "But it's only Tuesday."

After Brett left, it only took Penny twenty minutes to decide there was no point staying in bed since her mind wouldn't stop buzzing. She reluctantly left the warmth of Brett's sheets and walked down the hall to use her own bathroom. It was more convenient with all her stuff there.

After changing into yoga clothes that she now knew Brett appreciated, Penny chopped up the leftover chicken, whisked four eggs, and tossed it all together with a handful of spinach, grape tomatoes, and feta in a frying pan. Brett would appreciate coming home to that, too.

Penny's mind churned with all the different ways she could

make his day better, and she yanked hard on the reins. No. She wasn't going to let herself fall into that trap again. Yes, she noticed everything. Yes, she knew exactly what people wanted. Yes, she knew precisely how to give it to them. But with Brett, she couldn't fall into that same pattern of making herself indispensable.

She needed to leave in five weeks, not only to help with the anniversary party and go on their family trip, but to learn how to be on her own. These weeks with Brett could be like a cheat day on a diet. Something to get her through since it was impossible to sit in front of a flourless chocolate cake and *not* have a bite.

When the omelet was finished, she set the pan off to the side and took her half, then sat down and prepared her notes for the day. She journaled, prayed, and started yoga at seven on the dot. For fun, not because she had to.

Brett gratefully ate the omelet she made and ogled her with zero shame from his perch at the kitchen table. She loved it. Men had made it clear they appreciated her body before, but with Brett it didn't feel like that was all he was looking at. When his eyes were on her she felt desired, but also adored. Like he couldn't wait to pick apart another piece of her brain or hear another story about her growing up. It was like her body wasn't enough for him, and that was a sensation she had *no* experience with. It made her stomach swoop and her hands tingle. *She hoped he wouldn't be disappointed.*

They made love before Brett left for work, then Penny showered and got ready for her first client. When Jordan arrived, she met him outside and walked to the back, making small talk. He told her about a new bakery downtown, then asked, "How's Brett?"

Penny did her best to act nonplussed. "Good. He's good."

"Glad to hear it."

After settling him onto the treatment table, Penny took an inventory of body changes since they'd last met, then dove right into the sequence of exercises she'd planned for their session.

First, she had him lie on his side, supporting his injured arm with a small pillow.

"Start by lifting your arm to a ninety-degree angle," Penny instructed, watching closely as Jordan moved his arm slowly, the muscles in his bicep and forearm tensing with the effort. "Now, keeping your elbow bent, rotate your hand upwards until it's parallel with the ceiling. Good, now bring it back down."

Jordan followed her instructions, grimacing as he felt the stretch in his rotator cuff. This part was tough, but in her experience, athletes never wanted to admit the discomfort they felt. They'd grit their teeth and bear it.

"Next, I want you to try some external rotation exercises," Penny continued, handing him a resistance band. "Hold one end of the band in each hand, with your elbows bent at a ninety-degree angle. Now, keeping your elbows against your sides, pull the band apart as far as you can."

Jordan again obeyed, the strain evident on his face as he stretched the band taut between his hands. His muscles quivered under the pressure, beads of sweat dotting his brow.

"Nicely done," Penny praised, taking a few notes. "Now, let's finish up with some pendulum swings."

Jordan raised his eyebrow, and Penny laughed. "I know, these are your favourite in and out of treatment."

He smirked as he positioned himself and allowed his arm to sway lazily beneath him. When he finished, Penny handed Jordan a towel to clean up.

"Brett's lucky to have you at his disposal. Seems you have a magic touch."

Penny's cheeks warmed. *If only he knew.* "Flattery will get you nowhere, Wheatfill." She grinned. "I'm not doing any extra sessions."

He chuckled and set the towel on the table. "You don't work on the weekends, do you?"

Her eyes narrowed. "Why?"

"You haven't lived here long, and I know you have Brett and

probably friends on the team, but there's this concert Saturday—Delia Melise. Small venue. She writes all her own stuff. A bunch of us are going, and I thought you might be interested."

Penny considered the invitation. First, she was impressed that Jordan valued artists who wrote their own music. Second, besides her Snowballs friend group, he was the first person to invite her out to something since moving here. And third, she hadn't been to a concert all summer, and with Brett away for the weekend, she didn't have any plans. She tapped her fingers on her arm. "I have a few lacrosse games I'm contracted to be at—"

"The concert doesn't start till eight."

She nodded. "Can you send me the details?"

"I'll text it to you. Even if you come late, it's a small place."

Penny thanked him for the invite as her next patient walked up the drive.

The afternoon sun streamed in through the open garage door, casting long shadows on the polished concrete floor as she worked.

"Alright, one more set of shoulder presses. Make sure you keep that elbow straight. I think you have one more set in you . . ."

When the last player finally left, Penny quickly picked up her phone. She'd received a few text messages from Brett, but hadn't been able to respond.

> How's your day going?
>
> Got to mop up a sewage leak this morning, so I'm winning
>
> Did Jordan make a pass at you yet?

Penny's cheeks flamed at that one. Jordan hadn't been making a pass, had he? He was just being nice.

> Want to go out for dinner tonight? Unless you already have plans

Penny wrote back.

> I see how it is. We get to go out on your assigned dinner night?

LOL. I'm paying

The rest of the week fell into a blissful routine. Mornings filled with slow kisses and Brett's hands on her skin, then errands and work during the day, and hours of laughter and conversation accompanied by good food in the golden summer nights.

Penny ignored Kelty and Emma's invitations and Brett barely responded to his teammates. They wrapped themselves in their cocoon and only contacted the outside world when forced to. Then Friday afternoon hit, and Penny found herself standing with Brett at the front door with his packed bag.

"I'll see you Sunday night then." Brett adjusted his hold on the strap to his duffel. He'd already stowed his tent and air mattress in the trunk of his car.

Penny nodded, swallowing the lump in her throat. This was ridiculous. She was acting like a lovesick teenager. Brett was only going to be gone for two days total, and she'd be working the lacrosse games anyway.

"What did you decide about the concert?" Brett asked, glancing down at the floor.

Penny exhaled. "I'm not going to go. I don't know anyone else there besides Jordan and—"

"Thank you." Brett sighed and reached for her.

She laughed and tried to meet his eyes, but he crushed her to his chest. "You said you didn't care!"

"I lied."

She pushed back and fixed him with an indignant stare. "Why didn't you say something?"

"So you wouldn't think I'm a jealous bastard."

Penny wrapped her hand around the back of his neck and

pulled him down to her lips. She kissed him, then whispered. "I kind of like it."

"In that case, I wouldn't hate it if you ditched Jordan as a patient."

She gave his left butt cheek a squeeze. "Not going to happen." Brett groaned and tried to hold onto her arms as she stepped back. "Have a great trip with the fam."

"I wish you could come."

Penny smirked. "So you can keep tabs on me?"

"All the tabs. Also my hands." Brett wet his lips, and Penny's stomach dropped like she was stuck at the top of a rollercoaster. "Sunday."

Brett nodded then opened the door and walked out. And then Penny was alone. Thankfully, the game that night was out in Chestermere, so she had a bit of a drive to fill the time. She cleaned and prepped food for the weekend, then went early so she didn't have to keep wishing Brett was home.

The game was entertaining, and though she'd never wish an injury on anyone, she hated twiddling her thumbs on the sidelines. When she returned to a silent apartment, she turned on the Xbox and practiced Halo against the CPU until her eyes burned, just like she had as a kid. When she went to bed, she couldn't even bury her face in Brett's pillow since he'd taken it with him, so she settled for the hoodie he'd tossed over the chair.

Brett texted in the morning.

> You'd love the lake this morning

> Yeah? Describe it to me

> The sun came up burnt orange. Made the trees look like they were on fire and the water like it was melted copper. My new favourite colour

> That was my nickname in high school

> Do you turn turquoise in the rain?

> I guess we'll never know, especially since I've been deemed irrelevant by my own country

lol. I miss you

> Miss you, too. Enjoy the romance

She got up and visited the farmer's market hoping the vibrant colors and bustling atmosphere would be a worthy distraction. She listened to an audiobook while she cleaned the apartment, then headed to the lacrosse practice.

A player rolled her ankle and Penny worked with her on the bench, which made the time fly. By the time she got home, her body and mind were so exhausted, she ate, stretched, and went straight to bed.

Her heart leaped when she woke and realized she'd made it to Sunday. Emma and Kelty insisted that if she didn't show up for Sunday Supper, regardless of her claims that Brett was out of town, they'd be forced to call and report her as a missing person.

Penny chose to make spanakopita as her contribution, purely because she loved it and it took at least three hours to make properly which would help pass the time. The familiar scents of lemon, garlic, and oregano filled her home as she meticulously chopped vegetables and reduced sauces, losing herself in the process.

By the time she drove over to the Thompson home, she was counting the hours until Brett would arrive. She also spent the entire ride prepping herself to play it cool if anyone asked about him or why they'd both been MIA for the past week.

He's slammed with work.

I've got more patients than I can handle.

I caught a cold—don't worry, I'm past it now.

Brett's focusing on physical therapy and it's taking a lot out of him.

Penny was confident she had plenty of alibis when she knocked on the door. She smiled normally as Emma swung the door open, then walked past everyone in the living room to drop her pan in the kitchen. She was about to pat herself on the back when Kelty appeared from the hall, caught sight of her, and stopped dead in her tracks.

Her friend's eyes lit up. "Ugh. Finally!"

Penny gave her a questioning look. "What? It's only been a week, Kelt."

Kelty stalked toward her. "When were you going to tell us, hey?"

"Tell you what?"

"That you and Brett finally decided to stop torturing yourselves and get together."

Penny's face went blank. It took her so completely by surprise she couldn't begin to drum up her explanations. "Wha—how did you—"

"It's written all over your relaxed and contented face. You got laid, and Brett did the laying. Or is it lying?" Kelty grabbed her arm and pulled her to the hall. "C'mon. Emma's going to lose her mind."

CHAPTER
Twenty-Two

PENNY CRISS-CROSSED her legs on the floor of Emma's childhood bedroom. "No, I'm still going back." Emma and Kelty stared at her like deer in headlights. "What?"

"You realize Brett hasn't been in a relationship for years, right?" Kelty hugged a decorative pillow to her chest.

Penny ran a hand through her hair. "Yeah. I get it."

"Pens, I don't think you do. Brett has been through hell, and he's convinced he's never going to be good enough for someone. If you leave—" She shook her head.

Penny leaned back against the bed. "So I'm supposed to stay so he feels worthy? I don't have that power, Kelty. Trust me, I've killed myself trying to conjure it."

Kelty pursed her lips. She knew exactly what she was referring to. At UBC, she'd seen Lucas at what they both thought was his worst. They had no idea then how much farther he had to fall.

"I'm not saying you need to stay. I'm only saying . . . maybe it isn't a good idea to do this. If you aren't planning to stay, maybe—"

"Don't you think I know that? Why do you think I fought it

so hard?" She closed her eyes and groaned. "It turns out it was impossible because Brett is . . ."

"Amazing." Emma finished. "You should hear the stories Tyler has. It's like Brett doesn't see the world through the same lenses we do. He'll be late so he can sit down on the street and talk to homeless people. Tyler told me one time they were downtown and Brett gave a guy his shoes. Walked to the car in socks. In February."

Penny opened her eyes and stared at her. "Do you think this is helping?"

Emma grimaced. "Sorry."

Kelty twisted the tassels on the pillow. "I mean . . . do you have to go? If this is good, wouldn't it be something to consider at least?"

Penny bit the inside of her cheek. It was good. *It was so good.* But every relationship felt that way at the beginning, and she had a one hundred percent track record of running them into the ground.

Brett's heart hammered in his chest as he walked up the steps to the apartment. The door swung open before he could reach for the handle, and Penny threw herself into his arms. He dropped the sleeping bag on the landing and shuffled inside with his lips never leaving her skin. She smelled like honey and warm spice.

"Were you cooking?" he breathed.

"Spanakopita. For Sunday Supper." She pulled at the straps of his backpack as he pushed the door closed and locked it with the sleeping bag still outside. If someone stole his gear, he didn't give a damn. "How was the lake?"

"Not as good as this." Brett snuck his hands under her shirt and felt her lower back flex. Penny slipped the tip of her tongue into his mouth, and molton heat pooled at his center.

"Kelty and Emma know about us," she breathed.

"You told them?"

"No." Penny kissed along his jaw, then moved to his neck, nipping at the skin. "Kelty just knew. Said she could see it on my face."

"Damn right, she could."

Penny hissed a laugh. "You don't care?"

He worked to unhook her bra. "I'm glad. It also explains the cryptic messages from the boys on our team chat." Brett pushed her toward the hall, glancing at the container on the counter holding some kind of golden pastry. "I want some of that later."

Penny pulled back. "Are you hungry? I can—"

"Get your ass in the bedroom, Penny."

She grinned and fisted his shirt, then pulled him down the hall. "Yes, please."

Brett spent another week regretting every minute he had to sleep and work while drinking in every breath, every touch, and every second with Penny. He had tunnel vision, and once he admitted that to the guys on his team, they stopped trying to get a feel for his mental health.

He texted Tony, which was how he received a "called it" message right before:

> We're hanging out Thursday before the concert right?
>
> Btw Leanne said crashing at your place wasn't romantic enough. Got a hotel

Brett sat up in bed and stared at the screen. What day was it? *Wednesday.* He checked his calendar, and sure enough, he'd put Tony's visit on the twenty-second.

"Everything okay?" Penny turned onto her side and threaded her leg between his.

"I completely forgot a friend is coming into town tomorrow night for the Mother Mother concert."

Penny's eyes lit up. "What friend?"

"Tony. He used to live here in Calgary. He's my sponsor for AA." He watched Penny for a reaction, but her smile didn't falter. Maybe he wasn't giving her enough credit. He'd stopped at a meeting Sunday afternoon before coming home so he didn't have to bring it up.

"Do you have plans?"

"I thought we could go out with him and his girlfriend to the Stampede if you're up for it."

Penny nodded. "Of course I am. You sure you want me to come?"

Brett lowered his head and kissed her forehead. "I want you to come with me everywhere."

———

The next evening, they met Tony and Leanne at the entrance to the midway. Penny wore a linen jumpsuit, and with her golden skin and soft waves, she looked like summer personified.

"Hey, buddy." Brett grinned as Tony walked toward them already holding tickets. He clapped his arms around his friend, surprised at the lump in his throat. Tony coughed and blinked as he dropped his arms and put out a hand to Penny who ignored it and wrapped him in a hug. Leanne joined in the greetings, and once they'd embraced all around, they waited in the short line and entered the grounds.

It wasn't dark yet, so the rides and game booths weren't lit up, but the air was thick with the smell of cotton candy, roasted nuts, and popcorn. Brett was glad for the excuse to come since, given the option, he'd choose to stay tangled up with Penny at home and avoid the crowds.

"So Penny, you're brave enough to be this guy's roommate?" Tony asked.

Penny didn't correct his word choice, and Brett grinned. "Brett's pretty easy to live with."

"He's making it worth your while, eh?" Tony waggled an eyebrow, and Leanne smacked his shoulder.

"I swear, Tony." She pointed at a booth selling pulled pork sandwiches and they headed that direction.

Penny grinned. "Oh, he definitely is."

Tony laughed out loud, and Leanne's cheeks flushed. "Thanks for that." He gave Brett a pointed look. "I like her already."

Brett pulled Penny out of the way as a group of teenagers rushed past, then led her to the line. They ordered and took their food to a picnic table in the grass.

"How's the physical therapy going?" Tony asked, and Penny waited for Brett to answer before she realized he was directing the question to her.

"Oh. Good. Thanks to Brett, I have a lot of hockey players coming in."

Brett put extra pickles on his sandwich. "I don't think I told you, Sean found out you're helping Jordan with his shoulder."

Penny snorted. "Oh, I know. I got an earful from Kelty."

Leanne grinned. "Who's Jordan?"

"Our archnemesis," Brett answered, and Penny rolled her eyes.

"They look like men in their thirties, but they're really still sixteen."

Leanne laughed. "Preach, sister." Tony looked a little too proud of himself as he loaded vinegar slaw on top of his pulled pork.

"Have you seen Mother Mother before?" Brett asked.

Leanne shook her head. "I'm dying. I've heard their set is unbelievable."

Penny took a drink of her water. "I haven't been to a concert in forever." Brett gave her a sideways glance and she winked. "I did see Mother Mother at a festival in Vancouver, though. Years ago. Before the rest of the country knew who they were."

"Their tour is international. It's insane they've gotten this big," Leanne said, then turned as a woman in jean shorts, a red bandana for a shirt, and a cowboy hat asked if they wanted drinks. They ordered pop and lemonade, and she pranced back toward the bar.

"So Brett tells me you two met through AA?" Penny asked, and Brett's jaw tensed. It wasn't that he was ashamed of his journey, but it had been a long time since he'd needed to explain it to someone who wasn't in recovery. With Penny's history, he didn't know what she'd think when she heard what he'd been through.

"Do you know anything about the program?" Tony asked, dropping seamlessly into his role as advocate.

Penny nodded. "A bit. My brother went to meetings off and on."

"Did you ever attend Al Anon?" Tony asked.

She shook her head. "I don't know what that is."

Brett leaned over. "It's a group for people supporting people in recovery." He thought of their first conversation in the kitchen when Penny told him she'd never been to a support meeting. His hands clenched under the table at the thought of her having to navigate the relationship with her brother on her own. At least his family had people to remind them they weren't insane.

"Well, AA changed my life. Not only because of the steps, but because of people like this guy." Tony nodded at Brett. "Watching someone else work through their shit is inspiring."

Brett exhaled. "You worked through it before I did."

Tony put an arm around Leanne's shoulders. "Never done though, eh?"

Penny leaned forward and clasped her hands on the table. "What does that mean? I've never really understood why people keep going to meetings when they're sober. Like, years sober. I get the short term."

Tony drew a deep breath. "I know, it seems like there should be an endpoint. Maybe for some people there is, but most of us need to keep working those muscles. To remind ourselves what skills we should be using. It's almost like a spiritual lifestyle."

"And when something gives you your life back, you can't help but want to support others taking their first steps," Brett added. He put a hand on her knee and squeezed. He was glad he'd mentioned to Tony that she lost her brother a few years ago so he didn't ask something stupid, but as the waitress brought them their drinks, Brett wished he could snap his fingers and make everyone else around them disappear so they could continue this conversation in private.

Even that thought made his ribs squeeze. *What could he say to make her believe that he wouldn't end up like Lucas when he couldn't guarantee that for himself?*

"That's beautiful," Penny murmured. "It's amazing that there's a community like that for people who need it."

The conversation shifted to Leanne's work as an elementary school teacher, then to Tony's habit of wearing socks to bed, which then somehow morphed into sustainable wool shearing practices. Tony had thoughts, and when they finally parted ways and drove home, Brett's stomach muscles ached both from laughter and their poor choice of midway rides.

Brett thought about broaching the AA topic. He thought about starting at the beginning and telling Penny how one of his hockey teammates offered him his first drink in high school. How he'd always been socially awkward and that night he'd felt untouchable. How everyone paid attention to him the following Monday at school, and how he quickly adopted the belief that the girls he was interested in only wanted that version of him. Funny Brett. Confident Brett. How he started drinking a beer before he left the house in the morning.

But when Penny twined her fingers in his and smiled up at

him as they walked up the sidewalk to their steps, the words shriveled on his tongue. He wasn't that person anymore, and maybe if she didn't know he'd ever been there, she wouldn't look at him any differently than she did in that moment under the streetlight.

CHAPTER
Twenty-Three

PENNY STOOD at the end of the bed barely able to keep her feet on the floor. "I made the money." Brett looked up from his phone. "I just paid Andrea. So you get your wish. I told Jordan this is my last week seeing patients." *Two weeks.* It was two weeks until her parents' anniversary, and it was a huge weight off her shoulders to get that money posted.

Brett's jaw worked, and Penny knew what he was thinking. Their timeline was ticking down in his head just like it was in hers. She braced herself for him to ignore the comment, or worse, acknowledge it, then look back down at his screen. Instead, his face split into a smile and he reached for her, setting his phone on the comforter next to him. Penny launched herself onto the bed and slid against his side where she already fit perfectly.

"I had no doubt you'd hit it early. Did she wait until now to book everything?" Brett asked, wrapping his arm around her and pulling her close.

Penny shook her head. "No, she put everything on her credit card and we've been paying her back."

"What if you didn't pay her?"

"Then she'd blame us forever for her interest payments."

Brett chuckled. "That's faith right there." Penny counted his ribs with her fingertips. "Are you excited to go?"

Penny wasn't sure whether he meant Vancouver or Greece, but she chose to respond to the latter. "I haven't been to the Mediterranean since I was a kid. I don't even remember my aunt and uncle who still live there."

"You'll be there for two weeks?"

"Ten days." She breathed him in, closing her eyes and sinking deeper against his chest. *Maybe you don't have to go?* Penny had been thinking non-stop about that moment when she'd walk out the door of their apartment for the last time. When she'd load her boxes in the back of a moving van and drive away from this block.

She didn't want to go. Not permanently. Her resolve to force herself to ride without training wheels was quickly crumbling. Each time Brett held her. Each time a message popped up on her phone. Each time they laughed late into the night. Each time they made love.

This was different.

This was good.

She could find a job here or, as scary as it was, open up her own business for real. Brett had an MBA. He'd offered more than once to help her figure out the logistics, and she already had the paperwork done. She had a connection to the hockey and lacrosse crowd, and with some elbow grease, she had no doubt she'd be able to expand her reach.

Her family, while excited to have her home, was used to her being gone at this point. They'd be happy for her. Probably nervous at first given her history, but once they met Brett—once they saw how they were together—they'd get it, wouldn't they?

Brett's grip tightened around her, and the beat of his heart thumped low and deep against her ear. "Do you want some of that vegetable bean soup I made yesterday?"

Penny lifted her chin and grinned. "It's called Minestrone."

Brett set his bag next to the door and slipped off his shoes. Penny's car was gone, and that sent his heart racing. All week he'd been walking around with a needle in his chest, and none of his skills were releasing it. Give it to God. Accept the things you cannot change. He repeated these things to himself hourly in the hopes that his body would get the message, but it didn't.

It was like standing in front of a loaded weapon with a timestamp on the trigger pull. Every word, every touch, every kiss, brought him closer to the muzzle. Why didn't he just ask her to stay?

He would. He just needed to wait for the right time. The right words. She'd started to build a good life here, hadn't she? Penny had friends and work if she wanted it. Daniel had sand blasted her, but there were plenty of businesses she hadn't applied to, and with word of mouth on the hockey boards, she wouldn't need to contract with an office if she didn't want to. She could get her own space. His team could do the build out. He'd make her the best damn office in the northwest if she wanted it.

> How're you doing?

Tyler texted, and Brett stared at the message. *Not great. Happiest I've ever been and I can't enjoy it because I'm too scared to lose it.*

> In my head, buddy

> Meeting tomorrow?

> Yep. I'll pick you up

He set his phone on the counter and glanced down at the

notepad and pen in front of the stool. *Pick up pizza. Call florist. Fill out tax form online. Rent truck and tow kit?*

Shit. Shit. Shit. Brett gripped the edge of the counter and sucked in a breath. She was serious. If the boxes she'd brought in the other day weren't enough of a sign. But there was a question mark at the end of that last item. Was it there because she didn't know if she wanted to book it or because she wasn't sure if she already had? He felt like he was strapped into a runaway car heading straight over the edge of a cliff.

The front door opened, and Brett jolted. Penny walked in with a pizza box in her hands and thankfully didn't look up at him right away. He smoothed his features and turned his back to her, pretending to be focused on getting a glass of water.

"Hey!" she chirped. "I got pizza tonight."

"Oh perfect."

"Did you have to wait for me long? I wanted to be home before you got back from work, but they're redoing part of Stoney Trail and I got stuck in the longest merge lane known to man." Penny padded into the kitchen and set the box on the counter, then wrapped her arms around him and buried her face in his chest. "How was work?"

Brett set his glass on the counter and held her. "Great. Had to rip out some ductwork that was put in wrong, but they almost got it replaced by the time I left."

She looked up, keeping her arms looped around him. "You're still being careful with your knee, right? I know it feels normal, but it's not—"

"I'm being careful." He pushed her hair back from her face and tucked it behind her ear.

She grinned up at him. "Speaking of which, we should do a session. After dinner?"

Brett nodded, not sure how he was going to force himself to eat. "How are things going with the anniversary prep?" *Feel it out. See if she says anything.*

Penny sighed. "Good. I think my parents are getting suspicious though." She let go of him and turned to open the pizza box.

"Oh yeah?"

"Apparently my dad saw a friend of his who Andrea invited to the party, and he said 'see you next week' and Dad asked him why they'd see each other next week and the guy wasn't a good actor." She separated the two paper plates and handed him one, then lifted a slice from the box.

She wasn't upset. Why wasn't she upset? She was leaving in seven days—driving back to Vancouver and out of his life—and she was standing here prattling on about it like she was heading to the grocery store.

"Can we do our session now?"

Penny looked up. "Now? Before we eat?"

Brett set his plate on the counter. "I'm not feeling hungry quite yet."

Penny took one bite of the piece of pizza in her hand then set it back in the box and closed it. She washed her hands and dried them on the towel next to the sink. "Sure. Let's go."

Brett followed Penny down the driveway like he'd done three times a week since they set up her equipment. When she opened the door, he saw boxes at the back and half her props gone from the mats.

"You're not seeing patients this week?" he asked.

"Only my favourite one." She smiled at him, and the knot in his chest cinched. She led him through some stretches, then moved into single leg squats. Brett positioned himself beside the parallel bars for support. He flexed his right leg, feeling the muscles tighten and release. Two weeks ago he'd barely been able to do four of these, and now they felt like nothing.

"Good. Now, try some lateral step-ups," Penny suggested, pointing to a low bench. Brett complied, stepping sideways onto the bench, his knee bending and stretching under his weight. This felt like hockey, and even the hint of being able to return to the ice lit a fire in him. It sat in stark contrast to the dark void that had kept him company since Penny announced she'd made all the money she needed for her parents' anniversary.

As they moved to hamstring curls with resistance bands, Brett's muscles tired, and his motions became more mechanical. Penny corrected his form, and the reaction his body had to her touch felt like a betrayal.

"You're quiet today."

Brett grunted. "I'm focused."

Penny gave him a look that said, *I don't buy it.* "You're always focused and we still talk."

"Maybe I don't feel like talking right now." He hadn't meant for it to come out snippy, but it did, and Penny's smile faded.

"Did I do something to—"

"You didn't do anything." Brett pushed against the band, sweat beading on his neck and forehead. That was the problem, wasn't it? She wasn't doing anything to stop this. She'd made a decision before they got together, but didn't their relationship change the variables?

"Okay." Penny pursed her lips and let his comments go. She took him into calf raises and balance exercises on a wobble board next. After forty-five minutes, he was slick with sweat and breathing hard. Penny motioned for him to take a seat on the table. She took out some Icy Hot and slipped his ankle between her thighs so she could massage his calf and hamstring.

"You don't need to do that."

Penny looked up, hurt evident in her eyes. "It helps the muscles relax."

"You don't do it for everyone."

"Because *everyone* isn't . . ." She trailed off, dropping her eyes.

"Everyone isn't what?" Brett wanted to hear her say it. To label their relationship and give him a damn clue as to where she saw this going.

"Isn't you."

Brett hissed air through his teeth. "That's not good enough."

"What isn't?" Penny's fingers dug into his muscle, and Brett winced. He muttered something and leaned back to prop himself up with his elbows on the table. Penny worked in silence a few moments, then said, "I think you should try getting back on the ice. Nothing crazy. Just a simple skate around the rink. We can add that to your weekly routine."

We. There wasn't going to be any "we" after this week. She'd given him a printout of the exercises she'd planned for the next two months, never explicitly stating that he'd be doing them on his own, but he understood.

"If you keep this up, I can't promise you'll be ready to practice in October, but it could happen." She smoothed her forefinger and thumb through the soft tissue on either side of his kneecap.

"I won't have you to push me."

Penny scoffed. "You've never needed me to push you. And you're recovering so well, I don't think you'll need anything from me to get there."

The simmering heat in Brett's chest boiled over. "That's bullshit."

Penny's hands froze. "Excuse me?"

Brett swallowed hard. "That's bullshit. That I don't need anything from you." His pulse ramped up making everything in his body tingle.

Penny stepped back, releasing his leg. "Brett—"

"You've walked around for the past week acting like nothing is out of the ordinary when you're—" he motioned to the boxes behind them. "You're reserving a moving truck, Penny. You're packing up and driving across the damn mountains in six days. Don't you dare say I don't need anything from you because that's—" His voice caught and he clamped his mouth shut.

Penny crossed her arms over her chest. "I didn't want to talk about it." Brett exhaled but didn't trust himself to speak. "I don't know what the hell I'm doing, okay? I just know that I need to go back to my family for a bit. I'm not saying it's forever, but—"

"Not forever? Well that's comforting."

Penny's eyes grew glassy. "How can you say that? You know what I've been through, and I told you—"

"I'm not them, Penny! I know you're scared that this is going to end up like that, but I'm not your brother, and I'm not Danny—"

"*Well you're sure as hell acting like him!*" Penny sucked in a breath, and Brett's stomach dropped to his knees. Penny was shaking as she took a step back to the open door. "I just need time, Brett." Tears broke free and dropped onto her cheeks as she whirled on her heel and jogged down the driveway.

CHAPTER
Twenty-Four

PENNY THREW her clothes and toiletries in a backpack and ran to her car when she heard Brett's bedroom door close. She knew she should be a bigger person and talk to him about what happened in the garage. It was something about what he'd said, how he'd looked at her. The idea of starting up a conversation made her feel like she'd swallowed a handful of rocks.

> Heading your way

She texted Kelty. Emma had offered for her to crash on her couch, but Penny didn't need just a place to sleep. She needed someone to talk to, and Kelty had known her longer than anyone here.

Penny wasn't ready to text Andrea or anyone in her family for that matter. After the way Andrea connected with Brett, she had no doubt what kind of advice her sister would give. The worst part was that she knew the advice was probably good. Brett wasn't like Danny, and he wasn't like Lucas. But when she'd told Danny she was leaving, all the kind words and tender moments had disappeared in a snap.

Deep down, she knew that's not what Brett was trying to accomplish. Hadn't she wanted Danny to care? To be upset about her leaving? Now Brett was showing her exactly that, and she accused him of being the same.

He wasn't the same.

He wasn't anything close to the same.

And yet the response inside of her was eerily familiar. Penny wanted to give everything up to make him happy. She wanted to cancel the truck reservation and unpack her boxes and tell him she didn't need to go to the anniversary party. She didn't need to go with her family to Greece.

But that narrative, to use Brett's vernacular, was bullshit. She absolutely needed to be at that party, and she'd been looking forward to this trip for over a year. The fact that a few sentences from someone she loved would make her erase the board? That reality—both that she loved him and that she was so easily swayed—dragged claws down her spine to the point that she wanted to throw up.

She couldn't trust herself. That was the issue, and she'd known that from the second she drove away from her apartment with Danny. Until she grew a damned spine, she shouldn't be allowed to be with anyone.

Tears streamed down her cheeks, blurring her vision as she made her way to Kelty and Sean's.

She did love him.

She loved Brett so hard it felt like someone was reaching into her chest and crushing her heart with their bare hands. She loved him, but she'd thought she loved Danny, too. *And oh, how she'd loved Lucas.*

Love didn't solve the problem. For her, love *was* the problem. A sob ripped from her throat as she clamped her hands tighter over the wheel.

By the time she pulled up to Kelty's, she'd mostly dried her tears, but she wasn't going to fool anyone even though her cheeks were dry. Kelty was there standing on the driveway, and she wrapped Penny in a hug as soon as she stepped out of the car.

"What happened?" Kelty whispered. Penny shook her head as fresh tears sprang up in her eyes. "Well, we all knew this was going to suck balls."

"You've been spending too much time with hockey players."

"One could say the same about you." Kelty squeezed her shoulders and opened the back door to grab Penny's backpack. "Come on, let's go inside."

She and Kelty talked for an hour while Kelty cleaned up dinner. Sean was home, but either he was working on something or was wisely hiding out somewhere in the house far from any potential drama.

Kelty's niece was out for the night, so Penny was at least able to use her bathroom to take a shower. By the time Penny had braided her hair and put on pajamas, Kelty had wrapped sheets over the couch cushions and brought out a pillow and quilt.

Penny thought about texting Brett every second until she finally turned out the light and closed her eyes. What would she say? Even talking things through with Kelty hadn't made her emotions any less convoluted.

She loved him, *and* . . .

This was still something she needed to do. Brett, as much as he tried, didn't understand that. But the ache in her chest didn't come from her feeling unfairly judged. It came because she knew that he was hurting *just like this*. Her choosing to leave had punched a hole in his heart too, that's what he was trying to tell her on the treatment table.

Never in her life had she *chosen* to make someone feel that way. Never in her life had she walked away when she knew she could do something to make a person feel better. Never. In. Her. Life.

She clutched the quilt to her chest and squeezed her eyes

shut, trying to drown out the voices in her head screaming that she was wrong when she knew at her core she was right.

―――

Penny awoke the next morning surprised she'd slept so deeply. The sun was high in the sky, and Kelty was already gone. She'd left her a note on the counter telling her there were boiled eggs and yogurt in the fridge. Penny gladly partook.

She was halfway through her key lime pie Yoplait when Sean walked down the stairs.

"Oh, hey."

"Good morning."

He strode into the kitchen. "I forgot you were here."

"I don't see how. It's not like we didn't have this planned for weeks."

Sean chuckled and walked to the fridge for a Dr. Pepper. He pulled the tab and took a drink, then stood there awkwardly in the middle of his own kitchen.

She scooted her chair closer to the table. "You don't have to say anything, it's okay."

"Good because I wasn't going to say anything." He took a step and winced, then flexed his toes against the floor and kept walking.

"Is your leg bothering you?' Penny asked.

"No," he answered. She nodded and looked back down at her spoon, but Sean paused by the stairs. "I think I might've tweaked my hamstring."

"Oh, yeah? How long ago?"

He shrugged. "I don't know, a month?"

"And it's still bothering you?"

"Not as bad as it was."

Penny tapped the edge of her yogurt cup. "Do you want me to take a look? That *is* what I do for a living."

"I don't want to—"

"Sean, I have no plans today besides sneaking back into my apartment and packing while Brett's at work. So I'd be happy to see what's going on. In exchange for the couch space."

Sean nodded once, then stalked back toward the kitchen. Penny motioned to a chair and set down her yogurt. When he was comfortable, she gently lifted Sean's leg. "Let me know if you feel any pain." Penny pressed along the muscle, feeling for abnormalities. Sean winced slightly as she reached a spot midway up his thigh.

"Right there," Sean murmured, his brow furrowing.

Penny paused over the spot. "That's it, isn't it? Feels like a strain, possibly a minor tear." The muscle fibers bunched under her fingers.

Sean nodded. "So, what do I do?"

"Stop going to practice for one thing."

He scoffed. "That's not happening."

Penny pursed her lips. "You're telling me that you have a player who's been working out in the bleachers for months so he can be healthy for next season, and you're not willing to do the same?" Sean looked chagrined, and she sat back in her chair. "A couple of weeks. That's all it should need, but if you keep stressing it on Monday nights, you won't give it a chance to fully heal."

Sean exhaled. "That's it?"

"Ice it once a day, then do a couple of stretches before bed. Like the one you just did over there."

Sean nodded. "Thanks."

"No problem."

Sean moved to stand up, then hesitated. "You know if Brett did anything . . . if he treated you like—"

"Brett didn't do anything."

Sean's lips drew into a line. "You know we'd back you up,

though. All you need to do is call. I don't care if he has a knee injury. I'd be happy to show him what's what."

Penny laughed under her breath. "I think in this scenario, he probably wishes you'd shake some sense into me instead."

Sean gave a lopsided grin. "Brett hasn't learned yet. That's not how it works."

Penny laughed as Sean stood and picked up his pop. "Thanks."

"You're welcome."

Penny threw out her trash and washed her spoon, then folded the quilt and used the bathroom downstairs. She didn't take the sheets off the couch because she was planning to use it one more night. The thought of staying at the apartment still filled her with dread.

But she did have packing to do. Penny got in her car and drove back home. She breathed a sigh of relief when she arrived and saw that Brett's car was gone. *Four hours.* She rushed inside and got to work.

Penny moved back to her own bed the next day. She and Brett didn't talk about dissolving their dinner rotation, but they both read between the lines and did their own thing. Besides accidentally passing him once when she walked out to get something from her car, she'd successfully avoided being in the same room as him.

It was childish, but she still didn't have any explanation that would make the situation better. Nothing she said would reverse the hurt, and that would only drag her deeper. She just had to white-knuckle it until she could drive back home and sort herself out.

This was why it wasn't a good idea to date roommates.

Housemates. He was there on the other side of the wall at all times, which only tapped the little ice pick further into her heart.

On Friday evening, Penny hadn't heard the front door open and was positive that Brett had gone out after work. Her mind wanted to run wild with that one, imagining all the places he could be or people he could be meeting up with. She shut it down and walked out into the kitchen to heat up the last of her chicken fajitas, which she'd taken home after stopping at the Ranch House for dinner on her way home from Kelty's the other night.

She stuttered a step and pulled up short when she found Brett leaning against the counter looking at his phone. Penny froze as Brett looked up. The sadness was back. All of it.

"Hey." His voice was low.

"Hey." Penny didn't know what to do next. If she stepped toward the refrigerator, she'd be dangerously close to him, but if she didn't do something, he'd wonder why she came out here in the first place.

She wanted to ask him a million questions. The last five days felt like a thousand, and she wanted to hear every thought rolling through his head. Every problem he'd come across at work. Every clip on his phone that made him laugh out loud. Every second he thought about her. *Every time he'd wanted her.*

Brett's hair hung in loose waves to his shoulders, and he was still wearing his slightly dusty T-shirt and work pants. "I did it," he said. "Laced up my skates and got on the ice."

Penny's heart bubbled over. "You did? When?"

She hated that she'd missed it. She hated that he'd gone over to the rink without even telling her. But what did she expect? She'd been avoiding him like that guy at the office who asked you out and you said you'd check your schedule but never did.

Brett nodded. "I felt like Bambi in that scene when he's on the ice with his legs all splayed out."

Penny laughed. "I'm sure it wasn't that bad."

"The team had a good laugh."

They were all there. *Of course they were.* "I'm really happy for you, Brett."

He looked up with what seemed like a hundred words waiting on his lips. As Penny stared into those baby blues, that invisible thread attached to her spine stretched between them, tugging her in the only direction it could. Forward.

Her legs moved before she could intervene, and she reached for him. Brett dropped his phone on the counter and pulled her into his arms.

"I'm so sorry," Penny whispered, her breath already coming in short bursts.

"No, I'm sorry." Brett smoothed his hand over her hair. "I never should have said those things."

"You weren't wrong. I just—"

"I know. I know." Brett kissed her temple and brushed his thumb over her cheekbone, sweeping away the tears already spilling over her cheeks. Being held by him felt like sinking into a hot bath, and her legs wanted to give out. It was true that nothing she said or did was going to change anything, but if they both had to feel this way, at least they could sink together.

She stood there for what felt like hours, pressed against him as their breathing slowed and synced, their hearts settling into one consistent beat.

Brett exhaled. "Do you need something to eat?"

Penny nodded against his chest. She leaned back and ran her palms over her puffy eyes, then opened the fridge and pulled out her leftovers. Brett pulled out an almost identical takeout container and grinned.

They took turns with the microwave, then stood next to each other while they ate. When they finished, they threw away the containers and put their forks in the dishwasher.

As Penny straightened, Brett grabbed her hand without a word and pulled her down the hall. He threw his sheets open and they climbed into bed together. As soon as they were settled,

Brett scooped her against his chest, curling around her until she couldn't tell where he ended and she began.

Penny closed her eyes, gripping onto his hands and letting go of every thought about tomorrow. She had twelve hours—they had twelve hours—and she was going to steep in every last one of them.

CHAPTER
Twenty-Five

THE NEXT MORNING, Penny awoke alone in Brett's bed. She jolted up and checked the time on her phone. *Seven thirty.* She peered into the bathroom, but there were no sounds coming through the open door and no lights were on.

It was a Saturday. Had Brett decided to go to the gym? Penny frowned and threw her legs off the mattress. She walked to her room and freshened up, then stowed her toiletries in her backpack.

This was happening. The truck was parked out front, and she was going to drive away from this apartment. Somehow it didn't seem real. Had she only left Danny eight weeks ago? It felt like an eternity. It felt like she didn't remember her life before Brett. *She didn't want to.*

Penny drew a deep breath to try and force feeling into her limbs. She'd finished packing before she walked out into the kitchen the night before, and all her tubs and boxes, which weren't many, stood in a neat line against the wall. She stripped the sheets from the bed and tucked them into her bedding bin, then started shuttling all her belongings to the entryway.

She'd only taken two trips when the doorbell rang. Penny

adjusted her hair clip and opened it to find Tyler, Sean, Country, Suraj, and Fly all standing on the front step.

She gaped. *Had she told the team what day she was moving?* "How much stuff do you think I have?" She gestured to the small moving truck parked against the curb. With all of them helping, this was going to take less than half an hour.

Tyler pointed to the driveway. "Is your equipment all ready to go?"

Penny leaned out the door. "You remember the code, right?"

Tyler gave her a thumbs up and took Fly with him around back. The others started grabbing the boxes she'd stacked next to the door. Penny had overestimated. Within fifteen minutes, the Snowballs had loaded everything into the back of the truck, and Sean was already working on hooking up the trailer to tow her car.

"You sure you're going to be okay driving this thing?" Tyler asked.

Penny stood on the top step of the porch and rocked on her feet. "People do it all the time, right?" Truthfully, she was nervous to drive this behemoth over the pass. When she'd voiced her concerns to Brett, he said that meant she probably shouldn't do it. She should probably just stay there. They'd laughed then, but after their conversation in PT the other day, those comments packed a punch.

Penny had gone down a rabbit hole at Kelty's, double and triple checking her route. At least the weather looked clear, but there was always road work to contend with, and forecasts over the mountains were never a hundred percent.

She was actually most nervous about crossing into Vancouver city limits. On the open highway, people were used to navigating around RVs and campers. In the city, people were just going to be annoyed.

Penny glanced down the road hoping to see Brett's car coming back from the rec center. *Where was he?* He knew she was loading up, or he wouldn't have told the whole team to show up. Though, that could have been Kelty.

Maybe he didn't want to be here when she left? She couldn't blame him for that, even though it made her want to smack him.

"Where are your keys?" Sean called.

Penny turned and snagged her waist pack from the floor of the entryway. She descended the steps and handed it to him.

"Are you okay with me pulling it up on here?" Sean pointed at her car.

Penny held up her hands. "Please do. I don't trust myself to get the wheels in the right position."

"I doubt he's a better option," Tyler teased, and Sean flipped him the bird. Penny stood on the sidewalk and watched as Sean inched her car up onto the trailer. As soon as he got it in the right spot, Tyler got to work securing it.

"It kind of looks like your car is getting a piggyback." Fly walked up next to her, his hands on his hips.

"Or it's up on its hind legs rutting." Country grinned, and Penny rolled her eyes. "Hopefully she'll enjoy the ride."

"It's too early in the morning for this," Fly muttered, and Penny laughed. Then her toes started tapping. There wasn't much left to do, and she could only stall for so long. *Was Brett really not going to show up?* After holding her while she'd slept, he wasn't going to say goodbye?

Fine. Penny grabbed her backpack off the step and threw it in the passenger seat of the truck. She had just closed the door when she heard a car coming up the street. Her heart jumped into her throat as she turned and saw the car slow after swerving around the truck, then stop against the curb.

Her hands started to tingle, but when the passenger door opened, Penny's mind went blank. That was Brett's car, which meant . . . he was with someone? He'd left her that morning to go to the gym with—

The woman turned, and Penny jolted into a run. *Andrea?* How was it possible that Andrea was getting out of Brett's car?

Her sister spun, and her face lit up as she saw Penny barreling toward her. "Slow down, you're going to—"

Penny slammed into her, gripping her so tight, she squeezed the air out of her own lungs.

"Penny? I can't breathe."

Penny let go and stepped back, scanning her to make sure this wasn't a mirage. "How are you here?"

Andrea's grin was so wide, Penny could barely see the colour of her eyes. Andrea pointed to Brett still standing next to his open door.

"You did this?" Penny breathed. He gave a slight nod, and her head snapped back to her sister. "You're here to see me off?"

Andrea held out her arms like Penny had just unwrapped her for Christmas. "I'm here to go with you. You know, so you don't drive off a cliff and get eaten by bears or moose or whatever fungus is killing the trees in Banff right now."

Penny jumped up and down. "You're driving with me?" Andrea nodded emphatically. "The whole way?"

Andrea laughed. "Yes, the whole way! Why didn't you tell me you were nervous, by the way?"

Penny's words caught in her throat, and she looked back at Brett. He'd called Andrea and picked her up at the airport, all so she wouldn't have to be alone. *She'd mentioned her nerves one time.* Penny bit her lower lip to stop it from trembling.

Brett dropped his eyes and closed the car door, then rounded the back of the vehicle and greeted his teammates still standing on the sidewalk.

"Are you ready to go?" Andrea asked. "Do you need help with anything else?"

Penny shook her head. She'd scoured the bathroom while the guys were loading up. "I just need to vacuum the rug."

Brett turned his head. "You don't need to vacuum anything. I can take care of it."

"But—"

"I'll take care of it, Penny."

She shivered at the sound of her name and wrapped her arms around herself as she walked with Andrea past the guys to the moving truck. Kelty appeared from who knew where and handed Penny a grocery sack. "Snacks for the road."

"How long have you been here?" Penny frowned, then glanced inside the bag to find dill pickle chips and at least two bars of dark chocolate. She groaned. "You're the best."

Kelty flipped her hair. "I know."

"From me and Emma." Tyler handed her a card.

Penny's throat grew thick. "You guys didn't need to do this."

"We're going to miss you, Pens." Kelty threw her arms around her shoulders.

"Thanks for helping our boy get back in shape." Tyler clapped Brett on the back.

"No thanks for helping Jordan," Sean muttered, and Penny snorted.

"I'm equal opportunity, Sean." She raised an eyebrow, and Sean flexed his toes against the concrete.

The guys said their goodbyes and mosied back to their cars. Kelty gave her one last hug and followed Sean, leaving her, Andrea, and Brett standing on the sidewalk.

Andrea held out her hand. "Keys, please. I think I'll take first shift."

"I didn't list you as a driver on the—"

"Oh, give me the keys, Penny. If we get in a wreck, we'll just shift spots."

"I don't think that's a thing," Penny muttered as she handed the key ring over. She waited for Andrea to round the hood before looking up.

Brett's hands were shoved in his pockets, and his shoulders were tense. "Brett, I can't thank you en—"

"Stop." He shook his head and the muscles in his jaw worked.

Penny didn't know what to say. She couldn't make it better, and she didn't know what the other options were. "Brett..." her throat clenched so tight, no words could come out. She gritted her teeth and clenched her hands until her nails bit into her palms.

Brett stood like a statue, his brow furrowed. His eyes fixed on the logo of the side of the truck.

Penny's eyes welled with tears, and the only words that tumbled from her lips were, "Can you forgive me?" She wanted him to say yes, to tell her that he understood and that she could take all the time she needed. But Brett didn't answer, and Penny's chest felt like a Coke bottle with a Mentos dropped into it.

With a shaky hand, she reached for her door handle and escaped inside the truck. "Go."

Andrea didn't ask questions, she just started the truck and lurched away from the curb as Penny started to shatter.

Brett tried to draw a breath and nearly choked. He watched the truck turn the corner then disappear from sight, and it felt like a steel beam had landed across his chest. *He needed to get inside.* Kick a wall, break something.

It was moments like this where that black demon inside of him no longer whispered.

You can make this all go away.

Just forget for once.

You don't have a problem anymore, so why are you making yourself suffer?

Brett gasped for air as he clomped up the steps and threw his door open, then slammed it closed behind him. His apartment already felt like an empty shell. *She was gone.* Penny had packed up her things, his friends had loaded them in the back of her truck, and she'd driven away with no plans to come back.

Of course a part of him was holding out hope that she'd change her mind. She hadn't said this was forever. But she also hadn't said it wasn't, and that possibility was the one that got all the airtime.

Brett leaned over the sink and turned on the faucet, then cupped his hands and lifted them, splashing water over his face. He'd known it would end like this from the very beginning, and yet he still jumped in with both feet. He splashed another handful of water over his face, then froze when he heard a knock at the door.

He turned off the tap and reached for the towel next to the sink. It still smelled a little like Penny's lemongrass hand lotion. *Who would be coming to his door right now?*

Brett thought about ignoring it and retreating to his bedroom, but another knock came, this time more forceful. If this was someone selling Stampeder tickets, he was going to—

His breath caught as he flung the door open and saw Tyler, Sean, Suraj, Country, and Fly huddled together like they were posing for a Christmas card. He glanced down at the pillows they clutched in their arms. "What the hell is this?" He asked, his voice raw.

"You didn't think we were going to leave after that, did you?" Tyler asked, motioning for him to move out of the way. Brett stepped back and they filed into his living room, swinging sleeping bags underneath the pillows

"You guys, I don't—"

Sean held up a hand. "Shut your damn mouth, Bouchard."

Country kicked off his boots, and Tyler hung his coat on the hooks. "We're staying the night."

Tyler nodded. "We have wings and nachos coming at noon and then barbecue coming for dinner." He turned to Fly. "Do you have that ice cream?"

Fly pushed his feet back into his shoes. "Totally forgot it in the trunk. Oreos and chips, too"

"Mint or peanut butter?" Suraj called out.

"Both! I know you, Surry." Fly grinned and stepped back onto the porch.

Tyler turned to face Brett. "We're all staying the night."

"It's only nine in the morning," Brett grunted.

"Right, we're staying the day and the night," Country said, plopping down on the couch. "This lighting from your window would make a good video."

Sean shook his head.

"What about Emma and Kelty? Jess and Rashi?" Brett asked. He knew how much of a sacrifice their wives and girlfriends made during the season, and he doubted they were thrilled about these guys spending the weekend at his place.

Sean rubbed the scruff on his chin. "Kelty's the one who suggested it."

Brett leveled his eyes at Sean. "You're the one who planned this?"

Sean's cheeks coloured. "The food was Tyler's idea."

Tyler reached out and grabbed Brett's shoulder, pulling him into a rough hug.

"What game are we playing first on this old ass console of yours?" Suraj asked.

Brett and Tyler looked up and said in unison, "Not Halo."

CHAPTER Twenty-Six

BY FIVE O'CLOCK, Brett's apartment looked more like a bachelor pad than his old university dorm. Dirty plates, cups, and rolled-up socks were strewn across the living room, floating in the sea of sleeping bags.

Brett sat with his teammates around the table, revelling in the smell of smoke and barbecue sauce as they dug into smoked chicken, ribs, and brisket.

"Y'all are out of your minds if you think Smokin' Saddle's got anything on Big Al's." Country wiped the sauce from his chin with a napkin.

"Big Al's?!" Suraj scoffed, shaking his head. "That place is all hype. Are you tasting this sauce right now?"

Sean dropped a clean rib bone on his paper plate. "I've cooked better ribs than Big Al's on my grill at home."

Suraj grinned. "Thank you."

Country shook his head. "I can't help it if you city boys have poor taste. They smoke their meat over cherrywood. That changes the game."

Fly reached for another cornbread muffin. "My favourite is still Ember Trails at the Stampede. Their sauce alone is legendary."

Brett's chest compressed. That's where he'd eaten with Penny the night they went to the Stampede with Tony and Leanne. Their sauce had been good, and the pickles possibly better.

Fly sighed. "Jess got me a smoker for Christmas. Can't wait to try it out."

Tyler laughed. "It's already July, and you haven't tried it yet?"

"There are barriers to entry."

"That's what your momma said last night." Suraj put up a hand, and only Country was kind enough not to leave him hanging.

Fly tsked. "How are you one of two married guys on the team, and you're the one making 'your momma' jokes?"

"Your momma jokes don't age. I refuse to be shamed by you, Gramps."

Country took another half rack of ribs. "When are *you* getting married, Fly? Haven't you been with Jess for almost a decade?"

"He's still making up his mind," Sean teased.

Fly took a bite of his now honey-buttered muffin. "Our love isn't labelled like that."

"Said the guy who doesn't want to pay for a wedding." Country raised an eyebrow, and Fly grinned.

"All I'm saying is you both better hurry up. Curtis has you beat by four kids already," Brett added.

"Anyone following the draft picks?" Sean changed the subject. His tone was gruff, and Brett tried to get a read on his expression. He'd been with Kelty for at least four years by his count. Maybe not his favourite topic.

Country leaned back in his chair. "Axel Johansson's the best choice for defence. Kid's a tank."

"Nah, it's all about speed these days," Suraj cut in. "Viktor Kuznetsov's stats are off the—"

"He's impulsive," Tyler cut in.

"Exactly like a player should be, eh?" Suraj shot back.

Country shook his head. "Where's André when you need him? This is the one thing we've ever agreed on."

Brett was content to eat and let the conversation swirl around him. His head was still filled to the brim with thoughts of Penny, and at least this helped keep them from flooding his heart.

When everyone was stuffed, they grabbed pop and Oreos and moved back to the living room without putting the food away so it was ready for second dinner at ten.

"I still think NHL '94 was the best," Fly said, grabbing a controller.

"That's because you're prehistoric." Country shoved onto the couch next to him. Brett laughed, mostly because Fly was only four years older than most of them.

Fly scoffed. "It's because it's the best."

As the game loaded, Sean argued, "Nope, it's NHL 07. The skill stick feature changed everything."

Suraj held up the game case. "NHL 10. *Fights*. Mic drop."

Brett took the second controller when Tyler offered it to him. Normally he wouldn't care about playing or watching, but watching gave too much space for his thoughts to creep in. Right then, he wanted to watch small digital men swoop across the screen. He wanted to laugh at Country's commentary and focus on something he had even a little control over.

Because that meant he didn't have to think about the fact that the second bedroom was empty. Or that he'd already noticed Penny accidentally left her shampoo bottle in his shower. He didn't have to think about eating dinner alone or not having Penny's smile there to greet him when he got home from work.

Not thinking was what he needed, and playing video games with friends was better than booze.

Penny cried for the first hour of their drive and Andrea let her. She didn't ask questions or try to make her feel better. She did hand her a box of tissues that Kelty had been wise enough to throw in with the snacks.

When she was finally able to talk without breaking down again, they busted open the bag of dill pickle chips as they wound through lush pine forest.

"When did you decide to fly out here?" Penny asked.

"It was on Wednesday, I think?" Andrea frowned, and Penny did the mental math. That was when she was at Kelty's house. "Brett texted me that morning and asked what the chances were that I was free."

Penny had just been thinking what the chances were that Brett had texted her weeks prior when their relationship was going smoothly. "What did he say?"

"He said you were worried about driving the truck by yourself, and he wanted to bring me out."

Penny's brow furrowed. "Wait, bring you out?"

"Yeah, he offered to pay for my flight."

"Did he? Did you let him pay for you to fly out here?"

Andrea nodded. "Of course I did. Are you kidding?"

Penny swallowed hard. *Brett had done that for her?* Not that it was way out of left field for him to be thoughtful, but this was more than bringing flowers home. He'd done something that didn't benefit him at all on paper. *Unless he was hoping it would?*

Andrea pointed. "What's in that envelope?"

Penny glanced down at the card in her hands that Tyler had given her. She opened it up. Inside was a cash card with the letters G-A-S written across the front in black Sharpie. Penny grinned. She was guessing that was Tyler's contribution to the gift. On the card itself, Emma had written her a note in neat handwriting.

Andrea craned her neck. "What does it say? Read it to me."

"Maybe it's personal, Dre."

Andrea scoffed, and Penny started to read.

. . .

Loved getting to know you, Penny. I hope we have many more Sunday Suppers together (or unannounced gambling takeovers). And since you never really get to know somebody until after you sit in the stands for a hockey game, that will be the next step in our relationship. Come back and visit in October!

Love, Emma

"Who's Emma?" Andrea asked.

"She's Sean's younger sister, the captain of their hockey team. She's dating Tyler, Brett's old roommate."

"How long were you living up there? Only a couple of months, right?"

Penny nodded.

"That's cool. Seems like you made some good friends."

Penny slipped the card back into the envelope and put the gift card into her wallet. She had made good friends. Surprisingly good friends. As an adult, it felt like it took forever to build relationships, but these ones had fallen into her lap. She only knew the team and their significant others because of Kelty. She only knew Brett because of Kelty.

But once she was in, she hadn't only seen them at team events. The Snowballs et al. cared about each other. They showed up. They put forth effort for someone who was *just* Brett's roommate.

"So . . ." Andrea tapped her fingers on the steering wheel. "Are you ready to talk about Brett? Or should we wait until we pass through Banff?" Penny exhaled, and Andrea jumped back in. "I don't want to wait too long because this is only a ten-and-a-half-hour drive. I think it's going to take a while to unpack, and if we're not finished talking about it by the time we pull into Vancouver, I'm going to be ticked."

"Because we couldn't just keep talking about it at home."

Andrea scoffed. "You know you're not going to talk about it when everybody else is there."

"We're going to have plenty of time to hash things out now that—"

"Not while it's fresh! Road trips bring out the good stuff."

Penny sighed in defeat and started at the beginning, which for Andrea was before she came into town to visit. She wanted to know everything. What Brett had said when she looked over the apartment. How they'd interacted when they were living together but not living together. How they kissed for the first time.

It was torture, and with every sentence, the ache in her chest grew. She was driving away from him. *Why was she driving away from him?*

Penny's lips trembled as she finished. "It just seems like I'm not meant to be somebody who gets a love story right now."

"How so?" Andrea gave her a skeptical look.

"Because I still have too much of my own stuff to figure out."

Andrea laughed out loud. "First of all, nobody 'gets' a love story. That's a fallacy we all chewed and swallowed from the time we were in diapers."

"People do, though," Penny argued. "Look at couples like Theo and Amy, Tyler and Emma, Mom and Dad. They found someone, and it was a match made in heaven."

"I love how your brain skips over everything hard in those scenarios. I can't think of one person who's been together for a long time who hasn't had to fight for it, Pens."

That was fair. "But I did fight for it. I've fought for it so many times. I guess I don't know how to fight for it the right way, or maybe I don't know how to figure out what's worth fighting for."

Andrea pulled into a gas station as soon as they left the national park, and Penny handed her the gas card. "Maybe that's the only way you figure it out. By fighting for something that isn't."

CHAPTER Twenty-Seven

PENNY AND ANDREA made their way through the mountains, stopped at D Dutchmen Dairy for ice cream, then continued on to the Okanagan Valley where they stopped for the night in Kamloops. The next morning, they shopped at two different fruit stands, then spent forty-five minutes picking fresh blackberries in a ditch on the road when Andrea spotted them and insisted Penny pull over.

By the time they hit the outskirts of the city, they were halfway through Abba's Gold album, using empty water bottles as microphones. Driving through the city was just as annoying as Penny had anticipated, so she made Andrea do it, then gasped every time it looked like they were going to scrape up against a parked car.

By the time they parked in the driveway of their parents' house, Andrea looked like she'd just been electrocuted. She yanked the key from the ignition. "I hate you."

Penny laughed and handed her one of the dark chocolate bars they hadn't eaten through. "Does this make up for it?"

Andrea snatched it from her. "Hell, no. But it's a start."

Penny jumped out of the cab when she saw her parents

walking down the front steps. She ran across the interlocked bricks and wrapped her arms around both of them.

"You're here!" Her mom kissed her cheek, and her dad kissed her forehead. She felt like she'd just gotten off the kindergarten bus. They embraced Andrea, then ushered them both inside where her mom had a lunch of leftover pot roast and fresh buns set out.

They ate and caught up on each other's lives, though Penny left out anything about Brett. She hadn't told her parents about him, and hashing things out with Andrea in the truck had left her on empty.

"Theo and Marco are coming over later to empty out the trailer into the garage, so just take your personal things up to your room," her father instructed.

"Are the purple blinds still up?" Penny asked.

Her mom scoffed. "We took those down last year, you know that."

Penny did not know that since she hadn't been home. Standing there in the kitchen unlocked a hundred memories linked to the smell of her home, the familiarity of the countertops and cabinets, and the sound of her parents' voices. It felt like someone had wrapped a warm fuzzy blanket over her shoulders.

Andrea caught her eye. Penny rinsed her dishes and loaded them into the dishwasher, then followed her into the hall. Andrea grabbed her hand. "C'mon. We've got work to do."

Brett moved through his life in a haze. He woke up each morning and went for a swim, then drove between his job sites and worked with his team. At night he found any excuse he could to not to be home alone for dinner. Either eating after practice at One Place or meeting up with any of the guys who happened to be available, which was usually Country, André, Darcy, or Boyd. It was good to get to know them better off the ice, and the more questions he could ask about their lives, the less he had to talk or think about his.

On Thursday he showed up to the job site and saw Daniel sitting in his Mercedes waiting for him. Fantastic. All he could think as he parked was that this a-hole got years with Penny when he only got six weeks.

"Morning." Daniel was as chipper as a goalie with a shutout, and Brett had never wanted to punch him in his Botoxed face more.

"Good morning, Dr. Ascott. Another walk-through today?"

Daniel nodded. "Once a week isn't too much, is it?"

It was too much. "Not at all. Let's take a look." Brett ignored his passive-aggressive comments about the amount of progress happening now that he was back on-site. He answered his questions and showed him enough samples to satiate a teen girl buying makeup for the first time at Shoppers.

It wasn't until they were walking back to the front doors that Brett's world snapped into laser focus. One of the guys answered his phone and called out, "I need to take this. It's my wife," as he ran to the back doors.

Daniel chuckled. "Women are always there when they want something, never there when you need them, eh?"

Something clicked in Brett's brain, like a breaker tripping and then being reset. *Never there when you need them, eh?* Penny had always been there when he needed her. She was there for his PT even before she knew him. There to drive him to work. There for dinner, and there waiting for him when he got home from a long day.

Had she ever asked for anything? Had she ever complained about him not giving her enough? Not once. He, on the other hand, had asked for plenty. Brett's ribs ratcheted around his lungs. When Penny had finally verbalized a need, he'd acted just as entitled as this egotistical puck boy.

What was it Andrea had said on their drive from the airport? That Penny hadn't been back to see her family for over a year? Danny had guilt-tripped her into working the holidays after she'd already used her summer vacation to go with him to a conference in Vegas.

Was he any different? He'd asked her to stay. Of course he never meant for her to miss time with her family, but did she know that?

More than that, had he even once considered leaving Calgary and going with her? That question made him nauseous. *No.* Because his life was here. *His* team. *His* work. *His* friends. Everything he needed to be stable and functional.

He was asking Penny to give up her stability back in Vancouver. Again. He was asking her to fit into his life because his needs took precedence. Because he didn't know if he could hack it if his ducks weren't perfectly in a row.

"Is something wrong? You look like you just saw a stripper's cooch!"

"Shut the hell up, Daniel."

"Excuse me?"

"You heard what I said." Brett broke into a jog, ignoring the twinge in his knee. He pushed through the doors and dialed Tyler before he got to his car.

Penny folded her last summer dress, a vibrant turquoise piece, and tucked it neatly into her suitcase. She folded it closed and kneeled on the top to zip it up, then hid it behind the bed just in case her parents peeked in.

She glanced at her watch. Andrea had entrusted her with

picking up flowers and photos for the party, and she wanted to leave plenty of time to drive to Andrea's apartment and put the frames together before she needed to be at the restaurant.

Penny grabbed her backpack and car keys then dashed out the door. Traffic wasn't bad, and it only took twenty minutes to get to the flower shop. A bell jingled as Penny entered the white screened porch door that oozed whimsy. She breathed in deeply, inhaling the heady perfume of fresh blooms.

"Good afternoon." A woman with kind eyes and a warm smile greeted her. "How can I help you today?"

"Hi! I'm here to pick up an order for Andrea," Penny replied, unable to stop her eyes from flitting through the pastel arrangements behind the counter.

"Ah yes, the anniversary flowers!" The florist disappeared into the back room for a moment, then reemerged with a box full of bouquets, each wrapped carefully in delicate tissue paper.

Penny's eyes widened in awe. They were stunning. Now all she had to do was keep them happy until they could drop them into the vases at Winnleton. Penny paid, then lifted the bouquets from the counter. She carried them to her car, grateful for the careful packing so she didn't have to worry about them falling all over the backseat.

She stopped on the way to Andrea's and picked up two dozen prints of her parents, then took everything up the lift in two trips and settled in to finish her prep. Andrea had left the frames out for the photos, and Penny got to work.

She stared at each eight by ten, most of which she'd seen at some point growing up, but some she hadn't. The fashion choices. The hairstyles. All of it changed from year to year, but the smiles on their faces were consistent. They were always holding hands. Always close.

How did they do it? Her parents weren't perfect people, but they'd built something beautiful. They'd found a way to love each other through job losses, financial struggles, teenagers, and even losing a son. She'd grown up with their example, and yet after fifteen years of relationships, it felt like she didn't even speak their language.

Penny slid the last frame into the bag, and when Brett's face flashed in her head, she squeezed her eyes shut. She should text him.

She stood up and pulled out her phone, then searched for his number. Her thumbs hovered over the keys.

> Hey. Just wanted to let you know how much I appreciated having Andrea on the drive.
> Thank you

Shame filled her realizing she hadn't sent a thank you sooner. She didn't know what Brett was thinking about her at the moment, but it couldn't be good. Penny thought of him standing in front of her on the sidewalk. His clenched jaw. His silence as she turned and left in the truck.

No, she wasn't going to cry. She needed to get ready and head over to the venue. Penny grabbed her backpack and stood in front of the full-length mirror in Andrea's bedroom. She used her sister's curling iron to smooth her waves, then applied a smoothing mask to make them shimmer.

She applied charcoal liner to her eyes, blush on her cheeks, and a bolder lip colour than usual. It helped dull the sting in her chest. Penny pulled her dress from her backpack and laid it across Andrea's bed, then took the frames and hydrated flowers back down to the car.

When everything was loaded, she went back up to the apartment and slipped on her dress. It was simple. Buttery cream with thin straps that hugged her curves and puddled on the floor without her heels. She'd save those for after setup.

Penny's phone buzzed. It was Kelty.

> Are you on your way over?

> Yep, just got my dress on

> Pictures and flowers were good?

> Perfect. I'm impressed, Dre

> 🖤 See you soon

It was good to be busy. Less time to think about how much her heart ached. She stowed her toiletries in her bag, then rushed down to the car and drove to the restaurant. As soon as it came into view, Penny felt giddy. *Good choice, Andrea.*

The charming villa was nestled among lush gardens, its stone walls draped in ivy and fairy lights. The inside was just as stunning with high ceilings adorned by crystal chandeliers and polished wooden floors that gleamed beneath her feet.

"Welcome!" Amy, her brother Theo's wife, ran to greet her with a hug. "We've missed you!"

"I've missed you guys, too."

Amy helped bring in the supplies, and Penny tied the bottom of her dress up so she could walk around in flip-flops. With the help of the staff, they filled vases and cut the stems on the bouquets, then arranged them on the tables and lit the candles.

"Wow, you've really outdone yourselves," Theo, her burly oldest brother, walked in dressed in a charcoal grey suit. Penny ran as fast as she could in her tight dress and hugged him. Theo squeezed her so tight she wondered if Andrea had let anything slip about what she'd been through the past few months, but didn't ask. There would be plenty of time to debrief once they were sitting in the Mediterranean Sea.

Her stomach clenched as she pulled back and smiled at her brother. *She didn't want to go.* She'd felt numb packing her clothes, but now, surrounded by the floral arrangements and flickering light—after looking at snapshots of her parents' deeply fulfilling love story—the idea of getting on a plane made her want to throw up.

She turned before Theo could see the expression on her face, then walked to the chair she'd set her purse on and grabbed her phone. Brett hadn't texted back. Penny's heart hammered in her chest as she typed out another text.

> I miss you. I miss you so much. I hate that I left

Penny stared at the message, her eyes blurring with tears. It was all true, but what would it accomplish? Was she going to load her stuff back in the moving truck she'd already returned and drive back to Calgary?

She deleted the message and shoved her phone back in her handbag.

"I think we're ready." Amy planted her hands on her hips and surveyed the room. It had been transformed into pure elegance, soft and beautiful. Long tables were adorned with crisp white linens, and as the staff strung the last strands of fairy lights, Penny's breath caught in her throat.

Romance. Brett would've loved it.

The first guests began to arrive fifteen minutes later, and Penny was swept up in her emotions. She hadn't seen the faces of their family friends in years, and her heart was full to bursting as they walked into the dining room and took their seats.

Penny texted Andrea.

> People are here. You have the parental units?

> Yes! Just picked them up. They still think we're just meeting you and Theo for dinner

Penny grinned and looked up to see Sophia and Marco walking from their car toward the entrance. She hadn't seen either sibling since the summer of 2021, though that wasn't all her fault. Since Soph had moved to Ottawa, none of them had seen her much, and Marco was almost just as hard to nail down. He was always jet-setting somewhere around the world. She might've been a little bit jealous.

Theo caught them first, and Penny queued up to greet them.

After embracing all around, they stood to the side while the staff ushered people to their seats.

"Is Andrea almost here?" Theo asked, nodding at Amy on the other side of the tables as she re-lit a candle that had gone out.

Penny nodded. "Anytime now."

"Do you think we should hide?"

Marco shook his head. "No, I think we should plaster ourselves against the glass. Let them get a good look the whole time they're walking up the sidewalk."

Penny snorted, then went to her table for a drink of water. Her eyes pricked at the corners. *This.* This was what she'd been missing. This was what she'd given up for effing Danny. *Ugh.* She hated herself for being so blind—for having no backbone.

"They're here!" Sophia squealed, and Penny forced herself to pull it together. This night wasn't about her.

They watched as Andrea walked with their parents from the parking lot, and Penny held her breath, waiting for them to look up. Her mom's eyes landed on them first–her and her siblings standing in a row in front of the glass. When her hand flew to her mouth, Penny couldn't hold back her tears.

"*Shit,*" she whispered, and Theo put an arm around her shoulders.

"Amy has extra mascara in her bag."

Penny laughed and forced herself to breathe as Andrea dragged her now-weeping mother closer to the door. *She wanted this.* She wanted this life. She wanted steady love and kids and fortieth anniversaries, and she wanted to wake up every morning next to the same person until they were grey-haired and changing each other's diapers.

Cheers erupted as they entered the room, and then Theo had to leave her side to keep their dad from collapsing. Penny walked forward and looped her arm through Andrea's as all the siblings crowded around their parents. Together, they led them through the room to greet friends and look at the photo display.

Andrea patted her arm. "Lucas would have loved this."

Penny nodded, not trusting herself to speak.

After laughing until their cheeks hurt through the three-course dinner, Andrea pulled all the siblings up to the front while the staff placed dessert on the tables. She pulled an elegant cream-coloured envelope from her purse and tapped it on her palm as she waited for the manager to get the microphone working. When he handed it to her, Andrea cleared her throat.

"Hello, everyone. I'm sorry to interrupt your meal, but we wanted to do something quickly if you'll bear with us." Andrea turned to their parents, who were sitting front and center. "You know none of us are capable of giving a speech without breaking down, so I'm just going to hand this to you. Happy Anniversary, Mom and Dad. From all of us."

Penny's heart pounded a staccato rhythm against her ribs. Their parents exchanged curious glances, then their dad took the envelope and pulled at the tab. Everyone laughed when he finally gave up on saving the delicate paper and tore it open.

All five siblings held hands, waiting for their reaction. When they pulled out the boarding passes and trip itinerary, both their parents' jaws went slack. "Oh, my babies. Oh, my—" Their mother started to cry again. Their dad pulled her close and kissed her temple, then looked up at them with tears in his eyes.

He opened his mouth to speak, but nothing came out.

Theo reached out and took the mic from Andrea. "A trip to Greece!" he announced, and the room erupted into applause. Love and grief, longing and regret, hope and gratitude all washed over Penny, and she reached out for the table next to her to steady herself. They did it. They pulled this off.

Andrea wrapped her arm around Penny's shoulder. "Thanks for your help, Pens."

She shook her head. "You did this."

"I kind of did, didn't I?"

Penny laughed. "All it took was six months of planning, working alone with a travel agent, endless text messages to hound your flaky siblings."

"Hashtag worth it."

Penny squeezed her sister's waist. "I love you."

Andrea turned and wrapped her in a hug. "I love you too, and you're going to figure this all out. You know that right?"

Penny's eyes stung. She nodded, even though she wasn't sure she did.

Andrea pulled back. "Remember in the car when we were talking about that Sharpie family portrait?"

Penny laughed, searching for a napkin to wipe her nose. "You mean when you were embarrassing me in front of Brett?"

"Not embarrassing, making you more charming and relatable," she argued, and Penny laughed. "No, but do you know what I remember about it?" Penny shook her head. "I looked at that picture and noticed that everyone else was big and you were the smallest one, even though you weren't the smallest kid in real life. But there you were, right in the middle, looking up at everyone." Andrea swiped a napkin from the closest table, and Penny blew her nose. "I've thought about that, you know? You might see yourself as small, but it's because of you that everyone else feels big, Penny."

A lump formed in her throat as Andrea gave her one last hug, then turned to go back to her table. Andrea's words looped through her head. She'd always seen herself that way—the least successful, the least powerful. But maybe that was her gift, to lift other people up. If only she could choose the *right* people, she—

Penny froze as movement at the back of the room caught her eye. She looked up, and her heart stopped beating. The applause, the sound of her dad's laughter, the candlelight—everything faded into nothingness as she stared at the man leaning against the door frame near the entrance to the kitchen.

CHAPTER
Twenty-Eight

SOMEONE PUT a hand on her lower back. "Well don't just stand there."

Penny glanced back at Andrea who was grinning from ear to ear. "Did you—?"

"I had *nothing* to do with this." Her grin somehow widened. "Besides maybe texting him the address."

Penny's head snapped back to Brett in his crisp white shirt and dark suit. *He was here? Brett was here? At her parents' anniversary party?* Penny walked in a daze back to her table and grabbed her handbag then made her way as inconspicuously as possible to the back of the room.

She stopped in front of him, her cheeks flushed, and her throat so tight she could barely suck in a breath. Brett's eyes travelled the length of her dress, then skimmed back up to meet her eyes.

"That dress should be illegal."

"Thank you." *Thank you? What kind of a response was that?* "You look . . ." She'd never seen him dressed up, and the way the suit hugged his frame made her mouth go dry.

"Thank you." The corner of Brett's mouth twitched. "Can we . . . ?" He pointed to the door behind them leading out to the gardens. Penny nodded, wishing she'd brought her glass of water.

The sun was barely setting over the trees as Brett led her down the stone path deeper into the blooming bushes. He stopped behind the pond and turned to face her. Penny didn't know where to start. Thankfully, Brett spoke first.

"You asked me a question."

"I did?" Penny breathed.

Brett nodded. "Before you left. I didn't answer, so I thought I'd do that now."

Penny tried to swallow the lump in her throat. "Did you fly or drive?"

"Drove. With Tyler and Sean." Penny looked around as if expecting them to pop out of the bushes. Brett chuckled. "They're back at the hotel."

Hotel. So they were staying the night. Penny wracked her brain, trying to remember what she'd said to him. That moment was a blur, but the words finally filtered back into her head.

Brett took a step closer. "You asked if I could forgive you." Penny nodded and bit the inside of her cheek. He drew a deep breath, then clasped his hands in front of him. "No. I don't forgive you."

Penny's heart sank like a stone, and she braced herself to listen to him tell her how much she'd hurt him. The pressure behind her eyes started to throb. "Brett—"

"I don't forgive you because there's nothing to forgive you for. You told me you couldn't do that again, and I promised you I didn't have a mould I expected you to fit, but that's exactly what I was asking you to do."

Penny shook her head and started to speak, but Brett held up a hand.

"Just let me finish. Please." He paced in front of the fountain. "I thought I was enough. In my self-centred head, I thought you could stay because you had me and you needed me as much as I needed you, so that made your sacrifice reasonable. But I'm not enough, and I'll never be enough because I shouldn't be. No human should have to limit their world to a singular point orbiting around someone else's life. I don't want that for you, Penny. I don't want you to stay in Calgary because I need you."

Tears filled Penny's eyes. "It's not that I don't need you, I do! Leaving and driving across the Rockies felt like I was ripping out a piece of myself and chucking it out the window. But I go all in, Brett. I go deep and hard, and I don't see when I'm drowning until it's too late. I can't—"

"I know how to tread water."

"What?" Penny gasped for breath.

"You taught me. You showed me how to keep my head up and not look like a dying cat."

She shook her head. "I don't know—"

"Nobody can see when they're drowning, Penny! That's why we don't swim alone." Brett stepped closer, and Penny fought the sobs threatening to reach up and strangle her. "You taught me how to tread, and I'm doing the work. I'll keep doing the work. I'm not going to leave you in the water, and I sure as hell won't let you drown. I know I'm not perfect. I know I don't have the best track record, but if I have to strengthen my muscles, I want to do it with you. I want to struggle with you. I want to hurt with you."

Penny tried to find something to do with her hands, and Brett reached out and grabbed them. "Look at me. Please," he whispered. "I will sell my half of the business, I will leave the Snowballs, I will sell my apartment and start over here if that's what you want."

"Brett, you fought for that life, I can't—"

"I *can*. I built a new life from scratch once, and I can do it again. I know how to battle, Penny, and I will crawl through that shit a thousand times over if it means I get to have you through it. All of you. Not just the part that's there when *I* need it."

Penny swiped the tears from her cheeks. *Was he serious?* She thought about her family here, the pieces of her soul that had snapped back into place since she'd come home. But then she thought about coming home from Greece and walking back into her childhood bedroom.

She didn't have a life here, not yet. She didn't have a life anywhere. "What if I don't know who that is?"

Brett swiped his thumb over her cheeks. "Please let me be there when you find her. Because you're already the most beautiful damn thing I've ever seen." He pulled her flush against him, running his hands over her bare shoulders and back.

Brett kissed her wet cheeks, his breath whispering against her skin. "I love you, Penny."

She slipped her hands inside his suit jacket and ran her fingers over the soft fabric of his shirt. "I love you, too."

The setting sun turned the garden to gold as Brett drew her lips to his. The clinking glasses and chatter inside the restaurant blended with humming insects and the first croaks of frogs in the pond, but Penny was worlds away.

Brett touched her like she was a bird that had landed on his arm and he didn't want to scare her off. Penny wasn't having any of it. She tugged against his back, letting him know how much she wanted him.

He didn't take much convincing. His hands grew insistent, tracing the shape of her under the slinky fabric. "When do you leave?" he asked roughly before pulling her lower lip between his teeth.

"Sunday," she breathed, her heart slamming inside her chest. "How long are you here?"

"Till the second you get on that plane."

"Good." She dragged her nails over his back as Brett wrapped her hair in his hand and gently pulled, exposing her neck. He dragged his tongue and teeth over her flushed skin, and Penny gasped as her eyes rolled back in her head.

"Okay, I see how it is."

Penny jolted and spun as Brett tensed next to her.

"Hi, Brett." Andrea smirked and gestured at her neck. "You may want to give yourself a minute."

Penny's skin burned where Brett had been seconds before. She blinked. They were in a public garden. "Did anyone else—?"

Andrea shook her head. "Mom just asked where you were, though. Are you coming back in or . . ."

Penny nodded, then turned to Brett as Andrea started back up the path. "I should probably stay a bit longer."

Brett nodded, his breath still coming in short bursts. "I'll hold that thought."

Penny laughed, her heart fizzing like buttermilk syrup. "Come in with me."

He straightened his jacket, then adjusted his pants. "I might need a minute." Penny grinned and ran her hand over the stubble on his jaw. "That's extending my time out."

"It's dark in there. I don't think anyone will notice."

Brett frowned. "That's not what a guy wants to hear, Penny."

She laughed out loud. "Fine, everyone will notice your huge—"

He clapped a hand over her mouth, and she fell into him, breathing in citrus and spice. "Are you staying with Tyler and Sean?"

"I got my own room," he murmured.

Penny lifted her head and nipped his earlobe before pushing back and dropping her arms. "Good." She turned and walked up the path and heard a muttered, "Not helping," as she reentered the dining room.

Brett waited in his car, tapping his fingers impatiently on the wheel as he watched for Penny to walk out to the parking lot. When he finally saw her push through the doors, his breath caught. She looked like a Mediterranean Goddess wrapped in platinum gold. As much as he loved the dress, he loved the idea of it lying in a pile on his hotel room floor even more.

Penny searched the vehicles, and when she found his car, she waved and pointed to the front of the lot. He pulled up to the curb and rolled down the window.

"Amy said she'd take my car home. Can I just grab my toiletries and ride with you?"

Brett's pulse somehow sped faster. "Please."

Penny grinned and sashayed to her car. She tossed her heels in the back and put on her flip-flops, then grabbed her backpack and held up her dress so it didn't drag on the asphalt as she ran back. She opened the door and jumped in. "Take me to bed, Bouchard."

Brett pressed the gas, not realizing the car was still in park. His cheeks flushed as Penny laughed and threw her bag in the back.

When they arrived at the hotel, Tyler and Sean were standing in the lobby. Brett tried to get on the elevator before they noticed him but failed. Tyler launched into twenty questions about the party, knowing full well what an annoying bastard he was being by the smug smile on his face. Brett finally hit the button and pulled Penny into the lift mid-sentence.

She laughed as he pressed her against the mirrors and kissed her breathless. When the doors opened on his floor, he pulled her down the hall to his room and whisked her inside.

"I'm so glad you're here."

"You're about to be gladder."

Penny hissed a breath against his lips. "Is that a word?"

"Are you seriously correcting my grammar right now?" He slipped his hands under the thin straps of her dress and dragged them off her shoulders.

Penny sighed as he pulled her dress lower and kissed every inch of skin he exposed along the way. "I missed you." She pulled out the elastic and ran her fingers through his hair.

"What time do you leave Sunday?"

"One o'clock."

"Are you packed?" He pulled her into his mouth and felt her back arch. Penny nodded. "Good."

Brett took his time reminding her he meant what he said in the garden. He'd had plenty of time to think on the drive, and then he'd stared at the tattoo on his arm in the hotel mirror before getting dressed and heading to the party. He hadn't known what her response would be with him showing up like that, but it hadn't mattered. Whether she accepted him or not, his old self had already been reduced to ashes.

Brett took a long, hard look at that cream fabric puddled on the floor as Penny worked at the buttons of his shirt. She'd transformed him into a new creature, and whether she was ready or not, he was hers.

But damn, if he wasn't ecstatic that she was ready.

CHAPTER
Twenty-Nine

MONDAY

PENNY 3:00PM

> Just landed!

BRETT 3:00PM

> What do you see? Tell me everything

> The back of some guys' head

> Riveting

> I caught the coast as we landed. Pretty cloudy today

> Cloudy here, too

> Liar. It's never cloudy in Calgary

> I might still be in Vancouver

> Without me???

You're the one who left remember?

> Low blow

I'll only rub it in a few more times. Promise

Monday

Brett 11:12pm

Did you take my Blizzard hoodie on your trip?

Penny 11:42pm

> Maybe...

That's my favourite hoodie

> I know. It's big and comfy and I love it

But I love it. And now it's gone

> But it smells like you

> You can't be mad that I knew I was going to miss you

Nope. Just cold

Tuesday

Penny 8:01am

> I want another name on your hate list

Brett 8:03am

Demanding this morning, I see

Are you prepared to pay the price?

> Seriously? Kelty made your ears bleed and you gave it up. I think I've already earned it. Especially with what happened in the hotel...

Don't want the details on record?

> If I get famous someday, this is the text they'll scrape from my hard drive

> Enough distractions

> Pay up

Andy from the Office

> What!?

You asked

Wednesday

Brett 7:15pm

Swam fifteen laps this morning

Penny 7:22pm

> Pictures or it didn't happen

BRETT 7:33PM

> Eggplant Peach
>
> Dammit. Voice texting
>
>

PENNY 7:56PM

> I just spit egg on the table

BRETT 8:42PM

> You're welcome

THURSDAY

ANDREA 9:02AM

> Can you please stop texting Penny? We're supposed to be on the boat, and she's sitting on the couch grinning to herself

BRETT 9:02AM

> Andrea, why are you on your phone when you're supposed to be on the boat?

ANDREA 9:03AM

> Remember when I flew out so you could make some grand gesture and win my sister back?

Brett 9:03am

> Copy

Saturday

Penny 10:22pm

> Hey, random question, but what did you do with that box of stuff Danny left on the porch?

Brett 10:31pm

> I made a life-sized voodoo doll. Been sticking pins in it daily

> Lol. I love you. But seriously...

> It's in my closet. Didn't want to trash it in case you wanted any of it after the initial rage wore off

> I was so grateful it wasn't staring at me when I woke up. Thank you. I don't want it

> I'll take it to Value Village this week

> At least try to sell the headphones

> I'll give those to Dominic. Then I'll make sure Danny sees him wearing them

> Might keep the wallet. It's nice

>> Shut your mouth Brett. But...I do have good taste

Sunday

Brett 11:47pm

> I miss you

Penny 11:54pm

>> Miss you more

> We've become one of the couples I used to make fun of

>> I won't tell anyone

Monday

Brett 2:06am

> You told Kelty didn't you

Penny 9:22am

>> You texted me in the middle of night for that?

> Your night is my day. And you didn't answer the question

> 😄

> You're dead to me

> You're . . . adorable?

> 😄 Trying to figure out how to leave my team chat

TUESDAY

BRETT 6:01PM

> You're coming home on Friday

8:42PM

> About to do another walk through with our favourite guy

9:57PM

> Just finished. Didn't mind him today since I know I won. I kind of wanted to tell him thanks

PENNY 11:10PM

> Thanks for what exactly??

BRETT 11:32PM

> Didn't I tell you? It was something he said that made me realize I was a selfish ass

> You're not selfish

> ...but I am an ass?

> You're not selfish or an ass. Most of the time

> That's a win

> See you Fri?

> I'll be there

PENNY EXITED the customs area with her family, and they walked to get their bags. She'd barely been able to sit still for the last leg of their flight from Toronto to Vancouver. Before that, she forced herself to stay up most of the way home in the hopes that she'd be less jet-lagged once she arrived.

Now that her head was woozy, she was beginning to regret her decision. Especially because all she wanted to do was stay up all night with Brett. At least she had the weekend in Vancouver to recuperate before driving back to Calgary.

They gathered their bags off the turnstiles and loaded up a push cart while her nieces fought over who got to sit on top of the bags. Penny couldn't keep the grin off her face. The trip had been incredible—more than incredible. Relaxing and soul-filling. But now that they were back on Canadian soil, she only had one person on her mind.

He was there at the airport, based on his text half an hour ago, and her eyes darted around with each turn they made in the hall.

"You seem a little antsy," Andrea teased.

Theo chimed in. "You're driving home with us, right?"

Penny would have made a rude gesture had there not been two children present.

"I like Brett," her mother said. "I think he's a very nice young man."

Penny grinned. Brett was going to eat that compliment up. They rounded the corner, and Theo and Marco pushed the carts toward the elevator. Penny and Sophia grabbed their nieces' hands and walked toward the escalator instead.

"Do you think we can beat your dad?" Penny asked, and Alana's eyes lit up.

"Don't run on the escalator," Amy called out as the elevator doors opened.

Penny gave a quick wave, then raced forward, careful to make sure Alana didn't trip as they stepped onto the moving apparatus.

When she was sure her niece was stable, Penny looked down to the next level, and that's when she saw him. Brett stood from the chair he'd been waiting on and shoved his phone in his pocket. His eyes locked onto hers.

"Is that your boyfriend?" Alana asked.

"Yes," Penny breathed. That was her boyfriend. His hair was down just the way she liked it, and he was wearing a pink shirt and jeans that hung low on his hips. *Have mercy.*

"He's handsome." Alana giggled, and Andrea coughed a laugh from a few steps above them. *She wasn't wrong.* Penny squeezed her niece's hand. "Do you think I'll have a handsome boyfriend someday?" Alana asked.

"Definitely," she answered.

Sophia snorted. "Don't tell Theo about that one."

As they reached the bottom of the escalator, Alana let go of Penny's hand and raced around the side wall to wait at the door of the elevator for her dad. Penny walked to Brett and threw her arms around him.

"There's my sunkissed girl," he whispered as Penny moulded herself to his chest.

"I can't believe you drove out here again."

"I can't believe I get to take you home with me."

Penny listened to the beat of his heart. He'd tried so many times to convince her to stay in Vancouver. To prove that he was willing to take the plunge. But ultimately, Penny wanted to go back to continue building the life they'd started. They could always change their minds later, and she believed him when he said he wouldn't let her lose herself. Each time Penny let herself fall, he was right there to catch her. To prove that he was paying attention and he wouldn't let her drop too deep.

That kind of trust was something she'd never experienced before, and her mind and heart still lurched, wondering if the ice was going to collapse beneath her feet. It would take time.

Luckily, time with Brett was exactly what she wanted.

The elevator door opened, and her brothers pushed the carts out.

Brett kissed her forehead. "Let me go get your bags." He strode over to the carts and clapped her brothers on the back. Penny made the rounds, giving all of her siblings and parents hugs.

"We'll see you for Christmas, right, Pens?" Andrea gave her a look.

"If she doesn't come, I'm coming without her," Brett called out, and her parents beamed at him.

"I didn't know he was an ass-kisser," Andrea murmured.

Penny laughed. "You better watch out. He might steal your place as favourite child."

Andrea rolled her eyes as Penny blew her a kiss and jogged to catch up with Brett.

"I think they're more in love with you than I am," Penny said, taking one of the roller bags.

"That's my play. Make the parents so attached, you can never leave me."

She swatted his butt as they walked through the door, then clasped onto his free hand. "And when do I get to meet your family, hey?"

Brett shook his head. "Oh, at least a few months from now. When I'm sure they won't scare you off."

"Coward."

"Absolutely."

They crossed the street, and Penny's stomach grumbled. Her body was sure it was supper time even though it was ten in the morning. "Want to go get breakfast? An omelet or something?"

He nodded to his car at the end of the aisle. "It's called a frittata, Penny. This vacation has changed you."

Penny squeezed his hand. She didn't care what they called it. As long as she got to eat it with him.

Epilogue

PENNY STEEPLED her hands in front of her lips, her whole body tense as Brett skated out onto the ice. *Please be careful.* Her silent prayer was ridiculous because of course he wasn't going to be careful. He was a hockey player. The word "careful" had probably never fully landed in his vocabulary.

"He's going to be fine." Kelty squeezed Penny's gloved hand.

"You don't know that."

"Nope, but we all say it to each other anyway to keep from thinking about the fact that the men we love are going to keep battering themselves against the boards day in and day out until they die."

Emma snorted next to her. "That's the best description of this sport I've ever heard."

Penny gripped the edge of the metal bleachers as Kelty let out a whoop. Their cheeks were already rosy from the chilled air in the ice centre, and Penny pulled down her toque. She wasn't ready for winter, but the first snow was already forecasted for that weekend. It wasn't even Halloween yet.

Penny locked onto Brett on the left wing. He looked good on the ice. Smooth and powerful. The puck zipped across the ice, and Penny held her breath as Sean passed it to Brett, who weaved past a forward on Stiff Sticks only to be slammed into by a defender.

"*Damn it*," Penny hissed, her heart jumping into her throat. Brett was already sprinting back over centre ice unfazed.

"I've got a trick for you." Emma reached out and pulled Penny's toque down over her eyes. Kelty chortled next to her as Penny rolled it back up. She found Brett just as Sean intercepted the puck from a Stiff Sticks player past their own blue line and tapped it to him.

Brett took a sharp turn, ice spraying beneath his skates. He danced around the same Stiff Sticks forward, then bolted center with Sean filling in behind him. The crowd held their breath as he shot the puck toward Country who flicked his wrist and sent the puck whizzing into the far corner of the net.

Cheers erupted from the crowd as lights spun at either end of the rink. Two to one Snowballs in the second. Tyler subbed for Brett and Mike for Suraj, all of them tapping mitts as they traded positions. As Brett sat on the bench, Penny exhaled. At least she could enjoy the game for a few minutes now.

The Snowballs held onto their lead and went up three to one in the third. More importantly, when the final buzzer sounded, Brett was still upright. Penny leaped to her feet and cheered, stripping off her gloves so her clapping actually made a sound.

"First exhibition game of the season, check. One Place?" Kelty asked, and both Penny and Emma nodded.

They crossed the street to the cozy pub. There wasn't much action there tonight since the season had just started, but Penny had already heard stories about it being packed to the gills during the playoffs. They walked to the back where there was already a long table set up for them. Kelty blew a kiss to the woman behind the bar, then rattled off a list of appetizers to the server who'd come over to greet them.

Emma brought over pitchers of water and beer from the bar,

and they settled into their seats. Rashi, Suraj's wife, showed up a few minutes later with Fly's girlfriend Jess, and a few fans filled up the tables up front.

Just as the nachos arrived, the pub door swung open and Penny's eyes snapped up. Her cheeks warmed when she saw Brett. His damp hair clung to his forehead and his skin was still flushed from the game. She'd never seen his eyes so alive.

He strode to the back with Tyler, Sean, and André following like ducklings, and when he looked up, his blue eyes locked onto hers. He broke formation and headed to her side of the table, sliding into the seat next to her. She lifted her chin and kissed him as he scooted closer so his thigh was pressed against hers.

"Hi," she breathed.

"Fancy seeing you here." Brett's eyes danced.

"You're just a little too pleased with yourself."

Brett chuckled and kissed her again. "I took plenty of subs per your protocol."

"You got hit."

"Not exactly avoidable."

"But your knee's okay?"

He reached past her and grabbed a chip. "Never been better."

"Liar." She slipped her hand down and felt along his leg.

"Never."

Penny raised an eyebrow, but didn't get a chance to respond because the table erupted with laughter. She looked up and saw the rest of the players were there, laughing uproariously.

"Speaking of scoring . . ." André turned to Country. "Nice goal, bud."

Country leaned back in his chair. "Merci."

Penny grinned. "I don't think I want to know."

"You don't." Brett laughed, throwing an arm over the back of her chair. "What the hell happened behind the net, Curtis? The ice turn to quicksand?"

Brett twisted a tendril of her hair around his finger as he

talked and ate. Penny filled her plate with hot wings and jalapeno poppers. Her phone buzzed in her jacket pocket, and she pulled it out before getting her fingers saucy.

> How'd his first game go?

Penny grinned at Andrea's message.

> At the pub now. He swears his knee's fine. Not sure if I believe him

"I saw that," Brett whispered, his breath tickling her ear.

"Good." Penny slipped her phone back in her jacket and ran her fingers over his scruffy chin. "I'll be doing a thorough assessment later."

He stared down at her, and Penny's insides turned to mush. "Be gentle with me, Penny."

She grinned. "I would, but we all know that's not what you want."

Available Now!
Find special edition e-books and paperbacks exclusively at www. CindyGunderson.com

About the Author

Cindy Gunderson is a voice actress and award-winning author. Since she has commitment issues, she writes both sci-fi and fantasy, as well as contemporary romance and women's fiction under the pen name, Cynthia Gunderson.

When she is not typing away in a quiet corner of her local library, you can find her traveling with her family, narrating audiobooks, or happily digging in her garden. She loves acting and performing, beating her kids in card games, and playing ultimate frisbee with her handsome husband, Scott.

Cindy grew up in Alberta, Canada, but has lived most of her adult life between California and Colorado. She currently resides in the Denver metro area. Cindy holds a B.S. in Psychology from Brigham Young University.

Cindy's first novel Tier 1 was awarded First Place in Science Fiction at the 2021 CIPPA EVVY Awards and her women's fiction novel Yes, And was honored with the Indie Author Award's first place prize for the state of Colorado, 2023.

Also by Cynthia Gunderson

Yes, And
I Can't Remember
Holly Bough Cottage
The New Year's Party
Let's Try This Again

Sugar Creek Series
One Last Christmas
Love in Audio

Canadian Played Series
Against the Boards
Called for Icing
Stickhandle with Care
On the Power Play
Guarding Home Ice

Find signed books and discounted bundles at
www.CindyGunderson.com

Instagram: @CindyGWrites
Facebook: @CindyGWrites
TikTok: @CynthiaGWrites

Printed in Great Britain
by Amazon